PsyEarth Quest

psy•earth \ sī'ərth \ *n adj* **1** the human soul, spirit, mind reconnecting with the Earth. **2** the principle of the mental, emotional, physical and spiritual life, the conscious and unconscious, merging with the primal essence of nature.

OTHER BOOKS BY CHARLES BENSINGER

CHACO JOURNEY
MAYAN VISION QUEST

PsyEarth Quest
A Prophetic Novel

Charles Bensinger

BEAR & COMPANY
PUBLISHING
SANTA FE, NEW MEXICO

Library of Congress Catalog-in-Publication Data

Bensinger, Charles, 1945-
PsyEarth quest: a prophetic novel / Charles Bensinger.
   p. cm.
Includes bibliographical references.
ISBN 1-879181-53-3
I. Title.
PS3552.E5476545P8   1998
813'.54—dc21   98-13071
                                            CIP

Copyright © 1998 by Charles Bensinger

All rights reserved. No part of this book may be reproduced by any means or in any form whatsoever without written permisssion from the publisher, except for brief quotations embodied in literary articles or reviews.

Bear & Company, Inc.
Santa Fe, NM 87504-2860

Cover art: © 1998 Bleu Turrell
Cover Design: © 1998 Lightbourne
Editor: John Nelson
Copy Editor: Sonya Moore
Typography and interior page design: Bill Pfau

Printed in the United States of America by R.R. Donnelley

9 8 7 6 5 4 3 2 1

To the teachers, visionaries, and wisdomkeepers of many cultures—past and present—who have gifted us with the seeds of an extraordinary, potential future.

CONTENTS

ACKNOWLEDGEMENTS	ix
PROLOGUE	1
1. An Unexpected Assignment	3
2. Challenging Chac	7
3. The Fragile Web	15
PART I THE PSYEARTH INSTITUTE	23
4. Preparation	25
5. Clarification	37
6. Communication	53
7. Expression	67
8. Application	81
PART II THE SOUTHWEST INTERCULTURAL COLLABORATIVE	93
9. Building Cultural Bridges	95
10. Restoring Balance	103
11. Holistic Healing	113
12. Life Out of Balance	121
13. The Beauty Way	129
14. The Vision	139
PART III THE INTERNATIONAL CENTER FOR APPROPRIATE TECHNOLOGY	151
15. Making a Better Choice	153
16. A Hard Truth	161
17. Appropriate Technologies	173
18. The Eagle's Cry	189
19. A Difference of Opinion	203
PART IV THE WORLD STEWARDSHIP COUNCIL	209
20. A Meeting with the President	211
21. Making the Invisible Visible	219

22. Global Allies	229
23. Saving the Tree of Life	237
21. Critical Balance	245
22. A New Story	253
Epilogue	275
BIBLIOGRAPHY	279
RESOURCES	282
ABOUT THE AUTHOR	291

ACKNOWLEDGMENTS

Much appreciation is due Bear & Company editor John Nelson, who provided key plot ideas and major editorial support. And many thanks to Barbara Hand Clow and Gerry Clow for their belief in the value of the text and their willingness to facilitate the presentation of the *PsyEarth Quest* ideas and concepts to the global audience. I am also greatly indebted to the many individuals, groups and organizations that have given me hope that many people care enough to work together to build a better world.

PROLOGUE

WSC Takes Vote

By Tom Westbrook

EARTHHOPE, BELIZE — Today's Global Policy Council vote will be critical. This is the most controversial decision the newly formed World Stewardship Council has considered in its short two-year history. At stake is the social, political, and economic stability of dozens of nations as well as the quality of life for billions of people throughout the world.

At the core of the debate is Resolution 636, the so-called "Share Tax," a surcharge to be levied against the sale of goods and services sold in First World nations. The tax rate will be based on the social and environmental impact of the product or service.

The proceeds of the tax are to be distributed to qualified Third World countries for debt reduction, social improvements, and environmental restoration. According to the resolution's sponsors, the tax is intended to distribute global wealth more equitably.

CHAPTER 1

AN UNEXPECTED ASSIGNMENT

It was a hot, humid June day in Albuquerque, New Mexico. My editor, Jack Major, a determined man in his sixties who's not afraid to speak his mind, called me to his office. As I sank into one of two well-worn chairs, Jack leaned across his desk and engaged me firmly with his dark, tough eyes. "Thomas," he said, "I like your work. With practice, you'll do well." He paused, allowing me a moment to absorb his compliment. I suspected something important was brewing. He always called me Thomas when it was a serious matter. "I want you to pack for Belize. You'll cover the special upcoming 'Share Tax' session of the World Stewardship Council. The event is likely to stir up an international hornet's nest."

I was stunned. Before I could respond, he continued, "I realize you're new here, but you know what we're after: people, projects, and programs that are visionary, radical, revolutionary . . . that fire humanity into a new orbit, ratchet evolution up a notch or two. If I gave the prime movers a name, I'd call them 'cultural pioneers'—men and women pushing the envelope personally, socially, politically, and environmentally. Navigator types. I want you to closely examine these people and their organizations. Tell our readers who and where they are, what they're doing, and why they're doing it."

I could feel the heat of Jack's expectations bearing down on me. This was my big opportunity. Now was not the time to display any doubt. "Great, Jack. I'm ready. Can you give me some criteria?"

"I want some in-depth, behind-the-scenes coverage. Intimate profiles of key players. Not the usual stuff. You'll be our man on the scene . . . in the eye of the storm, so to speak."

Eye of the storm? My heart skipped a beat, and I suppressed a flash of fear.

"The world is in turmoil, Thomas. I don't have to tell you that. Anything can happen. You'll start with the World Stewardship Council. Then I want you to look into the PsyEarth Institute. Their back-to-nature program is very unusual. Personally, I'm fascinated with their approach. Anyway, check with my secretary. She'll make all the necessary travel arrangements. And Thomas . . . good luck!"

Later that day, as I sat alone, brooding, nursing my beer at a local bar, I assessed the turn of events. I was now the paper's official environmental and social issues reporter. Sandy Miller, who usually covered these areas, had suddenly decided to take a sabbatical. So I was given her job, at least temporarily. A promotion was great, but what did I really know about the environment? Not much. I'd had a few college courses in ecology and social sciences, but I knew next to nothing about the complicated world of environmental politics.

Refusing the assignment was not an option. Having just completed a postgraduate course in journalism, I wasn't about to kill my career before it got off the ground. Quality journalism gigs are hard to come by these days. The global media industry is so monolithic and corporately biased . It's super-centralized—with the big guys lunching down the small independents. And I like independence. I had absolutely no desire to work for some international media conglomerate whose sole and not-so-hidden agenda is to make the world safe for nuclear power plants, energy-hungry appliances, and cheap running shoes from China. That's why I considered myself lucky to have landed a job with a publication like the *Earth Renaissance News*, one that specializes in covering critical, social-change issues.

And these things really interest me. I've always wanted to make a difference in the world. But, as an energetic, twenty-eight-year old, I figured I had some time to work on it. Initially, I thought I'd be covering the local stuff like cross-cultural conflicts and school dropout problems. Instead, I now found myself flying off to Belize to report on one of the hottest environmental stories of our time.

So, with good thoughts of sunny Belize in my mind, a suitcase packed with enough clothes to last for a week, and lots of film, notebook paper, and my laptop computer, I boarded an early morning jet out of Albuquerque. After a short layover in Houston, my international flight proceeded due south across the full length of Mexico and on to tropical and exotic Belize . . . and into the eye of the storm.

CHAPTER 2

CHALLENGING CHAC

Settling in my seat, I finally had a chance to reflect on where I was headed. Belize, which was once British Honduras, has fabulous beaches, psychedelic coral reefs, and a pristine rain forest chock-full of wild jaguars and unexplored Maya ruins. It's also a major tourist destination.

This was my first trip to the tiny country, notched in between Mexico on the north, Guatemala on the west, and Honduras to the south. Guatemala, though, I was familiar with, having once explored the pyramids of Tikal, a major Maya city abandoned some twelve hundred years ago. The ancient Maya have always fascinated me with their love for extravagant ritual and ceremony, their obsession with calendrics, astronomy, and mathematics. They had a dark side too—ritual human sacrifice. But then, we, too, have our own version of ritual human sacrifice—a history of intentional genocide of minority and indigenous populations.

One of the most intriguing characters of Maya mythology is Chac, the god of rain and lightning. His characteristic trunklike visage, meant to summon the rains, is commonly featured in the masonry motifs of Maya ruins in the arid Yucatan. However, Chac's behavior is highly unpredictable, and he can strike with great power when least expected. Thus, the Maya priesthood was very careful to extend to Chac the highest respect. Those who failed to afford sufficient honor to the all-powerful rain god risked suffering his wrath. In the 1980s, a famous U.S. archaeologist disturbed a shrine hidden deep inside a sacred cave dedicated to Chac. Soon after—on a clear day—a bolt of lightning fatally struck the archaeologist while he was standing atop the sacrificial pyramid at Chichén Itzá.

I knew enough about the complicated pantheon of Maya gods to know that one should not challenge them. The fact that over six hundred ancient Maya cities lay brooding in the jungles of Belize gave me little comfort.

Belize has a history of transformation. A million years ago, while its land was submerged, monolithic coral reefs were formed. Eventually, the sea receded, and mountains emerged that today rise above the sea to almost thirty-seven hundred feet. Over time, mighty rivers carved through the mountains, slashing gorges, gouging out caves, and collapsing into noisy, picture-postcard waterfalls that flushed tons of silt into the ocean. This powerful hydrology produced an ever-broadening, swampy floodplain that provided rich agricultural and fishing resources. Likewise, the inland rain forests offered plenty of shelter and food for an amazing abundance of wildlife. These natural resources attracted the Maya who built their giant cities there and extended their trading network in all directions.

Fortunately, these same natural resources are also appreciated by the Belize government, and consequently over sixty percent of the land remains in tropical forest. Desiring to set an example to the world, Belize set aside five hundred acres for the World Stewardship Council to use as its international headquarters.

A gentle tilt of the plane suggested we were slowly descending. I glanced at my watch. We would be landing soon in Belize City, the country's capital. The landing was routine, but as I disembarked the plane, I had to push my way through the packed crowds of visitors who were arriving for the upcoming WSC Council session.

I now needed to secure passage on a small local airline for the short flight to Earthhope Village, located in a rain forest wilderness area about fifty miles to the southwest. I had noticed dark clouds gathering in the west as we flew in, and I shuddered at the thought of challenging Chac in a light plane.

Challenging Chac

Finally, after many frustrating minutes of locating baggage and dealing with customs, I emerged from the terminal and prepared to board a small, twin-engine thirty-two-passenger prop plane. The eighty-five percent humidity hit me so hard that I barely noticed the first raindrops vaporizing on the overheated asphalt. I raised my head to view a mass of swirling blackness. As I stood there, temporarily paralyzed, other passengers passed me and went up the steps into the cabin to be greeted by the cheerful flight attendants. Was everyone in denial about the weather? Even the pilots, checking out their instruments, appeared oblivious to the menacing maelstrom. Had they made the appropriate offerings to Chac?

Just then the heavenly floodgates opened, and I quickly rushed aboard the plane and squeezed into my three-quarter-size seat. The man next to me, older by about twenty years, appeared perfectly calm. The cabin door closed with a chunk, and we began taxiing down the runway into the premature darkness. Streaks of rain skidded across the window next to me, blurring my last view of the terminal.

I took comfort in the thought that we were taking off rather than attempting to land in this torrential soup, but remained haunted by the fact that we'd need to alight somewhere—and soon. In the next few minutes, the plane climbed determinedly and leveled out as best it could. As the engines relaxed into a comfortable cadence, I turned to the surreally peaceful gentleman at my side. He was dark complected and smartly dressed in a casual, light-colored suit—a traveling official or maybe a staff member at the WSC, I thought.

"Is the weather always this bad?" I asked nervously. We made eye contact, and I caught a smile on my companion's face, suggesting that he found my anxieties humorous.

"Oh, yes, the rain," he said. "It's really quite normal for this time of the year. Are you visiting the WSC?"

"Yes," I responded cheerfully, encouraged that I might have the opportunity to talk with someone familiar with the organization. I noted his Spanish accent and concluded that

English must be his second language. "I'm Tom Westbrook, a journalist for the *Earth Renaissance News*."

"My pleasure, Mr. Westbrook. My name is Xavier Gonzales. I'm an information agent for the WSC."

"Please, just call me Tom."

"Tell me, Tom. Are you concerned about flying in stormy weather?" We both glanced down at my white-knuckled hands, which still gripped the seat arms. I quickly released my hold, embarrassed. Mr. Gonzales smiled compassionately. "Yes, sometimes these flights can be alarming, but I can assure you that we will arrive safely."

Thus relieved, to some extent, I pressed him for information regarding the WSC. I knew the basics, but I was curious to hear what he had to say. He explained how a group of wealthy social-change activists from the United States and other industrial countries had come together to create a global, independent environmental organization to take action where governments had failed. The first step had been to form a planning committee, which then solicited a range of visionary people to design and create the World Stewardship Council.

"Their mission," Mr. G informed me in a most gracious manner, "was to fashion an organizational body with the desire and the means to encourage fundamental global change through the authentic representation of all the world's people, not just the elite few." He paused, narrowed his gaze and continued, adding emphasis. "Moreover, this collective body was to hold paramount the highest ethical standards while also acting in ways imitative of the processes of nature. Its challenge was to discover within itself a primal source of inspiration from which to help guide the people and the governments of the world toward a far more equitable and dignified human presence on the planet."

"A formidable task," I commented.

Mr. G nodded. "The founders next solicited some of the world's wealthiest individuals, those who had profited handsomely from the global entertainment business, mega-successful computer software and fuel cell companies, and shrewd stock market investments. Eco-minded movie and sports stars chipped in hundreds of millions of dollars, as did a few unusually charitable Arab sheiks and large lottery winners.

"A billion-dollar seed fund was raised that enabled the initial staff, drawn from around the world, to implement the WSC concept and construct the headquarters complex here in Belize. Next to be established was the WSC endowment and operations fund, which supports projects, provides loans, and pays modest and appropriate salaries."

"What kind of people are attracted to join the WSC?" I asked a little absently, as the plane began to buck and roll.

Mr. G continued in a smooth, practiced cadence, infused with measured enthusiasm. "The WSC has tried to draw men and women of uncommon imagination and integrity, empathy and wisdom—people gifted with a special blend of intelligence and deep compassion for the Earth and all its beings. You might call them true 'planetary citizens,' people with a strong sense of global civic duty."

"And how does the WSC support itself?"

"The WSC doesn't accept general funding from governments or large, global corporations so as to avoid undue political influence and dependence. We must rely solely on financial contributions from individuals, donation of patent and license rights, and special support groups. This was a conscious choice: The WSC jealously guards its mandate to act as the impartial servant to all the world's people, especially those disenfranchised populations formerly without a voice in official decision-making councils."

"And which group is the primary decision maker?"

"The 64-member Global Policy Council creates and proposes policy, but the 260-member All Peoples Council must render any final decision, and will be debating Resolution 636, the Share Tax. The All Peoples Council's policy proposals and recommendations are usually directed toward specific governments and corporate entities."

"Does the WSC attempt to dictate to governments and corporations? And if they do, how do they respond?"

Mr. G paused, raising his dark eyes toward me. "Although the WSC cannot legally require anyone to follow its recommendations, it does receive considerable respect from the media and the general public, and thus commands a certain amount of global influence.

"Of course, many powerful special interest groups strongly resent the presence of such an independent, illuminating force in the world; they would certainly prefer to continue operating in their typical stealth fashion, unquestioned and unchallenged. On the other hand, those groups and institutions outside the global elite consider the WSC a champion of a more equitable and humane world order."

"So I would imagine that the WSC is cautious when sponsoring mandates that run counter to the interests of the powerful elite."

He smiled confidently. "WSC governing members are very well-informed regarding the state of the planet and the potentially explosive political confrontations certain actions might precipitate. I think WSC decision makers feel that, given sufficient and careful reflection on the matter, their collective wisdom equips them to make fair and accurate decisions that have majority support of the planetary community. And . . . they're not afraid to take risks."

Risks? What kind of risks? I was curious, wanting to know more about the people of the WSC.

My friend explained that from the start the founders believed that if unusually wise men and women did, in fact, exist, they would come forth—given the opportunity and the appropriate context, like the WSC.

Impressed, yet still skeptical. I said to him, "WSC goals are quite laudable, but orchestrating people and technology together smoothly on a global scale seems an almost impossible undertaking."

He smiled, gently tolerant of my disbelief. "For your typical, hierarchical institution—yes, I agree. But the WSC is a special kind of energetic body, determined to utilize human resources and technology in more effective, more creative ways than is usually the case. But, obviously, I'm biased.

You'll just have to see for yourself."

We talked together at least half an hour. And I must admit that I began to agree that the WSC must be something quite special. But Mr. G concurred that the overarching challenge—attempting to rescue a world on the verge of spiraling dangerously out of control—was especially daunting. Moreover, he conceded that the WSC had plunged into the thick of it in deciding to take on the highly controversial Share Tax. Even its members had found themselves divided and confused.

My companion lapsed into a contemplative pause and stared off into space. He then turned to me and said in a hushed, almost prophetic tone, "Something tells me we should expect trouble tomorrow. It's just a hunch. I can't really say what or why. But if you're curious, be there tomorrow."

I detected a certain evasiveness in his statement, but I didn't probe him further. I glanced out my window lost in thought. Down below, I could barely distinguish a seamless black-green landscape through the fog and mist. Over the next few minutes, we slowly descended as our pilot gingerly picked out a tiny airfield amidst the overgrown forest, and headed toward it.

The plane came to a stop on the runway, and the cabin door opened into a driving rain. Courteous attendants greeted us with large, colorful umbrellas, and quickly ushered us into the lobby waiting area. The attendants then separated the passengers into groups. As we shuffled around, Mr. G approached me, shook my hand, and wished me success with my visit to the WSC. As he walked off into the crowd, I experienced a twinge of loss. Something about his presence had provided me with a level of comfort. I stood there silently, watching him fade into the corridors of the airport complex.

I followed a small group to the chartered vans waiting to whisk us off to our respective housing units. After a short ride, we stopped at a settlement of two-story thatched-roof bungalows nestled comfortably under a huge and dense forest canopy. Several hundred yards away I could see what must be the sprawling headquarters complex of the WSC. Its broad, low-slung buildings slid stealthily and unobtrusively into the forest like a jaguar hunting its prey. I went to bed early to recharge my internal batteries and to be fresh and open for the next day's events. I had no idea what to expect.

CHAPTER 3

THE FRAGILE WEB

I looked up. A scalpel of sunlight decended, temporarily blinding me. The tropical brilliance cascaded through a labyrinth of beveled glass set between the polished wooden beams arching gracefully overhead. Multicolored murals adorned the spacious meeting room. Fabulous and detailed scenes depicted endangered plants, animals, and Native cultures—no doubt intended to remind the delegates of what was at stake beyond the broad walls. The interplay of dissonant languages generated an unintelligible chorus that overflowed the expectant space.

This certainly is an impressive hall, I thought to myself, as I moved into the main meeting chamber of the WSC, turning my body right and left, my eyes scanning hungrily, trying to take in all the images, sounds, and ambiance as quickly as possible. Clearly, no effort was spared to insure that the visual impact of the decor would reinforce the lofty ideals of the institution.

"Excuse me sir, would you please take a seat."

I turned to the young female courtesy attendant. "Oh, yes, of course," I responded timidly, as I found a seat and waited for the start of the session.

A single, confident voice pierced the sea of linguistic babel. "The council will now please come to order." All attention focused on Sari Singh, a statuesque, obsidian-haired East Indian woman, who was presently serving as president of the World Stewardship Council.

I had read that Ms. Singh's ability to resolve contention had recommended her for this position. She had recently distinguished herself by mediating a difficult political reconciliation between the Indian government and several dozen rural communities that were bitterly opposed to a huge, ecologically unsound dam-building project. Because of her efforts, the ill-conceived program was ultimately canceled. Instead, the needed electrical power would be delivered by an extensive grid of state-of-the art wind and solar plants, owned and operated by a consortium of Indian villages.

The charismatic president welcomed council members as well as the live audience viewing by satellite.

On cue, motorized shutters moved overhead to shroud the skylights, casting the room in darkness. As the massive sky-doors closed, the room rumbled with low-frequency vibration. Behind and above the speaker's podium, a large woven tapestry featuring stylistic renditions of exotic plants was retracted into the ceiling, revealing a twenty- by thirty-foot-wide, high-resolution video screen flush-mounted against the wall.

The screen flickered to life. Dramatic images of verdant rain forest appeared in brilliant colors. Simultaneously, the raucous cries of jungle monkeys and the dreamy drone of invisible insects permeated the hall.

An extreme close-up of tiger eyes filled the screen. The startling image—twenty feet tall—blazed across the room. The intense beast gripped the audience in its hypnotic stare. A child wailed in the distance, while a single tear gathered in the great cat's molten pupil. The bulging liquid sphere emerged fully formed, pushed slowly over the edge of the tiger's lower eyelid, then skidded downward and out of sight. The animal's face remained frozen, taut, proud, desperate, despite sounds of chain saws and falling trees painfully ripping through the air. The tiger disappeared and was replaced by an exquisite tropical hardwood table poised singularly in an elegant dining room. Then slowly, scenes of smog-blighted cities, smoke-belching power plants, skeleton forests, burning lakes, and idled, rotting fishing boats overflowed the screen. A woman huddled in a cardboard and plastic-sheeted slum dwelling, breast-feeding a vacant-eyed newborn. Barely

The Fragile Web

clothed children played in trash-strewn ditches running over with orange and black foaming water. In the background loomed piles of corroding metal drums.

As the industrial cacophony diminished, Ms. Singh reminded the global TV audience how cycles—air, water, animals, and human life—intersect one another and comprise the delicate web of life; how a seemingly innocuous personal act in one part of the world can drastically affect a distant rain forest and its native inhabitants; how a furniture purchase in New York or Tokyo can deprive a bird, insect, or mammal species in Brazil of its sole habitat or source of food; how indigenous tribes may depend utterly on certain trees and animals in their local area. She went on, "As old-growth trees are removed to become finished wood products elsewhere, a once diverse ecosystem becomes much less life-supporting, and formerly sustainable and self-sufficient local economies are soon rendered untenable. As more and more people purchase goods and services that require the use of toxic chemicals, the world becomes a more hazardous place for all to live. And, ultimately, inevitably, the fragile web of life collapses."

The big screen juxtaposed pictures of towering green rain forests with badly eroded, clear-cut hillsides. Pristine lakes and rivers turned chocolate brown as sewage outflow and pipes emptied their noxious contents upstream. The busy and various sounds of the once-healthy forest yielded to an ambiance of desolate silence. And the large audience hall was quiet, too.

The president's voice rang in urgent appeal. "Those human activities that endanger our environment, our global commons, can no longer be justified. Fundamental, planet-wide systemic change is our only option. We must define a new pathway of living, one that is sustainable for all humans, the world economy, and the environment. To fail in this important undertaking is to invite the certain collapse of civilization as we know it. Therefore, it is our task today to begin creating the means for a new global future."

As the scenes and sounds slowly faded, I felt others

around me grappling with their mangled emotions. My own heart beat too fast for comfort, and I inhaled deeply to quell my building anxiety. I felt stalked by an invisible, undefinable assailant.

President Singh wasted no time. Having completed her quick course on species interdependency and global consequences, she signaled the staff to reopen the skylights. I anticipated the beginning of the long-awaited debate on Resolution 636.

But then, the unexpected happened.

A red light began flashing on the president's desk. Ms. Singh's face betrayed a sudden rush of anxiety as she reached toward her private telephone. Long seconds passed as she listened carefully to the voice at the other end of the line. Upon replacing the receiver, she returned, grasping the podium's chrome-plated microphone in her left hand, seeming to relish its metallic chill. She paused one beat, then two. Ms. Singh appeared to be searching for the perfect words to cool the mounting tension in the room. A wisp of moisture on her brow suggested that forces had been set in motion that she could not control. A compressed hush settled over the audience.

As I scribbled my notes feverishly, I sensed the presence of new factors here. My interest, already high, increased further. I arched my back, straining to obtain a better view of the proceedings. Suddenly, I recalled Mr. G's words about expecting some trouble. Was this it?

The president spoke, "The council has been asked to allow a live video transmission regarding the upcoming debate of Resolution 636. Its source is the Pan American Peoples Alliance or PAPA. I seek the council's consensus on this matter."

A flood of spontaneous chatter forced Ms. Singh to ask for order. Following a short discussion, the council agreed to permit the rogue transmission—but with one condition— that the communication be private, between the council and the PAPA, at least temporarily. It would be taped for later broadcast on the global satellite feed.

Again the room lights dimmed and the skylights were closed. The video screen displayed a sea of silver static that abruptly cleared to reveal the scene of a carefully staged press conference beamed live from some secret wilderness base. Several men and women wearing ski masks were seated around a rough-hewn table situated under a log and leaf arbor. The man directly behind the microphone, dressed in generic military fatigues, introduced himself as El Aguilar (the Eagle), the present spokesperson for the PAPA. He was flanked by several Hispanic and Indian men and women, who conspicuously declined to identify themselves. El Aguilar spoke English flavored with a rich Spanish accent. His voice conveyed long-held frustration and anger. Looking directly into the camera, he delivered his terse and passionate words.

"We, the men, women, children, and elders of the Pan American Peoples Alliance greet you, and express our desire that your dialogue on this very important issue go well. Much is at stake as we find ourselves today besieged by a world order that wages a global war against people, nations, and cultures. It is a war directed from a handful of financial centers by agents without heart or shame. The battle is about money versus humanity.

"But we find allies who share our dissatisfaction, our rebellion, and our desire to bring about positive change. Thus we need no longer continue to tolerate conditions of unrelenting poverty, declining health, and worsening environmental conditions while elsewhere privileged others benefit handsomely at our expense. We need no longer stand by while the new international economic order systematically and purposefully cannibalizes the human and natural resources of the poor and the less powerful nations of the world.

"We believe this economic predation could be greatly lessened by responding forcefully and affirmatively to your Resolution 636, which speaks to the critical matter of global economic inequity. In this concern, we find common ground with the WSC."

El Aguilar paused, allowing several seconds for his remarks to settle. Then he continued, his voice steady and deadly serious. "The Pan American People's Alliance must also warn the council that failure to pass Resolution 636 in a timely manner will result in a series of continent-wide actions against large land owners, power plants, and dams; against coffee, fruit, and timber plantations, and against oil refineries and major industrial centers. The foreign-owned and -financed economic infrastructure of the targeted countries will be strategically dismantled until the full range of social, political, and economic needs of the indigenous tribes, urban poor, and peasant farmers of each region are adequately addressed. No delaying tactics will be permitted. We will, however, allow the world governments time—following the approval of this resolution—to pass the necessary legislation to implement Resolution 636. We are offering a twelve-month grace period. Then we will have no choice but to carry out our program of aggressive response."

Immediately, the transmission ceased, although the PAPA logo, an iridescent green quetzal bird overlaid on an Inca temple, remained on the screen for a long, vacant moment. I slumped down in my seat. Mr. G and my editor were both right. The storm had blown in, trouble had occurred, and I was witness to this unexpected and possibly historic event.

The crowd, however, upon the fading of the video transmission, erupted into chaos as voices emerged from all corners of the room demanding to be heard. The representatives from industrial countries cried "blackmail" and "intimidation." Most Third-World delegates and those representing indigenous cultures, on the other hand, remained silent, quietly mulling over their own position. Having themselves experienced the pain of chronic poverty and disenfranchisement, they could easily empathize with the PAPA's demands. The knottier question seemed to concern the appropriateness of using physical violence to achieve one's goals—even though the accused parties had a year to head off the threat. Violence or the threat of violence does draw attention to matters, however, and such was the central objective of the PAPA's strategy.

The president was hard-pressed to return the assembly to parliamentary order. She said, "As we know from experience, there will be no quick and easy resolution to this challenge. I cannot tell you what to do. But I can offer you some advice. Perhaps we are engaged in a rite of passage, enmeshed in the flow of an evolutionary process that forces us toward a new reality, a new stage of life. There is mystery here, and there is the unknown. To move forward, we must search for that part of ourselves that knows how to find truth. No doubt we will need to dig deep for answers. However, great power is released when truth is revealed. Those decisions that stem from truth will then—in turn—attract allies. And finally, clarity on the large scale will emerge. Of that I am confident."

Ms. Singh paused. "I recommend that we invite the PAPA, and the forces of economic coercion and predation of which it speaks, to join us as partners in this process of factual inquiry, self-discovery, and exploration of change. Because in the final analysis, the will to change must be based on a shared set of values, one that celebrates the richness of our diversity and the benefits thereof. Somehow, we must find common ground that is physical, moral, and spiritual . . . not merely economic. The task before us, then, is to establish a foundation for constructive dialogue and problem resolution. And we must begin now."

A masterful summary and charge to action, I thought. But when I looked deep within myself, I realized I needed more understanding of the issues. No, not just understanding—I wanted something more profound, like *wisdom*. But how to obtain that? Most people don't achieve real wisdom in a whole lifetime.

As I reflected on my inadequacy, I felt lost. Perhaps, I shuddered, I'm not the man for this job. My frustration began to gather momentum. I had to admit that I had little knowledge of the PAPA and even less understanding of the conditions to which they referred. But that was a surface thing, to be fixed by securing additional information. What I truly desired was to somehow increase my own depth of understanding and range of thinking.

I remained in my seat while contemplating my present mental and experiential inadequacies, completely oblivious to the increasing level of crowd noise building around me. Suddenly, I felt overwhelmed by the extent of my own ignorance. I felt myself profoundly alienated from the mass of men and women even in my immediate environment. Finally, I forced myself to move, following the crowd as it flooded toward the large, double exit doors. I departed the room, deeply disappointed with myself. I knew I would need more time to come up to speed, get a better handle on the state of the world and myself. But how and when?

PART I

THE PSYEARTH INSTITUTE

As human beings, our greatness lies not so much in being able to remake the world—that is the myth of the "atomic age"— as in being able to remake ourselves.

—Gandhi

CHAPTER 4

PREPARATION

"Twelve months! I can't stay here for twelve months," I protested. "I've got a job, other articles to write. My editor will go nuts."

During the pause in our conversation, I gradually became aware of the forest that surrounded me. Its sweet pine odors and distant animal noises rapidly absorbed my desperate words. I reflected on the fact that, only seven days ago, I had sat paralyzed with despair in the World Stewardship Council chambers in Belize. But now I was now back in New Mexico, with an assignment to do a story on the PsyEarth Institute.

My gaze remained fixed on my counselor, a neatly dressed African-American man in his forties named Jefferson Morgan. We were sitting comfortably in oversized wooden chairs arranged circular fashion on the flagstone-covered outdoor patio. Jefferson had moved to the PsyEarth Institute from Denver, Colorado where he had founded a successful recovery and rehabilitation program for inner-city gang members. Obviously, he had dealt with some tough cases.

His calm demeanor suggested an inner confidence not only in himself, but perhaps in me as well. He asked respectfully, "Aren't you here to use part of your time to write an article? Perhaps your editor will be understanding."

Certainly, that was possible, I agreed. One reason I signed up was to write an article about the institute. But I also wanted to believe there was something of personal value in their program for me.

"I'll speak to Jack," I said, "and let you know." This would also give me time to think it over. Jefferson smiled with approval as we shook hands and I took my leave.

The gravity of this particular commitment weighed heavily on my mind as I walked along a pine-needled path guarded on both sides by ancient pine trees. I inhaled deeply, drawing in the thick and sensual odors of the cool forest. The gently curving trail eventually led me into the spacious lobby of the PsyEarth Institute's main building. Here I found literature explaining that the name "PsyEarth" is intended to describe the potential for reunion of psyche and Earth: psyche being soul, spirit, mind, the principle of mental and emotional life, the conscious and the unconscious, and Earth the living organic being we inhabit. The PsyEarth Institute's mission, then, is to create an experience and provide an environment where the individual can reconnect his or her soul, spirit, mind, and consciousness with that of the Earth. To facilitate this process, the institute had acquired a collection of rustic, yet comfortable buildings and hermitages located within a ten-thousand-acre private mountain ranch near the Gila Wilderness in southern New Mexico. My plan had been to visit the institute for a couple of weeks to investigate its leadership training curriculum. I certainly hadn't intended to stay for the whole twelve-month program. But perhaps destiny had decreed otherwise.

The next program cycle at the institute was to begin on June 20, the summer solstice. It was now mid-June. But program participants would not need to report to the institute until August 1. The six-week prep period was intended to allow time for enrollees to reflect on their commitment to the process and place their physical affairs in order. This gave me enough time to sublet my apartment, take care of business, and communicate with friends and family. As I contemplated this rather vigorous undertaking I wondered if I had the "right stuff?"

According to Jefferson, beginning August 1, I would join a team of fourteen people and undergo six weeks of intensive training in wilderness living skills. Each person would be dispatched to a small, isolated cabin somewhere in the nearby wilderness area. There we'd each live alone in complete seclusion for three months. The purpose of Phase I, the "Clarification Phase," was to trigger a process of "directed personal self-examination." That, at the time, seemed to me to be the most difficult part of the program.

Phase II, the "Communication Phase," required the survivors of Phase I to reside at their forest retreats for another three months. During this time, however, we would work with other team members, meeting once a week in a central location. Our task would be to refine the intuitive skills we acquired during Phase I. We'd also learn to exercise special "mental communication techniques," taking us deeper into uncharted psychological territory.

In Phase III, the "Expression Phase," which lasts for six weeks, we'd trade our woodsy dwellings for dormitory space back at the institute. Then we'd begin the hard work of rooting out old psychological patterns that might prevent us from attaining our full potential. Next we'd team up with partners of the opposite sex to explore the benefits of properly balanced male and female energy.

During the final six weeks, the "Application Phase," we'd focus on taking ourselves to the next level of possibility—the "new man and woman of the twenty-first century." To help in our quest, we'd undertake the study of natural law and the lives of extraordinary men and women.

This, in a nutshell, describes the PsyEarth Short Cycle Program. In the more advanced, four-year, Extended Cycle Program, each phase lasts one year. After two years, I've been told, one is able to experience much more of the "Paleolithic Mind" and the "Millennium Mind"—the best of the past and the highest potential for the future. The Paleolithic Mind remembers the "Old Ways," the natural wisdom of our ancestors. The Millennium Mind, or "New Mind," on the other hand, conceptualizes and implements wholly innovative ways of thinking.

Later that afternoon, I called Jack at the office and discussed the situation with him. After he recovered from the shock of my request for a twelve-month leave, he somewhat reluctantly agreed to let me "go for it," assuming he could find a temporary staff replacement.

The next day I met with Jefferson in his office. He looked me straight in the eye and said in an unusually serious tone, "Tom, are you prepared to face whatever demons might be waiting for you out there? And can you trust?"

"Trust in what?" I responded, slightly unnerved by his remark, and consciously ignoring the first part of the question.

He relaxed as he sensed my tension. "In your ability to sustain yourself, physically and psychologically—come what may."

I took a few moments to consider his question, once again staring through the expansive picture windows at the dark pines outside—like the void into which I would soon enter. I relaxed my mind and body, realizing I needed to reach deep inside myself. There I found a distinct but tentative "yes."

"Yes, I think so."

"Good," he responded flatly. But I wanted more encouragement. Instead, I was forced to fall back on my own inner resources. Seconds later, I realized my training had already begun.

Back in Albuquerque, I began to put my affairs in order. Strangely, I felt like I was preparing people—and myself—for my own death. Was I going to disappear from the Earth forever, step off a cliff into darkness? I shivered at this prospect, but continued to press on with my departure-related tasks.

I'd been given a list of things I would need for six months in the wilderness and four and a half months at the institute—mostly clothes, a backpack and camping equipment, some good boots and shoes, and journals to write in. That was about it. When the car was packed, I stared at the gear I had gathered, surprised. I couldn't believe how little I was allowed to bring for ten and a half months. I would learn to live very simply indeed.

I arrived at the institute a day before the preliminary session was to begin. After spending the night in the guest units, our group was summoned for a morning session in the lodge. The high-altitude mountain air carried a sharp chill, heralding the fact that fall was waiting in the wings. Having just endured two months of hot summer weather, I welcomed the refreshing coolness.

Entering the lodge, I saw my team members for the first time: six men and seven women, several from foreign countries. Everyone spoke English, although for some it was their second language. I scanned the faces of my fellow psybernauts who were about to join me in diving off into the abyss.

After the institute's staff introduced themselves, they explained that following six weeks of preparation, we'd be assigned huts in the forest about three miles apart. A five-day supply of food, water, and fuel would be stockpiled at special bases. These were the rules: We would transport our own supplies by foot to our cabins; contact with others was prohibited except in an emergency; no books were allowed except those on the recommended list; no electrical devices were permitted except those already present in the hermitages or specially approved. We would learn to form a new kind of relationship—individual human with planet Earth—for the duration.

We were told that a major purpose of our time of solitude would be to challenge the notion of life and culture as solely human-centered. "What better way to confront such erroneous thinking than to remove other humans from the picture entirely?"

But, dissolving five thousand years of cultural programming could not be accomplished overnight, we were cautioned. Indeed, heroic measures are required to shatter the seductive trance in which we find ourselves. Our imminent experience, though, would provide an escape route—a kind of outdoor 12-step program to launch us onto a path of recovery from Western civilization.

During breaks in the meeting, we joked about the madness of our undertaking, although I sensed an underlying current of excitement. We viewed ourselves as pioneers, pushing the edge of the frontier, setting forth to explore new territories—at least by those of us born into contemporary Western culture.

At a quiet moment in the schedule, I reflected on what lay ahead. I felt a sense of foreboding. Was I ready for such radical change? Was I willing to give up personal patterns and ways of thinking and relating that were flawed perhaps, but still personally familiar and comfortable? I wrestled with this question for days. No definitive answers came. No resolution occurred.

I was also very curious to discover if I was alone in my battle with these concerns. Did anyone else harbor such doubts? During the introduction, my attention was drawn to one individual, a woman, and the only Native American in the group. She seemed about my age and was dressed in shorts and an indigo velvet blouse. A strand of finely crafted turquoise beads hung around her neck. Her name was Jenny Begay-O'Brien, half Navajo, half Irish. Her strong self-confidence attracted me, as did her clear, dark face which spoke of generations of ancestors born and buried in harsh desert lands. So, too, did I marvel at her cascading coal black hair that plunged unimpeded to her waist. The only hint of Irishness I could detect was an elfin sparkle in her eyes that spoke of independence, determination, and purpose.

I met with Jenny later that day, and following the usual fumblings of first-time conversations, I shared my misgivings regarding the challenges that lay ahead. For almost an hour, we sat together under a canopy of fir trees, the wind gently spiraling the scent of the forest around us. I remained mostly quiet, preferring to learn from her potent sense-of-self. I admitted shyly that I did not share her inner confidence, but hoped I would some day. Impulsively, she grasped my hands and looked deep into my eyes. "It's there," she whispered. "It's hidden within, just waiting to be released. Be patient."

My eyes began to moisten as her powerful words of encouragement struck home. Over the following weeks, I continued to meet with Jenny as time and schedule permit-

Preparation

ted. Her presence and caring served as an anchor, helping me to sort out my feelings. But most importantly, her company kindled in me a lightness, a newfound confidence and awareness that life could, indeed, be extraordinarily beautiful.

During the first week of our wilderness training program, we were introduced to the mental and physical skills we'd need to master to live safely during the upcoming winter. When one student complained about such prolonged isolation, a staff member named Loren described a truly extreme method of personal training: "Consider the Kogi Tribe in the remote highlands of Columbia. They'd place selected young children alone in a cave for nine years. Each child received a store of basic foods, but no meat or salt. This experience was to teach the child-student to intimately come to know the spirit world and the cosmic forces of Creation. After nine years in the cave, the young, supersensitive Kogi could communicate with a powerful guardian force known as *A-luna*, or 'the Mother' and her spirit manifestations."

Loren went on to explain that according to the Kogi, A-luna is fertility and abundance—the Mind Inside Nature. "A-luna," she continued, "is considered the inner reality of the world wherein resides the eternal, the void, and the place to which everything returns. The Kogi say the Mother has created the Earth, its people, and the guardian spirits of everything. While living in near total darkness, the Kogi child initiate learned to meditate on and honor these spirits. Later in life, the adult initiated Kogi would become powerful seers, accurately and wisely guiding the community in ways according to natural law.

"But now the Kogi say the guardians are seriously weakened—sick, ill, and dying as a result of several centuries of industrialization. Alarmed by local evidence of climate change, the Kogi have issued an ominous warning to 'Younger Brother,' the industrial man and woman. Younger Brother is carelessly violating fundamental principles, destroying all order and damaging the world. Younger Brother must change his ways immediately!

"The Kogi are now doubtful their prayers can continue

to hold the world in balance. They feel strongly about this matter and have tried to communicate their concerns to the world. Meanwhile, the Kogi believe it is critically important for them to maintain an intimate connection with the planet's guardian spirits.

"We are not the Kogi," Loren reminded us. "Still, we can utilize a modified version of the cave experience to achieve similar states of awareness and sensitivity. Our technological world is full of distraction, difficult and diverse people, and highly complex social, political, and economic problems. This is our own unique and daunting reality. Nevertheless, we share the same atmosphere and planetary environment as the Kogi. Since maintenance of all societies on the planet is reliant on the proper functioning of our planet's climate, we would all do well to heed the Kogi's urgent admonitions."

I looked around. I could see that at twenty-eight, I was a little younger than the average student. Most of the others appeared to be in their mid-thirties, although a few were fresh out of college and even more unsure of themselves. With some hesitation, we began to disclose our feelings about the coming time of solitude.

"I've never done anything like this before. I'm not sure how I'll handle it," I remarked, taking the lead.

"So much isolation. That'll be hard," said Osaki, an alert, bright-eyed woman from Japan.

"I'm sure I can handle the physical aspects of living in the woods," said David, a healthy, outdoors type from northern California with a full beard and mustache. "It's the interpersonal stuff—dealing with people—I'm not so good at."

"I'll miss my family very much," mumbled a shy, young Mexican woman named Alisa. "And I'm not used to cold weather and snow."

"This will be a rather different experience for me. I don't know what to expect, but I'm willing to try almost anything," said Björn, a thirtyish Swedish man, who appeared somewhat intellectual, but highly confident.

"I know I'll be terrified at night up there all alone," remarked Carol, a feisty, energetic woman from Boston. "But

Preparation

it can't be as dangerous as spending the night in our city parks."

"No cell phone. No CDs. No TV. No *Wall Street Journal*! I'll be glad to be rid of it all," said a young man from New York. His voice, though, betrayed a more covert emotion—anger. His forceful response quickly diverted the attention of the entire gathering. His name was Lawrence Sullivan, and I learned that he had recently graduated from an East Coast business school. His father, a highly successful but domineering man, had expected Lawrence to assume the directorship of the family's stock brokerage firm. But Lawrence had zero interest in stock markets. He told us that he had applied to the PsyEarth Institute program partly to escape his father's relentless pressure, but also hoping that the wilderness experience would provide him with a new personal direction.

"I'm afraid I'll become terribly lonely," admitted Lynne, a light-haired, fragile-looking woman in her forties who spoke with a British accent.

"Why do it then?" Margaret asked. "Why did you come?"

"I need to challenge myself. And I believe the planet needs special people now. I think I can do something to help," Lynne replied.

We moved around the circle and Jenny's turn finally came. All eyes fixed on her in hushed anticipation of her response. In a direct, but restrained manner, she spoke from the heart. "I want to become more intuitive and develop skills I know I have but can't completely access just yet. And I want to be able to share this knowledge with others."

A collective sigh of acknowledgment rose from the circle.

Finally, an older woman named Claudia closed the circle with her quiet remark, "I'm doing it for myself—and for the children."

Tears forced themselves into my eyes. A rush of emotion swept through me, uninvited, like an errant summer breeze. I was so proud of these men and women. They cared greatly. It was written across their faces. Scared, yes, of what was to come. They feared failure, of course, but they exuded a latent power of inner strength. I had no doubt they would push themselves to the limit.

Our guides offered constant encouragement. At the end of the day, they delivered their pep talk. "You'll soon have the opportunity to go deeper within yourself than ever before. For those of you more familiar with computers than nature, it's a chance to explore nonvirtual reality, *psyberspace*—with a P-S-Y, not C-Y. *Psy* is the deep self, the unconscious or, some might say, the soul. Your own and the Earth's. Nature's. And where you'll travel is not limited by computer memory, disk size, or CD capacity. We're talking about the greatest, most powerful database ever created—nature herself. You'll learn to access this infinite mega file and cosmic internet, navigate within it, surf across it, download important intuitive files . . . and make it your friend, your ally."

I looked at my team members nested comfortably in sofas, chairs, and on floor pillows spread about the lodge. No words passed between us. Yet I could read their faces—formerly radiant with innocent courage—first shimmer, then contract with nagging doubt. This sounds difficult, my own mind warned.

Our head guide, Margaret, an ex-Outward Bound leader in her forties spoke with passion and challenge in her eyes. "To put it another way, think of your mind and body as sentient technology, ready to interact with the Earth and nature. Remember, we are constantly surrounded by a multidimensional library chock-full of information and ancient wisdom. You can also regard nature and your environment as a repository of sacred knowledge, accessible when you sincerely and unconditionally open yourself to its gifts. Think of your surroundings as mentor or whatever works for you. But don't be afraid to ask for help—from within or without."

During the next two weeks, our guides taught us simple methods of meditation—how to quiet the mind and tap into the beauty and serenity of silence. How to invite communication with animals, the trees, the "Earthmind." The key, we were told, is to empty oneself. We were instructed to take all that we are, our sum total of personal psyche, our complete

Preparation

internal and external selves, and breathe it out into the space that surrounded us. Then to wait for the response. But our guides declined to tell us what to expect next. When we asked, they just smiled knowingly.

We were also taught Tai Chi, yoga, and other concentration techniques to help us maintain high levels of physical fitness and mental acuity. We had classes in cooking and basic survival skills. Though food, water, and fuel would be supplied, and assistance was readily at hand in case of an emergency, we were encouraged to be self-sufficient as long as possible.

Our six weeks of preparation came to an end. Now it was time to begin our odyssey of aloneness. Staff led us in a collective ritual to welcome the autumn equinox. As a slender, razor-edged first quarter moon lifted effortlessly above the grassy clearing where we stood with our hands clasped, we stared quietly into the forest that would soon become our home for the next six months. I wondered what lay ahead. Our counselors had recommended that we ask the creatures and the invisible elements of the forest, into whose domain we would soon tread, to be kindly received. From the look of all the reverent, lowered eyes, I concluded that each one of us, in our own way, actively solicited such help. The next day we would commence our journey into the unknown, the forest and wherever else our paths might lead.

CHAPTER 5

CLARIFICATION

The fall equinox arrived bringing the crisp cool air of autumn. It was harvest time for many traditional cultures, and a time when preparations are made for the long, cold months ahead. Summer's bright colors were fading as once-vibrant plant flesh turned to brown-gray parchment, soon to become compost for new life—nine months hence.

"Pay attention. Be aware of what is happening around you," we were gently reminded by our ever-vigilant staff. "The change of season is part of the learning process. Consider how your own lives might parallel what is happening in nature."

I found this advice encouraging for it showed me in a concrete way how the cycles of nature can be linked to the human process. It made sense that during fall and winter, nature's time of involution, I would also have an annual opportunity for inward reflection. Usually, I'm too much in high-speed work mode, but this year, I'd given myself the time and space to explore the human-nature-cycle relationship.

The long-awaited day arrived. Our time had come time to enter the wilderness. The morning of our departure had greeted us with cool, brilliant sunshine. An intense feeling of anticipation hovered over us while we gathered together in a small clearing near the trailhead. A truck had delivered our gear—fourteen bulging backpacks—into which we had packed our critical items, carefully and lovingly.

My pack, an older, well-traveled but adequate frame model, was one of the first unloaded, giving me an opportunity to observe my fellow team members. As they made final pack adjustments, they unknowingly communicated much about themselves.

David from California looked as if he had come prepared to pose for a camping equipment catalog—everything correct, neat, and state of the art.

Osaki, the diminutive Japanese woman, was dwarfed by her pack. I couldn't imagine her hiking very far with such a load. But she radiated staunch determination and disproportionate physical energy.

Lawrence, on the other hand, stood by himself at a distance from the group in the shade of a large cottonwood tree. He appeared lost. His catalog-fresh backpack was askew, gear not fastened properly, plastic wrapping still covering his foam pad. Lawrence seemed rather fearful but unable to ask for help. I watched several staff observing him closely, probably debating whether or not to intervene.

But I was most intent on locating Jenny. She was in front of the truck making last-minute adjustments to her purple Kelty pack. Fastened to the back of her hair, a suede-wrapped, six-inch gray-and-white-spotted eagle feather twisted randomly in the breeze. She looked great in her well-worn jeans, russet shirt, and turquoise necklace. Unlike all the rest of us, she had chosen special footwear—a pair of ankle-high leather moccasins. I exhaled slowly, moved by her exotic, otherworldly beauty. When I approached, she welcomed me with a warm smile.

"I wanted to see you off," I said staring into her dark eyes.

She smiled, bent over her pack, zipping open a side compartment. She removed an object wrapped in a scarlet velvet cloth.

"Here, this is for you," she said, gently offering me the gift.

Speechless and oblivious to all the activity taking place around us, I carefully unwrapped the package. The folds of soft velvet parted to reveal a single three-inch eagle feather whose base was wrapped in rawhide.

CLARIFICATION

Jenny then spoke to the power of the feather. "The eagle represents the Great Spirit. It is Eagle who flies high above and knows all that is happening below. Eagle can teach you about the realm of spirit. Eagle can give you courage, so you can call upon Eagle for help if trouble comes. If you place your prayers into the feather, the wind will carry them to the Creator. The feather is very precious, very sacred, so it must be handled with great respect and care."

"Thanks, Jenny," I responded, deeply moved. "I will keep it with me always."

Sensing the moment of departure rapidly approaching, I stepped forward and gave her a cautious hug, not caring what others might think. A powerful charge of electricity coursed through me. The voices of counselors summoning the group to assembly finally pulled us apart. I walked back toward my pack, clutching my eagle feather and vowing to retain the energy of the moment. Then with my own pack heavy on my shoulders, I joined the group to receive last-minute instructions and directions to our retreat huts. A final well-wishing ceremony ensued, and we began our trek into the unknown.

As the trail continued into the woods, our group withered: fourteen became ten, became five, became two. Along the way Jenny, her eagle feather bouncing with each step she took, disappeared alone down a remote creekside trail. Soon, I was on my own and finally on my way.

My directions had me crossing a small river of cold, clear water and through a broad swampy valley deep in high green grass. Next, I began a gradual three-mile ascent through a thick pine forest. The extra thirty-five pounds I was carrying slowed my pace considerably and I sweated profusely. Finally, late in the afternoon, as the forest shadows lengthened, I attained the mountain's summit. My spirits lifted as a dark stand of trees expanded to reveal a hundred yards beyond, a small stone cabin nestled in a clearing. The cabin would be my home for the next six months.

At first, time on the mountain moved slowly. I had settled easily into my sixteen-foot round, stone house, tucked neatly between several large boulders and an assortment of spindly pine trees on a dragon-spine ridge. Margaret had said that men were assigned to circular buildings while the women were given square structures. It was thought that each gender—born with a particular form of energy—would benefit from the opposite energy. According to the principles of energy flow, the circle evokes feminine forces whereas the square draws forth male energy. So, we were told, certain physical architecture can be utilized to assist men and women to more easily balance their internal energetic fields.

I had all the essentials: a small kitchen with wood stove and solar-heated water for washing and bathing. The cabin contained a good bed; decent sitting and lounging chairs and a table; and best of all a small porch with sweeping views to the east, south, and west. To the east lay a steep fir-covered ridge, which I hoped would function to direct lightning away from my area. To the west the landscape presented an unobstructed view of endless forest. To the south rose a large, bizarrely gnarled, weather-eroded volcanic pinnacle that jutted incongruous and naked above the forest floor. I found myself strongly attracted to the formation and wondered often about the source of its mysterious draw. I also had a free-running stream about a twenty-minute hike away.

Every fifth day, I walked the three-mile round trip to my supply dump where I collected food and water, then packed it up the steep trail to my cozy home on the hill. On each trip, I found the usual store of grains, beans, fruits, vegetables, and other essentials like toilet paper, and occasional treats of chocolate. I could leave messages as well for individuals to respond to or pass on to the appropriate parties. Drop-off and pick-up times were scheduled to avoid all human contact.

My daily routine began with rising just before dawn and performing a short sun-welcoming ritual. Staff had instructed us to direct our attention to each of the four directions, then to the Earth and sky, giving thanks for the gifts of life and another fine day. We were also encouraged to remember our families at this time, and if needed, solicit guidance and assis-

CLARIFICATION

tance in the form of prayers addressed to whatever deity or deities to which we subscribed.

Following the morning invocations, I prepared my breakfast, usually a granola or egg variation, and then began my daily routine of meditation, yoga, and aerobic exercises. Later I substituted chopping wood for my cabin-porch aerobics. Often, I spent several hours writing in my journal, the purpose of which was to help me track the movement of my inner feelings and personal process. After a lunch of cheese, nut butters, and fruit, I ventured out on a hike to learn as much as I could from my environment. A simple dinner in the evening usually consisted of boiled vegetables and grains. Occasionally, I received canned or smoked meat. Evening time was reserved for reflection on the day's events and noticings, reading of inspirational literature, more writing, or, for me, long hours of guitar playing.

My task during the time of sunset and dusk was to pay close attention to the subtle changes in light and forest activity and to relate these changes to my own movements in consciousness. Night was a time for traveling into the dream world and carefully noting in my dream journals, the nature, tenor, and substance of the images and stories that washed through my unconscious mind.

While this sounds very wonderful, I found the adjustment rather difficult. At first I had trouble sleeping. The many strange sounds of the forest were unsettling, especially the cacophony of coyote calls, the cracking of sticks in the forest near the cabin, the occasional random thump on the roof—of unknown origin—and the pitter-patter of little feet across the cabin's roof. We were told to expect regular visitations by large and small animals such as bear, deer, raccoons, mice, chipmunks, coyote, and perhaps an itinerant mountain lion. Consequently, I made sure I was settled into my cabin by nightfall. I took great comfort in the solid stone walls of my circular shelter and always made sure my food supplies were well-secured in the locking metal box outside the cabin.

I've always craved time alone, but about two weeks into my tour of duty, I began to experience increasing emotional turbulence. I realized how dependent I was on the high-stimulus environment of television, radio, newspapers, magazines, and constant human interaction. Suddenly, these diversions were gone. A gaping hole remained. I was alone with myself, my thoughts, and the immense silence of the vast forest.

On one hand, everything I used to worry about—how I looked to others, how well the job got done—became mercifully irrelevant. Worldly things no longer mattered. To my surprise, however, strong feelings of guilt, anger, frustration, and despair arose. I found myself relentlessly tormented, sometimes for days at a time.

Finally, there was no avoiding it. I was forced to assess my life. Looking back on many years of effort, I concluded that, on balance, I had failed my culture, corrupt as it was, failed my father's expectations, and failed myself. "What to do?" I asked myself one particularly gloomy evening, while staring out a dirty window at the departing sun. "What next?"

This was what our journals were intended to process. I would speak to mine, render my thoughts in writing, seek solace in pen and paper. And so I began.

Silence. Except for the gentle roll of the fire occasionally punctuated by random incendiary crackles, I hear nothing. This land is so quiet. In stillness, I sit paralyzed in my chair beside my stove, gazing outside into the dense infinity of the sleeping forest.

Scanning inside, I find only barren, lifeless soil. I ask myself, what have I to show for all my years on this planet? Have I accomplished anything useful that might be noted by the scribe of passing time? Has all this being, eating, doing, talking, writing, sweating, loving, crying, laughing, touching, expressing that was—that is—me, come to naught?

I sink deeper into the fetid swamp of No Answers. The burden of a life failed by the only standards that seem to count—material accumulation and professional accomplishment—close off all doors of escape. One by one, air passages are sealed. I feel trapped. I gasp for breath.

Clarification

I set aside my pen and reflected. An eighty-year-old friend had recently said to me, "Life is so quick. Why, I can remember what I was doing at eighteen like it was only yesterday!"

Could I do that, too? I wondered. I'd go back to the beginning, review my life, see if it had indeed served no useful purpose, accomplished nothing of import, had no merit.

And so I did, starting with my childhood and moving through each memorable era, stopping to relish those moments that held special meaning. I knew my remembrances would mean nothing to anyone else, would seem wholly trivial. But no matter. For me they evoked soft tears, feelings of quiet cherishing, private points in time I could share only with the Earth, with time, and my soul. I felt the value of these small things to be considerable, and I tried to take pride in them.

I traveled through time while in my simple wooden chair. My wilderness retreat provided safety from the harsh reality of phantom critics lying in wait beyond its walls. I tallied my experiences, my meetings with remarkable people, my technical knowledge, and my personal achievements. I went deeper: intimate affairs held and lost, the tears of pain, women dearly loved, and all that had been shared between each one and me. I reviewed the music I had played and the smiles on thankful faces. I remembered with intense satisfaction my brief forays into the wilderness, seeking release from a form that was not really me. I recalled how I had sought to free the primal, the unfettered spirit that lives deep within my shadow, that part of me finding safety only in the places of wild things and no one else.

I remembered articles written for small publications—travel pieces with heart, I liked to call them. No mean feat, I reminded myself. "These things are nothing to be ashamed of," my inner voice asserted. And finally, it said, "Realize where you are. If you'd not acted spontaneously, risking scarce savings and setting aside your present commitments, this rare and essential experience would not exist as part of your life. It is powerful testimony to the essential, fundamental rightness of your decisions and the deep determination you feel for exploring meaning in your life."

So, have I indeed accomplished something worthy? I asked myself. Perhaps I can be proud of my life, what I'm doing now and the path I'm headed down. But again, the doubts surfaced. Deep inside, I found myself lacking any semblance of inner confidence. I began to obsess on all the failures I remembered in my life: opportunities lost, major miscalculations, stupid decisions. The many times I let people down. How could they ever forgive me? A brooding fear and anxiety welled up, becoming a poison that rapidly spread throughout my body. I sank into a state of disconsolation. I needed to find its source.

I fed the stove another dry log. It belched approvingly. I returned to my journal.

All my life I've tried to do "the right thing," but I've not felt the kind of validation I would have expected, would have wished for. I've felt so alone sometimes—like an alien in my own home, my community, and on my planet. And there's always been this nagging desire, or sense of mission, that I must try and change the world. Why do I feel this way?

I looked deeper into my psyche and continued writing.

I see civilization as illogical. Most people seem to act from a place of self-centeredness and greed. Governments and corporations seem appallingly selfish and insensitive, merely interested in hoarding power and exploiting the public for power and profit. Mass media exist only to con people into purchasing unnecessary products, while force-feeding vulnerable minds with seductively packaged stupidity and relentless, mindless violence. And we wonder why children kill children dispassionately.

I've had to live in this insane world, a place I've wanted no part of, where I've judged myself an outsider. If I could have ignored it all and lived on my own island populated only with good, caring people, perhaps I wouldn't have minded. Let the rest of the world choke on its own toxic waste. They've fouled the nest. But I have not the luxury to live unaffected by the ignorance of my fellow human beings. For I, too, am part of the planet's six-billion-person dysfunctional family.

I reflected: Though I'd spent much of my life trying to save the ship while secretly searching for the lifeboat or escape hatch, I found myself still here in the midst of it all, grasping for meaning, probing for answers, and regurgitating a sense of personal failure. But where did I lose it? Where did I lose my confidence?

I recalled how, upon graduation from college, I felt I could do anything I wanted. The world was my playground. As an upper-middle-class white male, I would be accorded the keys to the hierarchy of political and economic power. But I never accepted that precious membership. Instead, I searched for a different world, one more humane and noble. But such a world was nowhere in sight. At least I had no awareness of it, I sighed to myself. And certainly, the events I had recently witnessed at the World Stewardship Council—the very real and critical concerns raised by the PAPA—served as powerful testimony to the failure of human leadership to design a more equitable society.

So, who's to blame? I asked my journal. *Is it me, my parents, my nation, my culture? Yes, it seems, all of the above. But the source of the error message is Culture—our collectively agreed upon worldview. And the messages of Western Culture completely dominate our thoughts and actions. If we fail to challenge its process, or to consciously acknowledge its insidious and psychologically destructive message, we become its passive victims. Thus, if we unquestionably accept the messages of Western Culture, which are all materially based, we will continue to live our lives desperately searching for some ultimate, but unattainable satisfaction. In the meantime, our life light slowly fades. Sometimes, it seems as if some unspeakably vile and sinister, vampirelike demon has pierced our very souls and will not cease until we are reduced to dry, lifeless, husks of flesh.*

I shivered and moved my chair closer to the stove. As I reflected further, I found myself sliding down a tunnel, into a forbiddingly dark place. I struggled to check my fall, but nothing worked. As I examined my uncontrolled mental tumbling, my worry intensified. What if I, an uncommon person perhaps, but willing to question and grapple with such difficult matters, am unsuccessful in my quest for understanding? What hope is there then for those men and women comfortably mired in denial and wed unknowingly to a flawed cultural mind-set or paradigm? Are we doomed as a species, then, if we blindly continue down this path of slow psychological degradation and physical destruction? It seemed so.

I searched for answers, but none were forthcoming that night. In desperation, I crawled into my sleeping bag, and allowed the darkness to enfold me. I wept for myself, for my fellow humans, for the animals and plants, and for the Earth. I slept uneasily that night, but images of Jenny's face flashed intermittently throughout my dreams, as if she sensed my bitter inner turmoil and strove to offer help from afar.

The next day I pondered my struggles of the previous night. We'd been warned about this in class, that painful emotions and difficult questions would rise from the depths to challenge us. The shadow would have its day, its nights, its weeks with us. Our guides had cautioned us to prepare for a blood bath, a fight to the death with no quarter given. The antidote, we were advised, is to *surrender*. I recalled their advice, delivered in voices heavy with the weight of experience. "When it comes, and it will . . . just surrender to it all. Allow the fears and horrors to engulf you, the pain to penetrate every cell of your body, the sorrow to shatter your sensibilities, the grief to grasp you in its asphyxiating grip until total exhaustion emerges victorious. Then just let go. Let it all go." I could hear Margaret's slow, solemn voice. "Let the old, worn-out self that used to be you simply expire. Bury the body quickly. Thank it for its support and offer it up to maggots for speedy composting."

This was, after all, the season of death. Winter-whipped winds had already begun to race through the pines that shielded my small stone shelter. The cottonwoods along the creek had shed the last of their yellow leaves, and squadrons

Clarification

of squirrels worked overtime to gather adequate food. A dimmer sun, barely skimming the tree tops, meant that night crept closer sooner. Winter solstice, December 21, the shortest day and longest night of the year, loomed nearer. I felt the growing darkness as my own shadow . . . closing in on me, revealing itself to me as inadequacy, confusion, incompetence, and failure. The venom of self-doubt worked its treachery until all seemed lost.

I continued to seek some bit of resolution to my mental concerns during my daily meditations and afternoon hikes. With no human communication and no distractions except for my daily duties, my sensitivity to my environment began to sharpen. I began to sense a growing terror in the trees, an anxiety in the plants, a worry in the water. Anger. I felt powerless to affect anything in the world. And I became even angrier and more depressed.

"Release and accept," they'd said. "When you hit the wall and can't go any farther, just let go of all your burdens. Accept the nature of humanity and the world the way it is. Love it. Send it compassion."

Release was hard enough, but *acceptance*, the acceptance of even myself with all my faults, failures, and dashed expectations and powerlessness, I found even more difficult. I wrestled with my unwillingness for days and weeks. Each morning I asked for guidance from the trees, the Divine, the sacred Earth, and the spirit world. I prayed for insight, for a perspective that could help me find release from my prison of self-imposed criticism.

Days passed, routine and uneventful. Day after day I continued to cling to my process, determined to break through my internal blocks and find a way to the other side. I thought often of Jenny, recalling her bright loving face and wondering how she was and what she was doing at that moment. I wished I could meet with her, but that was impossible. All I had was where I was. It was here, then, where I'd need to seek my solace, my solutions—if there were any—to the troubles that haunted me.

Each day I pondered my spectacular surroundings.

Proud pine, fir, and spruce trees stood tall, weathering the rain, wind, snow, absorbing whatever forces nature hurled against them. So too, the rocks on which my cabin rested remained unperturbed. They seemed always there for me, carrying out their service in silence, providing support. The stream below the ridge continued dashing down its rocky course, despite the imperialistic imperative of below-freezing temperatures that sought to halt in place the independent liquid, rendering its happy movement into enforced, stilled silence.

"Look to your environment, your context, for guidance," Margaret had said. I glanced at the eagle feather pinned on the wall above my bed. Into it I projected my prayer for knowledge, for liberation. I trusted that my petition was on its way to Eagle, to grant me a broader vision.

Days, weeks, a month passed; finally, I began to detect subtle changes. I began to see things differently. The trees outside my cabin took on new shades of color, the rocks appeared somehow friendlier, more available. The stream began to murmur more, almost speaking to me.

I wrote in my journal. *I sometimes doubt the messages my senses provide because I doubt the context in which I find myself. When I do this, I feel powerless and separated from reality. But when I credit the context in which I reside with meaning, with value, I experience connection, belonging, acceptance, a sense of purpose. And if I really value that sense of purpose, then the failures, lost opportunities, stupid decisions, and my perceived betrayal of others' trust are seen in a new light. I suspect there is a purpose to all of this—to allow me a chance to experiment, to learn, to grow, to understand what hurts and pains others and myself. I can then look back on my behavior and learn from it. I can discard that which is unhelpful and reinforce that part of myself I judge to be much more in resonance with what I truly want to be. In the context of purpose, I can begin to accept myself for what I am and look forward to what I am becoming. And once I can accept who I am, I can begin to forgive myself for my perceived failures.*

After I wrote these words, a weight seemed to lift, a veil

Clarification

was parted. Light was shed on troubling matters. Because I've often doubted the substance of my experiences, I've felt lost and without strength. But generally, I know that I've tried to listen to my heart's directions and "follow my bliss," as Joseph Campbell would advise. I've refused to live for others and for their expectations unless they were resonant with my own.

As I looked back on it all, I realized I had no choice, if I would be true to myself. I needed to make mistakes. I needed to render harsh judgments against myself. But through it all, I've felt the presence of an inner wisdom—the same wisdom that has placed me here in the dark of winter, in the depth of the forest. I have come to my wilderness cabin to find something I judged was missing, perhaps for a long time. I needed to make sense of a bewildering, often directionless, path on which I traveled. And finally, I thought, I needed to recover lost parts of myself and discover how I might contribute in some beneficial way to the beautiful world in which I live.

The next day it snowed. Torn white flakes drifted downward in a bleached fog that blanketed the landscape with silence, usurping my long-distance view. On a similar evening, almost twenty-eight years ago, there occurred another snowstorm. During that frenzy of snow and ice, I entered the world. Roads were rendered useless, so my father donned skis to reach the hospital where I was born. Like today, it was unusually quiet, as life mercifully relaxes when snow visits.

For hours I watched the snow fall tirelessly outside my cabin window. I've always loved the ivory stuff and feel a special attraction to its still beauty—its way of hiding the usual state of things and birthing a new reality, if only temporarily. Perhaps that's why I chose such a time to be born—to enter into a newer, purer landscape, laundered free of old tired forms.

Over the next few days a warm sun began to aggressively banish the brilliant frosting from the ridge top, exposed areas first. As the weather changed, back and forth, between sun and storm, warmth and cold, I listened to the creaking of the trees bent by wind, the wild rush of icy rain-drizzle cascading down a mountainside, the pumping of crows' wings overhead, the steady cacophony of my private stream chasing gravity downhill. The more I attended to the fine details of the land that enfolded me, the more my physical sensitivity increased. I opened up to air, wind, water, earth, fire, and spirit. Soon, I could feel the life force well up within me, making everything seem so much more alive. As I allowed the healing sounds, arising out of stillness, to roll over and through me, I concluded that to be truly human, one must learn to listen and listen carefully.

I say this because, as strange as it might sound, I do believe I was receiving messages. First they were quite faint, then stronger. I felt myself becoming privy to a kind of direct knowingness. This subtle intuition might take the form of sensing beforehand when I would encounter a special rock formation, an animal, or a change in the weather. Then, ideas and principles new to me began to present themselves. For example, I learned about referencing to the vibrations of my own heart and breath, and then matching those frequencies to the rhythm of my outer environment. The inner voice beckoned, "Don't think yourself through life, synchronize your way. Become part of the flow."

Of course, this was much easier said than done. I learned that the process requires an empty, quiet mind and lots of patience. But when I did manage to bring my internal self into resonance with my external reality, my subjective and objective realities also merged. Separateness briefly disappeared. Feelings of euphoria would sweep through me like a wildfire set by lightning upon a wide prairie.

I finally understood that as humans we have the ability to be one with Creation. We can possibly even influence or alter our existence. Deep listening, then, seemed a potent means of direct knowing, of gaining insight into matters of all kinds. And since I had plenty of time to experiment, I discovered an especially useful means to gather such information. I would practice making my mind a blank slate, like a wall of light shimmering on the surface of a pond. And insights, images, and ideas would slowly appear on my mental screen.

Clarification

I learned about the reciprocity of thought, how my environment would mirror my state of mind. On days when anger and frustration gripped me, a storm might mysteriously gather out of nowhere. If I felt joyful or unusually ecstatic, sunlight or rainbows would fill my day. Whatever my heart sent out, it got back.

One day, as I awoke with a new found sense of confidence and security, I knew the animals had noticed my change. Sure enough, a wandering bear crossed my path that afternoon while I was returning from my food supply base. I thanked him for his visit of acknowledgment and continued on my way.

Indeed, this effect was curious, but I concluded that it proved the interconnectedness of mind and matter: The communication medium was thought, rendered into vibration and transmitted as wave and particle. By generating thought vibrations from my feelings, I was often able to summon specific physical energies into existence. Form, I discovered, is the servant of idea properly imaged.

As a result of my experiments in conscious sensing and thought projection, I came to a new realization: If we could better understand how thought-vibration connects unconscious to physical reality, we might achieve a more intimate alignment with the natural order of things. I suspected that this state of high resonance with nature or natural law is also the source of "synchronicity"—the appearance of miraculously timed coincidences. Perhaps synchronicity is, in fact, the natural state of life, reflecting the base state of world in balance. It then occurred to me that if we could regularly clear our blocks and resistance to such states of mind, we might discover the full knowingness and joy inherent in being truly human. And then, surely, the world would change for the better.

I woke at dawn. It was three days until the winter solstice, I noted from my calendar. I walked outside; a pregnant glow of yellow-orange tinted the eastern horizon. I laughed to the trees, congratulating myself that I'd made it through the dark night and was now approaching my own personal edge of dawn. Like the light preparing to return at solstice, so too was I beginning my return. But as I readied myself to rejoin my fellow team members and share my revitalized and renovated being, I realized that I contemplated the imminent event with anxiousness and reluctance. Would my fellows perceive me as too different or really strange? Or not changed at all, and all my revelations revealed as merely fleeting and insignificant mental constructs? And how would I relate to the other members of my team and to staff? These questions, of course, remained unanswered until I arrived.

CHAPTER 6

COMMUNICATION

Reunion. Winter solstice. The year's longest night, time of solar return. The ten remaining members of our team gathered in a roomy log lodge, centrally located about three miles from the scatter of our individual hermitages.

I looked around. Clearly there had been casualties. Only ten remained of the original fourteen. Lawrence was there and Lynne, the British woman, Osaki from Japan, David from California, Björn from Sweden, Carol from Boston, Alisa from Mexico, and Wilson from Chicago. We soon learned the cause of the attrition. Some individuals had succumbed to intolerable loneliness and boredom while others found their minds imploding with frustration or confusion, or they simply couldn't handle the physical difficulties of living in the wilderness. I could relate; I had almost sabotaged myself! Some were able to recover from their emotional nosedives by sending rescue messages to headquarters and seeking emergency counseling. Following a few days, and in some cases weeks, of rehabilitation, some had reentered the wilderness to give it another try.

Apparently, Lawrence was one who had encountered trouble. He had suffered a severe fall while hiking back from his supply camp, and he had to be rescued and taken to the hospital in nearby Silver City. After two weeks of convalescence, though, he had insisted on returning.

It was the first time we had met since our one-way trek into the wilderness. We glanced uneasily at each other, not quite sure what to say or how to act in this strange, unfamiliar environment. I scanned the group, more aware than I'd ever been of the tremendous psychic impact of other human beings. Apparently the rarefied space of my solitary retreat had heightened my sensitivity. I was open to any and all energies, and I felt my fellow humans bristle with powerful invisible forces. I myself was reeling, senses overloaded, needing to cool down. I concluded that human energy is so much more potent, obvious, and presumptuous than nature's energy, which is generally—by comparison—subtle and ephemeral.

I noted striking differences between the men and the women. Male energy was especially strong, full of potential, and one-pointed like an arrow ready to take flight—a mountain of kinesthetic energy waiting to be focused for explosive action. The women, on the other hand, exuded an intense sensual, sexual energy. It felt round—surrounding, receptive, all-enveloping, diffuse, and highly attractive.

I immediately searched for Jenny. To my chagrin, she was not with the group. My anxiety increased. Didn't she make it? Had something happened to her! Disappointed and distracted, I returned my attention to the group.

At first, we stumbled along, tentatively reactivating our long-inactive language mechanisms. Words fell half-formed from our mouths. During our isolation, we had rarely exercised our voices. It was oddly different now, having to abide by rules of syntax and grammar once again.

Margaret stood before us, her face beaming with barely restrained pride, and congratulated us on the successful completion of our first phase of work. "I know how difficult this was for all of you," she said. "Many times I've challenged myself in the wilderness. And I find that even now, after twenty years of engagement with my own process, that internal work is never completely finished. It spirals round and round and takes one ever deeper. It's truly a lifetime commitment. Indeed, I believe it's a multilifetime undertaking of vast and multifaceted proportions."

About midway through the meeting, I looked around and, to my surprise, I saw Jenny leaning against a large wooden pillar in the corner of the room. She looked healthy and radiant, but her face portrayed a weathered maturity I had not noticed earlier. Later, I approached her, not sure of what our relationship might be at this point. Our eager embrace, mutually initiated, at least temporarily assuaged some doubts. We spent an hour describing and discussing our experiences, but hers were so different. And she revealed to me a special secret.

"You see, Tom, I'm not really a standard student. This is my second year here. My official title is 'Field Counselor,' but the true essence of my work I only discuss with the top staff. My task is to oversee the psychological safety of the program participants, and when needed, perform *spiritual* search and rescue missions."

"I don't understand," I said, confused but totally fascinated.

Jenny stared at me, a shadow of seriousness accentuating her dark, chiseled features. Then she looked away, momentarily, as if soliciting validation from some invisible source. "Most people only consciously operate on the physical plane. My real job is to monitor this plane from higher dimensions. I'm usually busiest during the night. At night, while people are finishing up their day's activities and preparing to enter into their dreams for emotional processing, I track the group's collective subconscious. My intention is also to provide assistance and protection to an individual if and when it's needed."

I raised my eyebrows in surprise and skepticism.

"Wait! Before you get the wrong impression, let me say I don't intrude. Rather, I hold the space for them; I maintain the center place. When a group of inexperienced people enters a wilderness program like this, lots of things can go wrong, people can get hurt. They are vulnerable on many levels."

"What do you mean?" I asked.

"Well, one man experienced a major crisis. I knew he would need extra help, so I monitored him. His mind-body awareness is somewhat underdeveloped. He's too much in his head, and he lives disconnected from his intuitive awareness. That's dangerous anywhere. When he's in the wilderness, it can be fatal."

"What happened?"

"Apparently, he wasn't watching where he was going, and he fell off a cliffside trail, injuring himself—a sprained ankle and lots of bruises. I found him in a canyon with a high fever and slightly delirious, alerted staff at headquarters on my cell phone, and we got him out. He'll be okay. In fact, he went back in after he recovered."

"And he's still with us?"

Jenny nodded and then turned the conversation to avoid identifying her charge. "You needed a little assistance, too, didn't you? I could tell you'd hit bottom."

I was embarrassed, but I admitted it. "I saw your face in my dreams. You were really there?"

"Yes, that's my job . . . to be where I'm needed."

I was impressed. "I don't really understand how you do this work, but I'm intrigued. I'd like to know more."

"You will," she assured me with a comforting smile. "During the next phase of the program, you'll explore some of these other ways of knowing."

It was meeting time again, and as we walked back, Jenny asked me about the eagle feather she had given me. "Did you find it useful?"

"Of course," I laughed. "I'm here and I'm well."

Thus began the second three-month program—winter solstice to spring equinox—the Communication Phase. The sun would now begin to return its light and heat to the Northern Hemisphere, and our group would begin to explore a new psychological and physical reality.

To start us off, staff led us in an all-night ceremony in which we invoked the incoming solar energies of emergence and growth. Each of us spoke of our newfound sense of self, of the hardships we experienced and what we did to overcome them. We discussed the joys of simple living and of old negative patterns recognized and hopefully banished. Then we each hurled a personal object, representative of our prior selves, into a hungry bonfire burning vigorously in a great stone circle outside the lodge.

The letting-go completed, our guides charged us anew. "During the past three months you've worked to cultivate skills of self-awareness and self-sufficiency. It's time now to go to the next level: human to other-than-human communication. We want you to collaborate with your environment. Slip into Stone, merge with Tree, travel with Hawk, fly with Cloud. Become Life. Life will become you."

We were told to consider everything as always fully sentient, with information shuttling back and forth without regard to physical distance or species boundaries. We were to imagine ants trading food information with fellow ants, trees gossiping with clouds, hawks delivering data about mouse ground movements to each other .

So, with our new agenda and a head full of instructions, we returned to the forest. Each day I tried my best to try to communicate with the trees, the rocks, the animals—any sentient thing that might respond. But no luck! I became seriously discouraged. No matter what I tried, I sensed no response. "They won't talk to me. Maybe they don't like me," I complained only half in jest during one weekly meeting.

"Have patience," Margaret assured me. "Let go of your logical assumptions and mental expectations. Follow your intuition. Trust. Relax your mind. Drift into the silence and listen for hours, if necessary."

I did give her recommendation a try, even though I was skeptical. By this point, I was almost ready to quit. I just wasn't making any discernible progress, at least to my mind.

Then it happened. As I was approaching a ragged rock ridge, an inviting promontory had called to me. After a heart-racing climb to the top, I found myself easily nestling into a niche in the stone, a perfect place to rest and contemplate the view, perhaps to meditate. I looked to the left. Barely twenty feet away sat a chipmunk on a ledge, surveying his domain or maybe meditating, too. Strangely, he seemed a mentor to me, saying in his chatter, "Begin now; open to the knowledge waiting for you. The spirits are here. You need only to recognize them. Remember how you have already learned to listen."

My thoughts settled as I began to relax. I raised my hands toward a towering wall of evergreens on the opposite side of the canyon. I offered everything I was to the space around me. Mysteriously the wind rose, as if to acknowledge my sacrifice. I stretched my arms back while sitting cross-legged and touched fingertips to the warm, brown-speckled stone that held me fast. I let myself go, imaging myself into the depths of the stone, allowing it to interpenetrate me.

The wind whistled approval. Subtly, at first just a tingle, then a current began to flow between my hands and arms, flashing across my chest. I had somehow created a powerful electrical circuit between the Earth and my body, but in particular with my heart as it intersected with the current's flow.

Yes! My mind reveled. I saw it all, now. We've been *outsiders* for too long, sorely disconnected from our true power source, the great wisdom archive—the Earth herself. We've severed ourselves from the primal loop of elemental life, the circle of sentient consciousness shared by plants, animals, wind, water, rain, and moon. Somehow we have to get ourselves home, "back into the garden" as Joni Mitchell's song beseeches us. We need to relearn the language of Tree, Rock, Mountain, Bear, Deer, and Wolf. I knew, truly, at that moment, that Wind is the breath of the land, that Eagle's cry speaks of the loss of the man-woman-animal connection. "Come home," Eagle pleads, "join us once again in the exquisite dance of life."

I remained in that Earth electrical circuit for maybe an hour, though it seemed like minutes. But it didn't matter. I sensed that I had broken through into a mythic realm and temporarily smashed the padlock of anthropomorphic or human only-based history. I had pried open the door to other-than-human perception. I had glimpsed that full-dimensional, multitudinous place of present-time, past-memory, and future-reality I consider the Earthmind. I had experienced my own embedded connection to the planet. I had become an *insider*.

Soon I began to see things differently, as long as I released any expectation of what I thought should happen. I found that a well-tuned consciousness and a strong desire to redirect my attention into other dimensions were the keys.

While in my best empty-mind state, I would gather my physical energy together, wait, and listen for anything—a tone, a color, a thought, an image. Sometimes a leaf would flutter into my lap from a nearby tree, or a rock would tumble spontaneously into a stream. A raven would suddenly begin circling overhead. Indications of communication? I like to think so. I also made an effort to be comfortable with not knowing, with allowing mystery to enter my consciousness. I began to watch my intuition lead me to a new kind of experience, one that seemed to transcend both time and space. I hadn't yet learned to totally access that unfamiliar domain, but I caught previews of it in the silent pass of the leaf, in the splash of the rock, in the sweep of the raven's wing—messages from the Mystery.

In our weekly meetings at the lodge, we discussed the animal reality at length. Margaret and Loren explained to us that human evolution would have flickered out long ago if not for the presence of our nonhuman brethren. Our survival down through the ages has been almost completely dependent on the gifts of animal flesh, fur, fin, feather, and bone. Our ancestor hunter-gatherers knew this well and accorded the human-animal relationship the highest degree of reverence. When aboriginal humans entered the forest, they knew they were setting foot in sacred space, an abundant domain with essential survival elements. To perpetuate themselves and their kind, they needed access to the web of natural intelligence. And so they developed many ingenious means of inter-species communication. The human hunter would ask if Bear would agree to provide food and life for his tribe. If Bear agreed, Human and Bear would begin the dance of giving and taking. And the hunter would always thank the spirit of the animal and pray that it would again return to physical form.

"Go meet Wolf," encouraged Margaret. "He's newly

arrived here, thanks to a local reintroduction program." Eyes widened with doubt and fear. "You need to meet Wolf and Bear. Consider that it was fear of the wild, the dark, and the unknown that drove the wedge between humankind and the Earth so long ago. Our mission here is to mend that break, heal the wounding, and explore the meaning of the human-to-other-than-human relationship.

"And how about your own experiences with animals?" Margaret asked the group. "Would anyone like to offer some personal stories?"

"I met Bear," I said. "At first I experienced fear, especially at night when I would hear a mysterious cracking of sticks outside my door, indicating that something big was walking around. But when I finally sensed a resonance between my self and Bear, my fear began to evaporate. I began to view all the animals as friends, allies. In fact, they seemed to know exactly what I was doing.

"One day, when I was feeling particularly sensitive, a big old brown bear sauntered across my path. He took a quick glance at me. I thought I even saw a smile on his face. Then he just kept right on going, like he had an important appointment. I'm sure he was acknowledging my newfound inner strength. Is this what you mean?"

"Yes," Margaret said, nodding. "It's this kind of initiation–response relationship we're trying to encourage."

Jenny spoke next. "Animals live in a plane of consciousness different than ours but they can communicate with us if we're willing to listen. In Navajo tradition, each animal plays a vital role in the formation of the world and the history of my people. Animals have different qualities, determined by their own histories. If we're aware of them, we can learn much from animals who decide to visit us. If we study these qualities, we will understand what messages they have for us."

Finally, several more of our group began to experience solid, physical results with our animal communication. Some, maybe with more natural ability, caught on more quickly than others. Right brain types led the pack. Lynne impressed everyone, but then she had lived with a tribe in the Amazon for five years. She would report impressions gathered from rocks, bees, slugs, snakes, ants, and anything else she focused her mind on. We learned a great deal from her.

One week our assignment was to query the environment as to the state of the world. "Ask specific questions," our guides insisted. "Ask Tree what it perceives is happening to it and the other species that depend on it. Ask Water where it's most polluted, what's happening with the Rhine, the Nile, the Mississippi. Ask Soil and Rock how they like serving as receptacles for toxic and radioactive waste. Where are the worst areas of contamination? Ask Eagle about air pollution and about the weather on the other side of the mountain."

David had an experience of complete terror. He unexpectedly tuned into a redwood forest while it was being clear-cut. "It took my breath away," he stammered. "I could see the chain saws coming toward me and I couldn't move, couldn't escape. I panicked and screamed. It was so real. And the pain as the saw cut! I could see my innards spilling out, my flesh disintegrating. And then the falling over and smashing to the ground! It was like the worst experience I've ever had. I'm afraid to listen to trees now. I just can't take it! It's too awful!"

His account shook us all. The implications were staggering. If trees, animals, and rocks do feel some form of pain or terror when threatened with annihilation, do we dare expose ourselves to that additional suffering? Would we open the floodgates to such overwhelming horror that we'd become psychically crushed? Was this the price to be paid for intimacy with nature?

We discussed the matter at considerable length. We finally realized that our separateness from natural processes relieves us of enormous amounts of discomfort and, of course, responsibility. Men and women who live in cities teeming with noise and crowds have no choice but to erect certain shields to protect themselves from unpleasant realities. We all do this to a certain extent. But what gets sacrificed? Silence, space, ability to listen, deep presence with ourselves, others, and nature—in exchange for short-term sanity? When we close ourselves down, we exclude things. We become less of who we are. Psychological compression is one way to endure a grim reality, but is this a practical survival strategy for evolution as a whole? Or does it quickly become a deadly form of denial that leads inevitably to self-destruction?

We had no reliable answers but were determined to do the best we could with what we knew. At the same time, we resolved to live at the edge of what we didn't know, to keep testing that edge, pushing it further into the unknown. Intuitively, collectively, we sensed that by going deeper, we would know more of the relatedness of the whole to its parts—intricately interwoven, the connectedness of all things.

January was a tough month. The weather remained very cold, with below zero temperatures three weeks in a row. We had to cancel the weekly meetings a couple of times because of near-blizzard conditions. After all, we lived in the mountains at close to eight thousand feet. Lugging our supplies in was no simple matter either. Our water froze and often the suppliers were snowed in at institute headquarters. Sometimes, everything just came to a complete stop.

I don't think I could have made it through those winter months without the survival training and the practice of living on the mountain during the fall—an invaluable learning experience. Besides mastering certain wilderness skills in this session, I learned how to read the weather, the woods, and the animals to some extent. Nasty surprises were kept to a minimum. I made sure I always had a good supply of wood. My solar electric charger kept me in batteries for flashlights, my tape recorder, and a single reading lamp, which really made a difference during the short nights. But warmer weather was on its way. March was not too far off, and the ice and snow were fast disappearing from south facing hillsides. Muddy trails had dried out, and I was more than ready to welcome spring.

The next intersecting reality we were to encounter was

COMMUNICATION

nonverbal or "nonlocal" human-to-human communication. Our guides waited until just past the halfway point to bring it up. But, I must say, I expected it. It was the logical next step in our intuitive investigation. "Mental networking," they called it—"mind modems and massively parallel human computing."

The idea, we were told, is to fashion a collective of single minds into one powerful group mind and then progressively assume more difficult tasks. In theory, problems that have defeated single minds might be solved by the increased brain- and heart-power of multiple intelligences. Humans often do this when working as a group. Nature, too, works this way—ants swarming, birds flocking, and fish schooling. Humans also informally swarm, flock, and school when following fads, political leaders, or rabid nationalistic trends.

Our group goal, however, was to move beyond the trap of "the blind leading the blind." The idea was to act as an integrated whole, yet do our work as autonomous units. For this, there is ample human precedent in tribal communities. Jenny described to us how men and women might assume individual roles such as shaman, healer, midwife, farmer, musician, or chief, while all members were bound together by clan ties, communal purpose, and a common overarching spirituality as expressed and maintained through collective ritual and ceremony. "In the tribal reality," she said, "everyone understands that the survival of the whole is critically dependent on the successful daily work and contribution of each individual. In addition, the entire group always remains referenced to their environment and acts accordingly. The shamans, medicine people, and elders see to that."

History and anthropology tell us that in preagricultural communities, people intuitively learned to match their populations and food needs to local or regional carrying capacity. This is group mind in action. The ideal group mind is nonhierarchical, egalitarian, vertically integrated, gender-balanced, holistic, and devoid of strife. It has the capacity to nurture, sense, elicit, and encourage individual creative inspiration. The group mind serves to speed the evolution of the whole.

One example our guides offered as a successful large-scale endeavor of a group mind project is the Anasazi community at Chaco Canyon, in northwestern New Mexico. There the remains of beautiful multistoried buildings, built between A.D. 850 and 1150, demonstrate evidence of design continuity lasting centuries. I was somewhat familiar with Chaco Canyon, having read about it years back. The Chacoans had mastered the judicious blend of radical innovation and pragmatic utilitarianism. Though millions of tons of local stone required quarrying, and hundreds of thousands of huge logs had to be transported from forests fity miles away, workers apparently operated without coercion or oppression, cooperatively raising one of the most spectacular, elegant, sophisticated, and architecturally imaginative settlements in human history. A vast road network, possibly twelve hundred miles in length, constructed without beasts of burden or the technology of the wheel, adds to the enigma of the undertaking.

Chaco Canyon has been called a "spiritual construction project"—the placing of each stone being a prayer to Creation. Not surprisingly, some walls still stand perfectly straight and true over eight hundred years later. This amazing accomplishment documents the power of the group mind creatively and positively employed. Archaeologists have pondered the mysteries of Chaco for decades. How could such an extraordinary event occur in such a hostile, barren, and remote location? And why?

Loren explained that the "Chaco Phenomenon," as it is formally labeled, is about energy coming together in an elemental, natural way. He suggested that an extraordinary confluence of singular events and factors enabled the phenomenon to occur. It could happen because the Anasazi were poised for a quantum leap forward. The Anasazi were a particularly innovative group of former pit-house dwellers whose population and cultural influence had spread throughout the Southwest by A.D. 1000. The canyon was a womblike receptacle of female energy that attracted the male force of creative manifestation. Shakti and Shiva forces (East

Indian female and male energies) merged into a perfect weaving of yin and yang, earth and sky, past and future, heart and head, spiritual and material. Margaret defined this gathering of energies as a "Neolithic Tantric Event," a great inbreath and outbreath of high-human, psycho-spiritual creative expression lasting until the end of its cycle—about 250 years later.

We were also reminded by Margaret that group force can be used for considerable harm. World history has much to say about how ruthless power mongers can manipulate large assemblies of people. A case in point is the lesson of Germany, Italy, and Japan during World War II, when fascists played to the basest human instincts of fear, paranoia, nationalism, revenge, and greed.

"But," she went on, "the highest expression of group mind requires conscious participation by all for the greatest good. And authentic collective collaboration rests upon a foundation of solid, balanced, and healthy relationships between human and nonhuman elements, including the Earth. Although anyone can provide leadership or information to the system, no elite hierarchy exists. All are of equal importance. Information may travel in any direction. True collaboration teaches how to share *power with*, rather than dominate with *power over*."

Having accepted the idea that we could work as one mind, we began our work. A thought would be initiated by a designated individual, then broadcast telepathically to the others at specified times. Theoretically, we could, as a group, edit and comment as one would on an electronic network, but we worked without wires or voices.

As expected, first results were poor. Back at our hermitages, most of us found it challenging to try to separate our own thoughts from those incoming from other sources. We simply could not distinguish the transmission signal from background noise inside our heads. I think that most of us actually had substantial doubts about the process; subsequently, any successes were greeted with healthy skepticism.

Nevertheless, small knowings led to larger ones—and we

began to experience the power of the process. At weekly meetings, we learned from each other what techniques worked. It soon became obvious that a great deal of trust was required to admit another person's thoughts into one's own. But, once we opened ourselves to the possibility of mutual trust, we began to sense each other's thought presence in our minds. We felt ourselves reaching out through the trees, across the miles of topographic separation to make contact, feeble as it was. I experienced such incoming messages as long-awaited letters from home, a welcome reunion that carried an extra spark of soul-felt recognition. I concluded there surely was potential in this type of communication for greatly enhancing human community.

The arrival of warmer weather and the spring equinox heralded our wilderness sojourn's end. It was time to depart our mountain retreats and begin the next cycle of our training: the Expression Phase. Reluctantly, I packed up my small assortment of belongings, smoked my cozy nest with a bit of burning cedar, and thanked my little cabin that had nurtured me so well for so long. I also took the time to bid a tearful farewell to a favorite squirrel who had become my confidant during the past few months. My furry friend seemed incredulous that I was leaving. We had connected, indeed communed. We had entered into the web of life together, our stories blending as one.

She followed me down the trail one last time and halted at the edge of her territory. She paused and remained motionless, head raised. Our eyes locked. I said, out loud, "I'll miss you. You've added much to my life. Let's stay in touch somehow. Okay?" She blinked, flicked her tail rapidly back and forth, then turned and quickly bounced up the trail toward home. The human-to-other-than-human communication grid was working, I thought to myself proudly. I had learned my lessons well.

CHAPTER 7

EXPRESSION

Culture shock! The silence of the forest had given way to the noisy rush of human activity. My canopy of trees had been traded for enclosed spaces made of fabric, beam, metal, and plastic. We'd moved back to institute headquarters for our final session. This period of study would last from March 22 to June 22—spring equinox to summer solstice, when the sun would reach its maximum generative mode.

I found the move a mixed blessing: no need to carry in supplies every few days, plenty of heat, light, and comfort; but something was missing that I'd come to cherish—my daily, intimate connection with wildness. Surely all humans, I thought, must, on some level, feel a separation from that original context which birthed and supported us for countless millennia. Surely, our collective psyche must still, in some remote cellular nook, harbor memories of wide, lush savannas, epic hunts, fabulous feasts, and suspenseful stories masterfully told around the campfire. I tried to fill my mental void with echoes of those ancient images: bodies locked together in the lush warmth of animal robes, grand rituals, first plantings, successful harvests. I entertained dim remembrances of old ones buried, and of new ones birthed and presented for first naming, of humankind lifting itself through the ages: the Paleolithic, the Neolithic, the Agricultural, and into the Industrial and Information eras.

My musings were of little comfort, however, as I recalled the hard-core world of the present. We do have more comfortable lives now with electricity, television, cars, aircraft, telephones, and the like. But are they deeply rewarding ones, full of meaning and purpose and knowledge of that which has imbued us with our miraculous lifeforce? Doubtful. Overall, we seem lost in a skewed, corrupted reality that daily threatens all life on the planet.

"Congratulations! You've reached the two-thirds point," Margaret informed us during our first group session. "You've had six months to make nature your ally and to explore new levels of awareness. Now we'll focus on helping you learn how to relate more effectively to your communities, institutions, and to the outer world. And to better integrate masculine and feminine energies. You'll also explore creative leadership models that harness the power of natural law. Any questions?"

I inhaled slowly and looked toward the rest of the group. That seemed a lot to accomplish in only three months. Surprisingly, I detected a certain measure of confidence in the air. We were steadier now, newly empowered. We would handle our new challenges with grace and self-assurance.

One of my first priorities, once I had settled in a guest cabin, was to contact Jack at the *Earth Renaissance News*. I was curious about developments at the WSC. Much would have happened there during the past eight months.

I was happy to hear his familiar gruff voice on the phone. "Yes, Thomas. The WSC did pass Resolution 636, but not without a prolonged and bitter debate."

"How's the rest of the world reacting to the Share Tax?" I asked.

"Well, governments need to ratify it, of course, before it can be implemented. Getting that accomplished is going to be difficult because most governments and international corporations don't like it one bit. They all say that foreign aid and private investment will eventually accomplish the same objectives. Banks, on the other hand, see big profits in the tax. They want to set themselves up as the official handlers of the money—trillions of dollars moving through their hands over the next few years."

"So what's likely to happen next?"

"Chaos and confusion during the process of ratification, which will require a major catalyst of some kind to push it through in most countries."

"What does the PAPA say?"

"To them, the ruckus over the Share Tax proves that global financial institutions are merely old-fashioned pirates in new gray suits, and that transnational corporations are hell-bent on controlling the world and converting it into one giant shopping mall. But the PAPA is standing firm to its time frame—high noon, ninety days from now. Will you be ready to cover it?"

"I should be," I said. "It's been a challenge here, but I've learned so much."

"Good. And I'm looking forward to your article."

So, the world keeps turning, with or without me. I'd been out of the loop—at least the outer world loop for eight months. I consoled myself that I'd had the opportunity to join a different circle, one that would provide me with increased abilities to participate more effectively in society. At least that's what I hoped would happen. The PsyEarth Institute schedule, though, permitted little time for pondering world events. Our attention was now directed toward learning about male-female energies.

Our second day back at headquarters we were requested to assemble in the Forest Lodge, a two-story round log structure located a few minutes walk from the main administration building. The lodge featured an arched cathedral ceiling and lots of glass on the south side. A porch overlooked a talkative stream bordered by well-tended herb and flower gardens. Several curving walkways led through the woods.

We assembled inside, lounging on large pillows arrayed in an arc on the well-padded floor. Our new instructors, a couple named Louise and Steven Darden, introduced themselves and the program. Apparently they had developed a highly acclaimed process for teaching men and women how to tap into their male and female energies, build trust, and work together more effectively.

They were in their fifties but looked ten years younger. I took that as testimony to the power of their process. Both were dressed in jeans and casual shirts. Louise had medium-length dark hair and a serious but compassionate face; Steven sported a close beard and had blond and wavy hair. They were full of energy and smiled often at each other. I felt these were people I could trust.

They began by saying that each of us would team up with a partner of the opposite sex. The staff who had already worked with us had preselected our partners. I, of course, wanted to work with Jenny, but I resigned myself to respect their choice, holding my breath as names were called. By some strange turn of fate, Jenny and I were designated partners! Whispering to myself, I thanked the gods.

Our schedule was demanding. Each morning we were up at dawn for an hour of meditation followed by an hour of yoga and gentle stretching exercises. Later, there were much more vigorous yogic breathing exercises, usually performed with our partners. The intention of these physical activities was to align our physical and mental energies. After we ate breakfast, it was back to work—more physical exercises with partners, and in-depth group and individual discussions skillfully led by Louise and Steven. These discussions focused mainly on our personal experiences with the opposite sex and what it meant to be male or female. Almost immediately we found ourselves confronting the trust factor—or lack of it. "Men and women," Steven explained, "often harbor a basic distrust of each other." He insisted we explore this issue with our partner, taking whatever time was required to go to the source of the matter.

On our first afternoon working together, Jenny exploded. She admitted she felt a great deal of anger toward her father for abandoning her and her mother. "It wasn't right!" she said, clutching a Kleenex to absorb her tears. "Family is so important to us. Even though he sent money to Mom, it was hard. He wasn't around much. I'm just so very thankful I have my grandmother, uncles, and cousins, but it's left a hole in me. So I'm extremely wary about men, I'll admit it. I see this pattern of men deserting the women and the families happening a lot on the reservation. Too often the men become alcoholics and the women are forced to throw them out."

Jenny impressed me with her ability to be so candid so quickly. I simply couldn't access or express my feelings quite so easily. She sensed this, was patient, and provided encouragement. Finally, after much prodding, I was able to discuss my resentment about growing up in the ever-present shadow of competition and economic expectations. It was always the same message for a man: Go out and compete and become a financially productive member of society, otherwise your life has no value, no meaning. If you're not powerful and successful, you're dispensable, not wanted, a failure as a man and as a member of society. Consequently, I spent a great deal of time battling the conflict between what my culture expected of me and who I really wanted me to be. I could also see that placing such expectations onto people with profound cultural differences could really be confusing, forcing many individuals into highly destructive coping patterns.

Day after day, the Dardens encouraged us to go deeper. "Dig below the surface stuff and find out what's there. Examine how you feel about each other at the archetypal level, not as individual personalities but as representatives of a specific gender."

After hours and days of soul searching, we discovered this: We men expressed a general fear of a woman's sexual energy and envy of her reproductive capacity. We also admitted that, despite our own usually superior physical strength, we coveted the formidable sexual and psychological abilities women seem able to wield to their advantage. Upon hearing this, Louise reminded us that Western European culture, generally a creation of male design, has had an eight-thousand-year history of political, social, and sexual repression of women.

The women in the group had little difficulty expressing their rage and anger toward men. They described the difficulty of living in an environment that failed to honor women and their needs, and that was filled with the potential for violence directed against them at every turn. This being the case, they would of course fear men. Steven then raised the question: Are men solely to blame for multi-millennia of violence and exploitation directed toward women?

Our discoveries about this "great divide" brought on many more emotional and tense hours of discussion. We all agreed there is plenty of blame to go around. But given a historical record so full of pain and suffering for both genders, we decided on a more productive response—to consider what actions would prevent these tragic patterns from perpetuating. We concluded that much could be changed if men would speak out against dysfunctional and poisonous actions by other men that pass for "normal male behavior." That the lack of healthy male psychological development demands redress by whatever means can be mustered. Clearly, women have no influence over sexual attitudes expressed in the locker rooms and board rooms of all-male enclaves. But aware and courageous males do. It is there that fundamental changes must be made. Man to man. If men no longer allow such denigration of women, then slowly, eventually, the world might be made safe for women. We agreed, too, that women can help by learning to appreciate men's contributions of economic and physical support and by honoring the unique and positive male ways of being and relating.

We tried to imagine how different the world would look if men and women were willing to address the oppression of men perpetuated in cultural expectations of competition and economic success and the physical standards women are forced to emulate. And how men and women would act if they were both able to more fully express their own true selves. Surely, both genders would profit greatly by mutual liberation from myriad culturally defined limits.

Jenny and I worked diligently to examine and expose those factors that prevented us from reaching a new level of trust with each other. The process taught us much about ourselves, far more than what would be revealed in the course of a "normal" relationship. Sometimes it seemed like we were x-raying our souls, and I think both of us became a bit scared of the level of disclosure that we were approaching. Anyway, I perceived Jenny beginning to withdraw. We discussed this, and she told me her wariness of males was being triggered by memories of her mother's pain and sadness regarding the absence of her husband.

As our first month drew to a close, I watched with fascination as Louise and Steven guided us skillfully through these very personal and often very painful matters. Along the way, we explored how men and women in contemporary U.S. culture are bound to tightly constricted concepts of maleness and femaleness, imposed upon each other due to our personal woundedness and previous gender conditioning. We began to examine how our individual and collective creative potential was severely limited by the extent of our mental distortions.

Recognizing these impediments, our guides encouraged us to find ways to shatter our embedded fears and conceptual blocks. "Define new ways of relating to each other," Steven said one rainy afternoon when we were all feeling that men and women would never reach a level of deep trust. "Remember that all humans embody both the masculine and the feminine. Move beyond your distrust, as difficult as that might seem, and regard each other personally, and in this present moment, with highest honor as God or Goddess in hiding. Consider that you stand before a being who carries some of life's most profound wisdom, a being who does not need to remain bound to old programmed ideas and cultural misperceptions. And treat your bodies as temples, places of worship, sacred spaces where head and heart might merge in an egalitarian, respectful, and deeply liberating way."

These sessions were hard work, bringing slow resolution, or none, at that time. We learned patience with the process—and ourselves—and planted many seeds for further harvest.

We kicked off our next unit on knowledge and personal responsibility in a comfortable meeting room with lots of large windows. Two sets of wide french doors allowed plenty of fresh air to flow throughout the classroom. The room filled with the perfume of spring wild flowers. Errant breezes would playfully reshuffle any papers lying about loose on desk tops. Large black and white and color blow-ups of the history of science and technology adorned one windowless wall. Our instructor was a colorful, roundish British gentlemen in his sixties, named Dr. Arin Fallows. Arin, as he insisted we address him, dutifully related his scientific background to us, but preferred to emphasize his passion for philosophy and ethics. His bushy beard and electrically charged shock of white hair caused us to quickly dub him Merlin the Magician. Indeed, he seemed to fit the role rather well. The only thing missing was a white robe. His command of facts, ability to render difficult concepts into plain English, and his cheerful wit soon won our hearts.

"So . . . you've learned how to get along with each other now?" he quipped on our first day together, his English accent giving his words an extra spin. "Perhaps you can teach me a thing or two. I just can't seem to the hang of it. My wife keeps telling me I still don't understand her."

He stretched himself over a desk in the front of the room, directed his sharp eyes toward us, catching us with his full attention. "You're the lucky ones! I suspect you've had a taste of the power of masculine and feminine energy properly aligned. Have you felt the magic in your heart and in your bodies? Even if but for a fleeting moment?"

Several heads nodded in agreement.

"Good, because now we'll begin to examine just how that energy and insight might be appropriately employed in the social and political world."

Over the next few days we explored the concept that certain knowledge comes with strings attached. Those strings could be read as a requirement that the carrier of the knowledge assumes some measure of personal responsibility for the possession and use of it. A good example of the principle is the ancient field of study called "alchemy."

"Alchemy has its origins in ancient Egypt as the Hermetic Doctrine. In medieval Europe the alchemist was a highly revered professional and was considered the scientist/doctor of the times. The best alchemists were always vigorously sought after by kings and nations. But what do alchemists actually do?" Arin asked rhetorically in his measured, booming voice, employing dramatic sweeping full-body gestures. We stared at him blankly.

"Alchemists investigated relationships of all kinds. They sought to understand the balance and wholeness inherent in the universe. Unfortunately, in today's world we usually categorize our areas of knowledge separately. We label them physics, chemistry, psychology, religion, ethics, history, and the like. The alchemical tradition, on the other hand, viewed all aspects of knowledge as *absolutely related*. Today, in the Western tradition, we'd call alchemists generalists or holistic thinkers. Native Americans would likely inform us in a polite but rather impatient manner that they have been thinking this way even longer than the alchemists."

Arin added that the study of alchemy is relevant to our study for at least two reasons: "One, a primary goal of the PsyEarth curriculum is the holistic investigation of interrelationships; and two, there is no comprehensive, information-based ethical system quite like the alchemical model in contemporary Western tradition. Furthermore, the alchemists understood well the critical importance of energetic polarities. In fact, no experiment was ever conducted without proper representation of both male and female. A true alchemist would insist that female energy be used to balance masculine-directed scientific experiments, thereby preventing incomplete, erroneous, and likely dangerous results.

At this point in the lecture, Jenny graciously pointed out to us that "the Iroquois Indians of pre-Colonial times embraced this principle as well. A council of female elders had the power to finally approve or disapprove any decisions made by the tribes' chiefs and warriors."

Arin acknowledged Jenny's contribution with a grin, and added that Native American women traditionally held both family and tribal power. He went on to say that although the transmutation of certain chemical elements was the immediate focus of many, the overall goal of the authentic alchemist was the transmutation of the alchemist himself. But, because their investigations into the nature of matter often resulted in the mastery of powerful forces, it became necessary for the alchemist to agree to act as a responsible steward and often observe a stringent code of secrecy. This agreement was called the 'Alchemist's Creed.'

"How did prospective alchemists learn about responsibility?" I asked.

"They'd be required to undergo a long period of study, and told that if powers gained were misused, there would be a high personal price to pay. The punishment varied from banishment to death."

"That seems like a steep bargain to me. But we could sure use some technological responsibility in today's world." I could see heads nodding in agreement.

Jenny's hand was up and Arin nodded in her direction. She turned toward the class. "Native cultures still observe such rules because they understand the possible negative consequences that can result from the wrong use of sacred knowledge."

Arin nodded. "In most tribal cultures, the concept of initiation was created to provide a proper context for the transfer and application of exceedingly potent information. The initiate would undergo special training to demonstrate that he or she could be trusted with the knowledge."

Jenny continued, "My people call their alchemists 'Medicine Men.' They take great care to protect the knowledge that has been passed down to them over many generations."

"Yes," Arin said, clearly pleased with Jenny's contribution, "and in pre-Christian times, my culture termed its male and female custodians of sacred knowledge 'priests,' 'magicians,' 'wizards,' and 'priestesses' and 'wisewomen.' Unfortunately, not all cultures are as enlightened as Native Americans and Pagans. History is filled with weak-willed and selfish individuals who've utilized their access to special knowledge to gain personal power, exploit others, subvert the democratic process, or even destroy entire civilizations.

This is knowledge abused. And perhaps science poses the greatest danger of all because the forces that it invokes are so extremely potent. You might say that much of today's science serves as an example of *knowledge wielded without conscience."*

Lawrence shifted uneasily in his seat. He asked to be recognized. Arin nodded in his direction. "It seems you're suggesting information should be censored and controlled. But how can you restrict the man or woman who puts new information to work in a useful way? That's the way civilization evolves. That's what's given us our cars, planes, phones, electricity, computers—our whole contemporary, technological society. You can't impose restraints on the pursuit of knowledge."

"I think now's a good time to define some terms," Arin stated evenly. "Information is just raw data. Facts. Knowledge, on the other hand, involves understanding, which usually results after a body of facts has been acted on by human consciousness. The mind must undertake to place the data or facts into a meaningful context. So we're moving up one level here. Choice, intention, conscience, and maybe even responsibility now become part of the picture. And things can become dicey. What do we do with what we know now? How do we use our newfound knowledge appropriately?"

"And where does wisdom fit in?" I asked.

"Hmmm," muttered Arin. "I was hoping somebody would ask that question." He paused and answered succinctly, "Wisdom requires the additional component of experience. Wisdom might be described as 'good judgment.' But it is only gained after much trial and error. So, to review: We begin with the accumulation of relevant facts. This is information gathering. Facts then are introduced into our critical thinking processes. Once the facts are integrated with our conscience and intuition, we have a body of knowledge. Then, after we've tested our knowledge in countless life experiences, and judged what works and what doesn't, we begin to develop what we call 'wisdom.' It's a long and tortuous process, but it's life. It's what we're here for. Right now, though, we're focusing our attention on how to handle our knowledge."

"So when did it change?" Osaki asked. "When did we eliminate the notion of the individual assuming personal responsibility for powerful knowledge?"

Arin was standing behind the desk. He moved to the windowsill and relaxed his body against it. The simple natural beauty of the forest scene outside contrasted with the complexity and weight of the issues we sought to resolve.

"In the area of scientific information, I'd say the shift occurred when the inquiry into the investigation of natural forces was intentionally removed from the rarefied and protected domain of the alchemist, wizard, and wisewoman. This happened because natural sciences became viewed as highly valuable commercial and political commodities. People interested only in profit and power quickly disregarded the ethical and spiritual training that normally accompanied the teaching of scientific knowledge. In Europe, the usurpation began with the coming of Christianity to Britain in A.D. 500, but it developed a full head of steam around the sixteenth century in most of Europe.

"Then is the Alchemist's Creed dead, at least in science?" Osaki asked.

"Not completely. But about sixty percent of the scientists in the United States are working on military related projects. A good portion of the rest are working for industry making things that often do damage to people and the environment. However, some scientists do appreciate the profundity of nature's secrets and the weight of responsibility they have taken unto themselves. A case in point: Years after the bomb he helped create destroyed the cities of Hiroshima and Nagasaki, your own Dr. Robert Oppenheimer, an authentic priest-scientist, admitted in a particularly candid moment that 'In a very profound sense and in a way that cannot be lightly dismissed, we scientists have sinned.' So you see, some find out the hard way. There's really no getting around it."

An important statement, I thought to myself. I took it deep within, drumming my fingers silently on the table in front of me, perhaps to work the insight fully into my being.

Over the following days and weeks Arin took us further into the nature of the quest for knowledge. "To acquire truth requires the embrace of balance and wholeness and the perfected union of polar opposites—male and female, earth and sky, light and shadow. No preconceptions and no tired, outdated dogma are allowed to intervene. Total honesty, deep humility, and an unquestioned respect for the sacredness of life—seven generations past and seven generations hence—are essential prerequisites. This is *knowledge wielded with conscience*."

"But how would we apply such standards to our daily lives?" I asked.

"By being aware of the effects of your actions. If you must drive a car, recall that its manufacturing required the use of a great deal of energy and many natural resources. Maybe walk or ride a bike instead. Frequently ask yourself how you use what you know. Now that you know how easily the environment is damaged, act as an educator to others of this fact, and live your own life in a way that minimizes your destructive impacts and maximizes your ability to enhance the world in which you live. Try to give more than you take."

There was a lot to absorb, and each day Arin pushed us further toward the edge. Yet, at the same time, he somehow kept expanding the edge. It was uncanny. On our last day in class, he bid us farewell with an eloquence that only he could deliver.

"This is your charge today, tomorrow, and for the rest of your lives: to pursue life-enhancing knowledge with a deep personal commitment, and utilize this knowledge responsibly, always, under all conditions. No exceptions, please. I, of course, can't force you to accept this challenge. But here at the institute, you have tasted the fruit of potent knowings. And it is our deep desire that you will permanently benefit from the opportunities your newfound awareness will provide for you and your kin in the world outside these sacred groves. I pray you will learn to appreciate the gravity of your individual destinies and the responsibility you carry to justly serve yourselves, your associates, your families, your communities, and your world. And may Spirit guide and protect you."

CHAPTER 8

APPLICATION

The day began supremely springlike—bright and clear, fresh mountain air urging all things into the celebration of new life. It seemed a difficult kind of day to spend in a classroom. Still, I felt an eagerness to learn about leadership. After all, producing students with effective leadership skills was the ultimate goal of the PsyEarth curriculum. Fortunately, this class met outside on a large patio adjacent to the classroom complex. We were thankful to be able to enjoy the open air and simultaneously engage our minds in a subject that interested us.

I was surprised and pleased to find that our new instructor was Jefferson Morgan. His work rehabilitating gang members and advising inner-city community development projects had taught him much about how to negotiate the treacherous mine fields of ego and personality conflicts. Through his own process of trial and error, he had learned how to bring people together, develop consensus and compromise, and get good things done. He seemed an ideal choice for a leadership instructor—he exuded confidence, inspired trust, and maintained a strong personal presence.

Following an introduction, Jefferson asked us to identify people whom we felt fit the role model of good leader. After a long period of silence, there were several questions for clarification.

"What kind of leader? Political? Artistic? Human rights? Scientific?"

"Any kind," Jefferson responded. "Can you name some?"

Soon, a list of well-known public personalities was drawn up. A discussion ensued on what kind of qualities might be expected in a typical leader.

Jefferson summed up the responses, "Respect seems to be a big one, and ability to listen, make difficult choices, and act decisively. And also trust."

"Can these things be learned?" I asked. "Or are good leaders just born?"

"I think both are possible, Tom. But leaders come in all sizes and shapes. Most will never be featured on the cover of *Time* or interviewed on television. You'll find them in small towns, on Indian reservations, in inner-city gangs, in public institutions, in government . . . just about everywhere. Our goal in this class is merely to provide you with some basic guidelines so you can be effective agents for positive change. So let's begin."

The first thing we learned was how to listen well to others. We honed our skills by spending many hours in role playing and then evaluating our behavior in group sessions. We also learned how to tune into what might not be immediately obvious or explicitly addressed—in other words, hidden agendas and unconscious denial.

"Can you suggest any special methods to help us become more sensitive to what people are really feeling?" I asked Jefferson.

"I would recommend that you draw upon the experiences you've had while living in the wilderness here at the institute. Did you discover that by careful observation, you received information on many levels?"

"Yes, I did."

"Good, well I suggest you apply that same technique to everything you do in life. You'll find this skill particularly helpful when you're called on to facilitate group process."

I shuddered with the thought of myself facilitating a group process. I was sure I wasn't ready for that just yet.

Jefferson continued, "It's always helpful to learn from the experiences of others. So we'll start there. I have a selection of books for you—mostly biographies of famous men and

Application

women. I want you to read the texts and come prepared to report and discuss what you've learned. Also, to insure that the material truly 'works' for you, we've designed a special meditation technique that will allow you to experience these biographies almost firsthand."

That moment began the final phase of our work, easily the most demanding. Our reading material included texts by and about an assortment of exemplary social, religious, and political figures of world history; selected Native Americans; a variety of twentieth-century feminist writers, and contemporary biographies of transformational luminaries such as Gandhi, Susan B. Anthony, and Martin Luther King.

Over the next few weeks, we were taught how to enter into the lives of these people, to become them, merge with their minds, and come to know the times in which they worked. We learned to share their struggles and the resistance they encountered from their respective societies and political systems. We experienced this time travel with the help of a special method of holographic meditation. It worked like this: Joining with our other-gender partners, we entered into a deep meditative state using techniques we had previously learned. We then allowed our egos to drift away, opening ourselves to a kind of universal energy field. Through the fusion of our internal masculine and feminine energies, we tapped into what we termed "the universal hologram." Here we learned that all information and knowledge are encoded in an infinite series of holographic patterns. It is then a matter of locating and accessing a particular pattern in order to experience a designated period of time or a particular historical personality. Once we had sampled the lifecycle of the person and his or her historical context, we returned to our normal state of consciousness and analyzed how that person's work and knowledge could be applied appropriately to today's world.

The experience of seeming to travel in time, of encountering the fear, trauma, joy, and power of the extraordinary lives and circumstances of others, was exhilarating. I found the realism and detail exceptional; it felt like a movie playing in my head. We experimented with ourselves as well—attempting to probe our own past lives. Once an initial scene appeared, I'd know everything that was happening—people's deepest feelings and the hidden agendas of the main characters in each life drama. I became the omniscient observer, able to fast forward, rewind, or pause events and circumstances at will. I learned much about my own self and possible sources of my idiosyncrasies.

As I entered the continuum of history again and again, I was reminded of the interconnectedness and the timelessness of human existence, as points to be held in constant and common reference. I had learned during my wilderness experience how to enter the Earthmind, how to work with the human group mind. Now I was traveling into the Universal Mind in which my own personal millennial history floated adrift as well. I learned that in this cosmic mixture, all events, all intelligence are contained—seemingly chaotic, but still accessible by utilizing my power of intention.

Like Arin, Jefferson reminded us that we do not merely observe reality. Rather, we have the ability to change it. "'We are what we think,' the Buddha has said. Cause and effect. Thought power consciously directed can become transformed into physical action. It happens all the time."

Jefferson was enthusiastic. "A leader needs a solid point of reference, a source he or she can trust and look to for guidance. I propose you consider this reference point as the most fundamental energy of the universe, which I like to call 'Creation.' And that which issues forth from Creation should, at least theoretically, be in resonance with it. Do you agree?"

This is becoming pretty philosophical, I thought to myself, but I'll hang in there.

"We know the physical universe operates within a given set of principles. These principles are commonly described as the 'laws of physics.' Should there not also exist a similar set of universal principles that govern human behavior?"

I nodded my head in agreement. Should be, I thought.

"Let's call these operating principles 'natural law.' Nat-

Application

ural law, if it is indeed the human parallel of physics and biology, would be a template of wholeness, like life itself. It would seek greatest diversity, ultimate simplicity and complexity, and maximum cooperation. It would enjoy a big happy family gathering in which many different stories are told."

"And how do we access this natural law or life energy of which you speak?" Lawrence asked, with more than a touch of impatience and skepticism in his voice.

"It's simple," Jefferson responded, a sly smile spreading across his face as if he was ready to deliver a prearranged punch line. "*Surrender.*"

"Surrender?" Lawrence asked, genuinely curious.

"Yes, surrender. You simply let go of your ego, which I will agree is no simple task, and open yourself to what I call guidance with a capital G."

"But," objected Lawrence, "I always thought a leader had to be strong-willed, strong-minded. Take strong actions. Make strong statements. It seems that's the only way you get respect in the world. You need to command respect. You don't command respect by surrendering."

"And how do you command respect?" Jefferson asked evenly.

Lawrence thought for a minute, then said, "With power, of course. Power is the best way to command respect."

"Well, Lawrence, I grant you, power will get you respect, but it's usually fear-based. But what is power? Must it be only political, monetary, physical, sexual? Or are there other kinds of power—quieter, invisible kinds, perhaps, that don't involve generating fear. Can anyone think of some examples?"

The class was quick to respond.
"Caring."
"Compassion."
"Friendship."
"Sacrifice."
"Generosity."
"Loving."

"Dignity."

"Service."

"Yes," Jefferson continued. "Some of the most impressive and effective leaders I've ever met come from the poorest families living in the most desolate parts of the city. On the surface, you'd think they had nothing in the world that would render them powerful. But, you needed only to spend time in their presence, meet those whom they've influenced with their work in the community, and you know that they have tapped into some kind of incredible power source."

"So, there's more to it than money, beauty, and politics," said Lawrence, clearly intrigued.

"Yes, I think so," responded Jefferson. "It's not an easy thing to define, but if there does, in fact, exist a source of guiding power—maybe called 'Creation'—with an agent on Earth we might call 'natural law,' then it seems that perhaps certain men and women have accessed it and put it to work in their lives.

"And to further aid us in our understanding of natural law, I have invited certain elders to speak on the subject."

We gathered the next day in the main lodge reception room, a large wood-paneled space with a roof of hand-hewn beams and a west wall of carefully worked stone inlaid around a broad, rustic fireplace. The entire institute was there. Our guides and counselors reclined in the large, overstuffed chairs while we students scattered ourselves about on floor pillows or casually leaned against the walls. The capacity crowd had come to honor two Native Americans willing to share their thoughts with us.

The years had scribed a definite history on the two frail bodies. The faces of these elders—a Hopi man and a Navajo woman—were deeply grooved and tanned. Both faces carried most vividly the tales of wind and weather, of decades spent mostly outdoors tending plants and sheep and harvesting a living from the land. The man was an acquaintance and the woman a relative of Jenny's.

Dressed traditionally, our guests sat in large soft chairs

with their backs to the expansive stone wall. The crowd, eyes wide with curiosity and expectation, had tightly packed itself close to the elders' feet. I noticed how the age differences portrayed a gulf of awesome breadth. Though of flesh and blood, this wizened pair seemed as solid as the masonry wall that rose behind them. They'd suffered life's challenges for nearly a century, yet their physical presence carried an aura of easy grace and wise compassion.

The first speaker was the Hopi man, popularly known as Grandfather David, who lived in a very traditional Hopi village. He had recently turned 100. Almost blind and unusually thin, he still traveled as much as he could to spread his message of world peace.

The room hushed and after a brief introduction by Jenny, the man began to speak. His voice was thin, his statements simple, but profound.

"The Hopi understand that the highest way of life can only be founded on a spiritual basis. This must be done through loyalty to the true religion of one's own tradition. For thousands of years, we Hopi have followed this guideline. We have survived to this day as proof of the strength and truth of a life based on spiritual forces.

"You ask about natural law. Natural law is the Creator's law. It is the way of peace. In fact our name Hopi, which was given to us by the Creator, means peace. We depend on natural law to survive. Though we live on high sandstone mesas, we grow our food in the valleys below where there is no surface water. We depend on our prayers, which must reach the giver of rain and food in the spiritual way. Otherwise no one could live from this land.

"We learned from our ancestors that man's actions through prayer are so powerful that they decide the future of life on Earth. We can choose whether the great cycles of nature will bring forth prosperity or disaster. This power was practiced long ago when our spiritual thoughts were one.

"Will this concept still work in today's world? It will if we rid ourselves willingly of hate, and put love within ourselves. And we must join together with renewed faith in our Creator so that we may be spared the destruction that results from trusting in weapons and other devices of our minds, and that we not forget the future of our children to come.

"Protest alone will not stop the wars and violence. Only a life lived on the basis of the natural order, which no person can alter, can avert the catastrophic pattern of events we have studied through the centuries. The Creator's law cannot be changed, so it will never break down. It can't be remade, as with the white man's law, even by the people in what they think is a democracy. This is why no central government can ever succeed. In this fact we can see the problem of the entire world: We may want freedom, but we cannot get it from any design other than the pattern of nature.

"People must learn how to work together for peace, regardless of race, color, and religion. The problem is we emphasize differences too much. Yes, we are different physically. We have different customs and different religions; but in the eyes of the Creator, we are all one. We are all the children of the Creator. Our task on this Earth is simple: to bring love into life, to share it with everyone, share it with all of Creation.

"We Hopi have tried to bring our message of peace, and our warning of great destruction to the world if it continues in its present way. We have tried to take this message to the United Nations as we have been told to do through our prophecies. We have tried four times now, but without success. People are not ready to hear our message. Still, we must all continue to work together for world peace and never tire of this effort. This is our great mission together."

For long seconds his words reverberated throughout the room. In silence we each pondered the wisdom of his words in our own minds and hearts. His voice had quietly carried to each corner of the room, and into the body of each person present.

Following a short break, the second speaker took her place in the large padded chair at the front of the room. Anita was Jenny's grandmother, a beautiful Navajo woman in her seventies. With Jenny acting as translator, Anita shared with us her views of life and the problems of the world.

"I live in a small house on the Navajo reservation. I have no TV or radio or electricity even though I can see the big power lines from my house. I do not speak or read English. But I know what is happening in the outside world. I know about the killing of the dolphins and the loss of many plants and animals. We the Indian people are not doing these things. We do not have the power to stop such things. But you do. You are the people with power. You know how to speak the languages of the world. You can travel. You have the education, the money, the knowledge of science. You can talk with the people in power.

"Our job as Indian people is to feed the spirits of our land, to maintain the balance of the universe in our own way. But you must wake people up . . . to see how they are destroying all life. I know this will not be easy, but it must be done. I am speaking about all the uranium and coal mining that is taking place right here in the Southwest, in between the Sacred Mountains. This is Holy Land. We all just take, take, take from Mother Earth. When you take something out, it must be replaced. A payment must be made for everything we get. To keep the balance of the world we must all live by the laws of Creation. If we do not, we will suffer. If we live a balanced life, we will find great happiness in all that we do.

"I am told you are learning many good things at this school—about nature, about how to get along better with each other. These things are very important. But don't forget your ancestors. They can help you, too. Pray to them for help. And remember that we are all one big family. We need each other. We need to help each other out. But I am concerned that we've forgotten how to do this. Many of our own young people do not respect their elders anymore. They do not talk with their parents. It used to be that people always helped each other. Now the young people ride around in trucks with the dark windows. You cannot tell who is there. There is too much separation now. There needs to be more love between people. And we must heal Mother Earth. We need your energy, your help. Only love will restore the balance of the world."

Following the elders' presentation, the crowd dispersed in an unusually quiet fashion. Obviously, the words of the speakers had touched everyone very deeply, and no one wanted to break the spell that had settled over us all. The next day we had a free morning, so I asked Jenny to meet with me. I had many questions regarding the issues the speakers raised. We sat together in a quiet circle of benches under a grove of large cottonwoods near the stream. It was another one of those magical New Mexico days. I felt very much alive.

"Jenny," I said, "I want to learn more about what your Grandmother said last night."

"Can you be more specific?" she asked, brushing her long hair from her face and directing her sparkling eyes toward me.

"Yes. She spoke of the necessity to wake people up regarding the mining destruction in the Sacred Mountains. She said that the world will go out of balance if something is not done about it. She talked about separation between people, and how we need to heal Mother Earth. How can I learn more about these things?"

I watched Jenny ponder my request for long seconds. She seemed to be debating something important inside her mind. Finally, she responded.

"The day after tomorrow I'll be leaving for Arizona to take my Grandmother and Grandfather David back home to the reservations. Would you like to follow me and spend some time there? I can introduce you to the people who are dealing first hand with some of these issues, and I can give you a tour of some new, rather exciting cross-cultural projects at SunSpirit Village."

I was intrigued. I couldn't pass up an opportunity like this, I thought to myself. But then the reality of my situation hit home. I was scheduled to return to Albuquerque in a few days. How could I fit this in? I really wanted to go. I paused. Perhaps this was what Jefferson meant when he recommended surrendering to the process. I'd just have to trust that if I was supposed to go, the way would be cleared.

"I'd love to join you. Thanks so much for the invitation, but I need to speak with my boss first. If natural law is agreeable, I'll be there," I assured her.

That afternoon, I called Jack to check in. Somewhat to my surprise, he was most supportive of my plan to visit the reservation. "Tom," he said. "While you're there, write me an update on the ecovillage project and the mining situation. Take a week so you can do it right."

I was greatly relieved. It seemed I was synchronized with natural law. It also struck me as an example of thought and intention manifesting itself in the physical world.

June 21. Sunrise.
As a fresh golden sun broke through the rocky niche on Solstice Mountain, we began drumming. Nearly two dozen bodies swayed in unison, voices lifting to the heavens, chants and songs marking the turn of the solar year. I stood in bliss, thanking the sun for its light, warmth, and heat, its gift to earth, and seed, without which all living creatures would perish. We prayed for strength and guidance to become better people and to find ways to share our talents and skills with others. The balance of the day was spent in outdoor group games, playing music together, telling stories, sharing great homemade food, and walking quietly in the woods—things people had been doing for centuries before television, cars, computers came along to isolate and separate us.

We spent our last night as a group gathered in a circle of power around a great yellow bonfire set amidst a dark canopy of ancient overarching trees. We laughed and cried and sang, and recalled the unfounded fears, unconscious missteps, and unexpected successes of our recent collective adventure.

I remained late with the fire, savoring the last traces of its intimate orange heat. I had given hugs and words of appreciation to everyone for their patience with me and for serving as guides during my challenging and strange inward journey. I singled out Lawrence and congratulated him for sticking with the process. He smiled shyly when I told him this, and confided that he had really learned a lot about himself and what he wanted out of life. "It was just the right thing to have done at just the right time in my life," he said, his voice cracking with emotion. I smiled in silent agreement and we hugged each other spontaneously.

I reflected. Another chapter in my life had come to a close. I still perceived the planet as floundering in endemic crises. Yet, I felt an increased optimism about the human potential for positive change and proud that I had acquired some powerful new skills. But most important, I believed I had a true friend and ally in Jenny, who I was sure would open my mind and heart to many more extraordinary experiences. And, indeed, that would soon prove to be the case.

PART II

THE SOUTHWEST INTERCULTURAL COLLABORATIVE

The best learning comes from the lips of wise elders and from the earth and nature.

—David Monongye, Hopi Traditionalist

All the suffering going on in this country with the tornadoes, floods, and earthquakes is carried on the breath of Mother Earth because she is in pain.

—Robert Blackgoat, Diné Elder

CHAPTER 9

BUILDING CULTURAL BRIDGES

Speaking in Navajo, she stood firm upon the Earth, her wide form starkly silhouetted against the emerging orange incandescence spilling across a panoramic horizon. Praying.

With hardly enough light to discern her facial features, I watched Jenny's grandmother Anita skillfully lead our small group of early risers in a traditional sunrise ceremony. Like many indigenous people, the Navajo believe the sun will not rise if it isn't daily prayed into rising. Thus, she thanked the sun for gifting us with its presence and gratefully acknowledged the four cardinal directions, the Earth and sky, the revered spirits of the land and the ancestors. She prayed for the health and well-being of all people and for the planet's pressing needs. Finally, she humbly asked blessings for her family, her loved ones, and lastly, herself.

As she continued to pray for our health and for the success of the SunSpirit Village Project upon whose grounds we stood, I drew my jacket collar tight against the early morning chill of the metallic desert air. So vast, so silent here. A coyote's distant wail skipped across the miles to our ears, as if powered by some mysterious vibrational force that could amplify sound without electricity. I savored the morning coolness. Soon, the air would crackle with frying-pan heat, the sandy ground underfoot struggling to absorb the full force of the incendiary onslaught of the midday sun. Meanwhile, towering sandstone mesas, looking like old guardian ancestors, stood by in silence. Their job, it seemed, was just to watch.

I glanced down from our small ritual space—a fifteen- by

twenty-foot ledge, a short climb up an orange rock cliff. Pecked into the stone above us, ancient petroglyphs, likely crafted by long-gone Anasazi hunters, depicted several splayed human stick figures and assorted animals—a few antelope, deer, and birds. In the growing light, I could also discern two spirals and a zigzag snake.

Our rocky perch afforded a hawk's-eye view of the huge complex below. How stunned those Anasazi artists of ten centuries past would be to gaze upon what now lay beyond these cliffs. They would recognize the pueblo buildings and the cornfields but little else. How would they mentally classify the two hundred acres of reflective panels, troughs, and parabolic dishes that track in unison the sun's wide arc across the sky? And those strange towers with rotating wings on them? And the three-acre translucent domes bulging with green plants and tanks full of water and fish? And the "herds" of square reflective objects gliding silently along dark paths—transporting men, women, and materials from one kind of odd-shaped structure to another? Would they likely report they'd beheld a vision from another world, another dimension? This was the stuff of myths.

The ceremony completed, our prayers for the day now on their way to the appropriate spirits, we thanked Anita for her leadership. But a part of me had drifted away, even as she was speaking. More than just words had passed into the growing dawn light.

An emptiness, a loss, tugged insistently at my guts like a deep hunger. The simple ceremony in the desert reminded me of my personal remoteness from the primal process of daily Earth connection that the Indian people seemed to have. I stood amazed that after all the assaults that European civilization and its industrial culture have wreaked upon the Native people of the Americas, some still retain that vital kinship with the land, the spirit world, and their ancestors, however tenuous. So blessings on these hearty survivors of plague, pestilence, the U.S. government, and television.

As the sun's golden disc began to etch its way through the mountains on the eastern horizon, I followed the others as they scrambled down the old cliff path partly hewn from solid rock. I was eager to learn more about the incredible village that lay before me on the desert floor.

After a short hike in silence, our multicultural group began to dissipate as individuals headed to their respective destinations. I followed Jenny down the trail. As we approached a rocky overlook near the village, we were joined by two members of the original group. I learned that Matthew, an African-American from New York, was writing a paper on sustainable communities, and Rinchen, a Tibetan, had embarked on a six-month journey through the Southwest to investigate how Native American tribes were adapting to twenty-first century technologies. I was impressed with the curiosity and strong presence of both men. Then Jenny encouraged us all to consciously absorb the beauty before us—the large vertical mesas that soared into the blue desert sky, seeming to serve as powerful energy attractors and protectors of the human treasure below. As Jenny's hand swept across the dramatic panorama, she described how men and women of several cultures have contributed to the success of SunSpirit Village.

"This is what the future can look like," she said with pride, "when the collective imagination of different cultures can be harnessed freely and creatively. That which is tried-and-true can be married to what is newly conceived. Here you see ancient and contemporary architecture, ideally suited to desert living, coexisting with traditional and modern methods of agriculture, and blended with high-tech, renewable energy generation technologies. People can live here year-round in harmony with nature in a highly self-sufficient and reasonably sustainable way."

"Do the Navajo still practice the traditional ways of living?" Rinchen asked. "The grazing and weaving?"

"Yes," Jenny said, speaking slowly. "Some of our people still graze sheep and do without electricity and telephones. But our population is now too large and our land resources too limited to support everyone adopting this lifestyle. In fact, some years ago, we were warned that overuse of our land and water resources plus rapid population growth would severely reduce our future lifestyle options. And most people, especially the younger ones, desire all the modern conveniences."

Rinchen laughed. "We have this same problem with our young people. We, too, are by nature herders, but now in exile, we are being forced to adopt the ways of the industrial society. Our children have the television, and they want the things they see there. They have no interest in working with animals. What is your response to this change?"

"We must not sacrifice our traditions, but our people need some modern technology and social services. Our goal is to create new infrastructure and employment opportunities that build on what we know works here. This village is the result of that vision."

Matthew spoke up in a highly excited voice. "The village is truly beautiful and reflects extraordinary creativity. I've never seen anything like it. How did this come about?"

"It's the result of a collaboration between us and our neighbors, the Hopi, and a non-Indian socially conscious investment group. The partnership is called the Southwest Intercultural Collaborative. The tribal governments sensed the urgency of our environmental and social problems and finally decided to take some action. The president of the Navajo Nation and the chairman of the Hopi called for emergency public meetings to address a variety of critical issues. Following months of discussion, both tribes found we could forge agreements without resorting to litigation. We also decided to seek outside financial assistance and technical expertise from the non-Indian community."

We all listened intently as Jenny explained how the investment group was actively searching for an opportunity to demonstrate how collaborative social/economic strategies could be applied to liberate indigenous cultures from the forced destruction of their own natural resource base.

As it turned out, the idea of a cross-cultural collaborative generated considerable excitement among all the prospective partners. The non-Indian investment group offered to collaborate with the tribes to create a model sustainable community featuring Earth-friendly enterprises that also honored tribal spiritual values. The new village would be located on reservation land, convenient to both Navajo and Hopi populations, yet with easy access to the off-reservation world. The project was designed to provide education, social services, health care, vocational training, and employment opportunities while generating substantial revenues for both tribes.

Jenny continued, "The tribes and the investors planned a complete village and support system. The facilities include a utility-scale solar and wind power plant and a water electrolysis hydrogen production facility, a hospital with a broad range of Eastern, Western, and traditional practitioners; a university with state-of-the-art telecommunications capacity and historical archives; a traditional and permaculture-based agriculture component with greenhouses for year-round organic food production, a biological sewage treatment facility and recycling center, and model energy-efficient housing complexes.

"The designers intended that the village generate one hundred percent of its internal energy and fuel, and grow most of its food. It reduced water use by seventy percent and solid and liquid wastes by eighty percent, as compared to a similar-size population in a typical urban setting. Also, the methane gas produced in the waste treatment process is captured and utilized as additional energy for the community. Finally, to insure that the project would benefit from the best knowledge, talent, and wisdom of both tribes, the village infrastructure and organizational design incorporates as many tribal, philosophical, and spiritual concepts as possible.

"And so here it is," Jenny said, facing toward the landscape in front of us. "In English, it's called 'SunSpirit Village.' As you can see, it's quite new. Most components exist separately elsewhere in the world. But this is the largest contemporary example of so many architectural, technical, social, and environmental elements designed into a spiritually meaningful context by traditional, indigenous cultures.

Already, the rest of the world is taking notice, especially developing countries who are trying to preserve their own cultural identities and avoid the 'Americanization' of their communities. We hope to make a strong international statement that communities can become self-sufficient in energy and food, preserve their traditions and their environment, educate their people, and provide essential services."

"It's something I surely want to cover in the *Earth Renaissance News*," I said.

"I'd like to work here for awhile if I could," said Rinchen.

Jenny smiled proudly. "I can arrange tours for all of you later. But any minute now, the sun will be high enough to activate the solar field. It's pretty exciting. What you see out there are two hundred acres of energy generation equipment and our hydrogen production plant. A certain portion of our solar- and wind-generated electricity is used to make hydrogen gas by electrolysis—the splitting of water into its components of hydrogen and oxygen. The hydrogen provides the necessary energy storage for nighttime use and during cloudy days. And the hydrogen can be converted back into electricity through fuel cells or used as a fuel for cooking and running vehicles. When in full operation, our power plant can produce fifty million watts of power each hour—enough for an average U.S. city of twenty to thirty thousand people." Jenny stopped, straining her ears to pick up a barely discernible sound. "Look, you can see the system is waking up now!"

We stared in the direction of the solar field. In the distance I could discern the first stirring movements of the huge devices. The magic moment had arrived. Whining motors nudged the massive solar panels and reflective mirrors into proper alignment with the newly arrived sun. Enormous energies were focused. Temperatures rose rapidly inside the receivers. The hissing of fluids exposed to 3,000° F heat saturated the once-still desert air. Pumps sprang to life to move liquids and gases into hot receivers. Spinning generators transformed mechanical into electrical energy that quickly surged into hungry transmission lines. Another day at Sun-Spirit Village had begun.

After Matthew and Rinchen left for their appointments, Jenny and I walked toward the Visitor Center. "Was it difficult to get everyone to work together?" I asked.

"It was. We found that right from the start, misunderstandings proliferated. Our two cultures—Western European and Native American—are so vastly different in physical history and spiritual orientation. Also, the Hopi and the Navajo have a long history of hostility. Our historical relationship has burdened people on all sides with varying degrees of guilt, suspicion, woundedness, arrogance, victimization, and dominance. We found that we simply couldn't gain enough mutual trust without first addressing the past and its impact on the present.

"In the beginning, the working groups, which were composed of both Indians and non-Indians, quickly ran afoul of differing philosophical worldviews, unexpressed emotions, dissimilar time values, and destructive patterns of relating. Much conflict has resulted from the dominant culture attempting to assimilate Indians into the European way of life. During this process of forced assimilation, Indian youth and elders became estranged from each other, and youth were separated from their traditions by many years of education under a different cultural mindset. Non-Indian people, on the other hand, had enculturated an unhealthy attitude of superiority and dominance toward Indian people. These attitudinal snags made planning acutely difficult and time consuming. Consequently, we had to call in interpersonal communications experts. Project planning was placed on hold while everyone took time to reexamine his or her own value systems, assumptions, and expectations. We asked ourselves: What needs to be modified, accepted, or eliminated? Were shifts in personal attitude and relating possible, or even desirable?"

"What did you come up with?"

"We all talked about our personal histories and how we'd

learned to think a certain way. How we got these ideas from our culture, our upbringing, and our parents. How our personal values and attitudes run deep. How they are so very hard to change even when we know they're dysfunctional and destructive. We talked for days. Then, in the final session, we performed a ritual together. We prayed for help to let go of our anger and our pain . . . to find our oneness, our common ground, and to forgive ourselves and each other. We brought in our singers and medicine men. Non-Indians summoned their priests, rabbis, and wisdom-teachers. All of us prayed together. We asked for help to learn how to become allies rather than antagonists and learn to collaborate on our visions for the future. I know we're nowhere near done with this process. It's going to reqire considerable healing. But still, something incredible happened. Change occurred. I know it. I felt it."

"What's the 'it'?"

"Hmmmm . . . maybe the beginnings of fundamental changes in our attitudes toward each other . . . perhaps even the faint possibility of a new kind of trust. And respect. Respect for each other as equals—different but equal. That's what's really critical. We concluded that even though we've chosen diverse paths as individuals and cultures, we sensed a shared destiny pulling us all along.

"Okay," Jenny said, turning toward me as we approached a handsome tan and glass building. "We're almost there."

CHAPTER 10

RESTORING BALANCE

Jenny had said that the Southwest Intercultural Collaborative was designed to answer a number of sensitive questions. Could cross-cultural economic development partnerships be created that worked for both groups, meeting basic needs while maintaining traditional values? Could Western technological and Native American nature-based worldviews be successfully joined? What models for other cultures might emerge from this synthesis? These kinds of questions greatly intrigued the collaborative's founders. The only way to discover answers, they concluded, was to build the village. And so they did. The financing accomplished, construction began on the SunSpirit Village early in the twenty-first century. It was fully operational within three years.

I began my acquaintance with the village at the Visitor Center, an ultraenergy-efficient, two-story building equipped with the latest in passive and active solar systems. Stepping inside this magnificent space constructed of local sandstone and large energy-conserving glass windows, I noticed a substantial temperature drop. An indoor-outdoor thermometer mounted conspicuously in the reception area registered 96° F outside and 65° F inside. The interior environment, a nearby sign noted, would remain naturally cool even during the hottest days. I could easily see that this temperature magic was accomplished by judicious use of earth-based materials—in this case, stone and adobe—utilized along with strategically placed insulation and intelligent building design.

While I stood there, transfixed by the beauty of the space, Jenny tugged at my shirt.

"I need to arrange some meetings for later today. You'll find plenty to do around here until I'm finished. Let's reconnect around 1:30 at the Agricultural Center, the next complex to the west."

"Fine," I said, as she disappeared out the doorway. Watching her, I made a mental note to savor whatever time we might have together.

I proceeded into a special theater containing an IMAX projection system. A three-story screen and multichannel sound system provided me with a forty-five-minute history of the local Native peoples. The wide-screen format effectively re-created the expansive panoramas of the indigenous landscape that so enthralls the senses. The presentation emphasized the remarkable ability of southwestern desert dwellers to survive and prosper for thousands of years in a nearly waterless and seemingly barren environment.

The camera surveyed a typical Hopi cornfield. A Hopi farmer stood alone in the foreground adjusting a ragged scarecrow. No verdant forest of man-high stalks surrounded him as one might expect. Instead, robust green clusters of bushlike plants dotted the otherwise sandy expanses. Each plant cluster was four to six feet from its neighbor and arranged in a slightly irregular pattern. But I saw no nearby streams or irrigation ditches. Just sand . . . everywhere. How could anyone grow corn in sand?

The film's narrator anticipated my question. I learned how ideally adapted Hopi corn is to its environment. Although only three feet high above ground, each plant has a fifteen- to twenty-foot root system penetrating deep and seeking precious moisture. And it works! Until the late 1890s, ninety percent of the Hopi's vegetable diet was comprised of corn—red, yellow, black, and blue.

Toward the end of the program, provocative documentation featured the Hopi Prophecies. The prophecies are depicted in a simple graphic inscribed on a large standing stone referred to as "Prophecy Rock," located near the

Restoring Balance

ancient Hopi village of Old Oraibi. In its present form, the inscription is believed to date to 1906 when a faction split from Old Oraibi and founded the village of Hotevilla to continue a life free from outside interference. (Apparently, an earlier version of the inscription exists elsewhere on the reservation.) The prophecy predicts the course of events when humans no longer respect the Earth as the source of spiritual truth. It has successfully foretold of two major wars and a so-called "path of inventions." Specific mention is made of the dropping of a deadly "gourd of ashes," a reference to the atomic bomb; the coming of a "house in the sky," the Skylab space station; the technologies of television, telephone, and computer; and "cobwebs in the sky," electric transmission lines. Two circles on the lower part of the graphic predicted two global upheavals linked to the symbols of the swastika and the sun—and yet to come, a mysterious third cataclysmic event. The future event can come about either wrathfully or peacefully, depending upon the choices humanity makes.

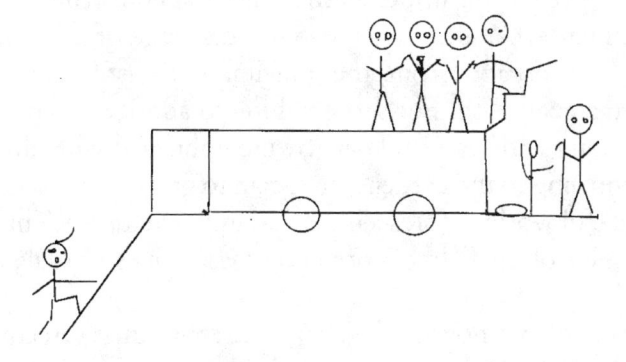

Hopi Prophecy Pictopraph

The oral transmission, handed down secretly by different Hopi clan members and made public in 1948, addresses the fateful choices. Two possible paths are described by the graphic. The first or upper path, upon which several stick figures stand, leads to a jagged line which interpreters define as the materialistic path—the path of inventions. A second or lower path, the path of eternal life, leads to a symbolic field of corn where *Maasaw*, the owner of the land, awaits, planting stick in hand. A long time ago, Maasaw invited the Hopi to share his land and taught them the proper way to farm and maintain balance.

The mysterious stick figures resident upon the upper path, whose heads were originally drawn on Prophecy Rock as separated from their bodies, symbolize humanity's often fatal tendency to sever mind from heart, logic from intuition, and physical from spiritual. When disassociation occurs at such a primal level, greed and materialism are able to triumph over love, compassion, spirit, and our connection with nature.

And all is lost, ending in annihilation at the end of the path of inventions.

If, on the other hand, humanity chooses to forsake materialism in favor of the path of harmony with natural law, divine assistance stands ready and willing to serve. To facilitate this transition, the inscription displays a crossover line extending from the upper path of ignorance to the lower spiritual path that affords a last-minute change of heart and subsequent escape from the inevitable disasters of the dreaded zigzag path. For those willing to adopt a life based on harmony with natural law—by metaphorically or physically returning to the garden once again to grow corn—a gentle, peaceful world is foreseen as an alternative future. This is the message of the field of corn and Maasaw, its spiritual gardener.

Where are we now on the prophetic continuum? According to the narrator, some Hopi traditionalists insist we have already passed the final point of spiritual reconciliation. They say we are entering the "Time of Purification," in which the human race will be winnowed down dramatically to only those practicing the "True Hopi Way"—"one who walks in the right direction" and lives a life of balance, peace, and humility. Following the cleansing, a new, corrected version of humanity will perhaps be given another chance.

Apparently, this isn't the first time humanity has

destroyed itself. Indeed, according to Hopi Creation Myth, humanity regularly runs amok and must routinely be purged and purified. Hopi history recounts three major purification cycles so far. We're now on our fourth attempt, which they refer to as the "Fourth World." As the story goes, the materially based Third World was destroyed by flood because the spiritual nature of life was forgotten.

I wobbled out of the theater, my head reeling from the implications of what I had just seen and heard. How should one relate to prophecy? How accurate can it be? Can we really know the future? Perhaps time does wrap around itself in ways most of us are not trained to understand. But some evidently are. They've learned to observe, record, and predict the great cycles of civilization. Amazingly, the Hopi—perfectly isolated for so long—seem to have psyched out the whole of Industrial Era history from the remote steadfastness of their mystic mesas.

Clearly, America's indigenous cultures, like others around the globe, able to evolve for millennia in isolation from the technological and political machinations of European-based civilization, have developed wonderfully rich and complex traditions. But recent centuries of destructive interference by outside cultures have taken a toll. Now, if what remains of Native American wisdom is to be preserved and perpetuated, aggressive and creative efforts will be required by both Native and non-Native cultures.

I left the Visitor Center, my mind filled with more questions and a renewed openness. Wherever I looked, so much seemed to be going on both visibly and invisibly. I sensed an intangible timelessness expressing itself in the sand and stone, in the broad turquoise sky, and in a subtle but earthy magic present in the air.

I stared across to the nearby Agricultural Center where I was headed next. A young Navajo man, perhaps sensing my confusion, approached unabashedly. "Ya'at'eeh," he said, offering the typical Navajo greeting. In a friendly tone of voice, he asked, "Where you headed?"

"Right now? I'm just exploring."

"Where you from?" he inquired again with surprising directness.

An interesting question, I thought. Did this mean where had I been born, or where had I lived for the past ten, twenty, twenty-five years? Was I from Pennsylvania, California, New Mexico? Or Planet Earth?

"Well," he laughed, sensing my bewilderment. "I'll start. My name is Roger Tsosie, and I'm from Chinle, a town about fifty miles away, near Canyon de Chelly. I am Diné. It means 'The People.' That's what we call ourselves. Navajo is the white man's word for us," he nodded with grace and firmness. "If you're looking for a guide, I can show you around."

"Sure," I said gratefully.

Roger led me to the agricultural area where we inspected hundreds of acres of Village crops, lovingly tended, many of them ancient and indigenous but some newly introduced. We stopped to examine a special plot demonstrating Hopi dry land farming of corn, beans, and squash—all traditional crops. He introduced me to a slight, weathered Hopi man who tended the field and would only give his name as James.

When I commented about the seemingly impossible feat of growing nutrient-intensive corn in sand, James paused for a moment, shifting his weight to the well-used digging stick he clasped between his furrowed hands. His ancient eyes lifted pensively toward mine. He told me how, at the beginning of the Fourth World, the Hopi god Maasaw gave the Hopi their planting stick—called a *sooya*—and taught them proper farming techniques. Thus, when the Hopi engage in the traditional planting process, as their ancestors have done for thousands of years, they are recalling or reexperiencing the creation of the world—"the time before there was time."

"For the Hopi," he continued, "growing corn is sacred. It's the coming together of earth and sky, above and below, male and female. The corn will grow only when Mother Earth joins with the rain. The rain feeds the corn, bringing life to the people. Without corn, there would be no Hopi."

His hand waved across the land that meant everything to the Hopi. His gray-white hair spilled over a red headband. "You see, the four colors of corn—red, blue, yellow, and white—are like the four races. Corn is life to the Hopi. The life in corn becomes flesh when eaten. It is the Earth Mother becoming human. When we eat corn we are then part of our Mother from whom we are born and receive our sustenance and to whom we return after death. The Hopi give thanks for the gift of corn through our dances and ceremonies. And we sing to the corn."

"Why do you sing?" I asked carefully.

"Corn is our relative, an essential member of our family. We want to invite them into the community. Singing to corn is like giving love, thanking them, praying for their health, encouraging them to be good and strong so we will grow strong and healthy too when we eat the corn. When we sing, we work our spirit, our energy into the corn."

"You see," James said, staring intensely at both of us, "growing food right is really about working with Spirit, working with Creation. Many things are happening here, many beings take part. You're working with life itself. But to be successful, you must know how to pray to the spirits, honor the land, and communicate with the wind, the rain, and the sun."

I thought to myself that this is obviously not the case with our contemporary process of industrial agriculture. "What happens if the community ignores the kind of spiritual connections between food, life, and nature that you say are so important?"

James paused, leaned heavily on his planting stick and stared solemnly into the distance. Finally, he spoke. "We have a word for this kind of condition. *Koyaanisqatsi*. It means 'life out of balance.'"

Well, there you have it, I mused. That describes our global situation pretty well. We stood together silently; a hot wind scurried across the desert and pressed hard against us. I welcomed the heat that brushed randomly across my face and arms. It seemed comforting and appropriate as I contemplated the thoughts James had put before us.

Roger and I then headed toward a demonstration area dedicated to land reclamation. He said that besides recovering drought-resistant crops, the village agricultural program focused on restoring degraded rangeland. Because dry southwestern lands have suffered badly from two centuries of abusive grazing practices, Arizona and New Mexico have experienced some of the highest rates of desertification in the United States. The restoration design system being explored at the village is called *permaculture*, or permanent agriculture, which seeks "to reconcile human communities and activity with the ecological imperatives of a living planet."

Roger explained to me that Australian ecologist Bill Mollison coined the term in the early 1970s to describe a comprehensive, integrated process of sustainable agriculture and land management, efficient energy use, sensible community design, and egalitarian economics.

"These techniques are particularly well-suited to restoring badly eroded lands and regional biodiversity. We build small earth, rock, and wire dams—called swales and gabions—into eroded areas to trap and redistribute rain water and soil nutrients. Almost immediately, nature can begin rebuilding damaged areas with new soil. This allows plants and grasses to reestablish themselves, and the animals and insects that depend on them to return.

"Permaculture is a comprehensive physical system of living in balance with nature. It puts everything to work. It teaches how to use trees for shading, cooling, and wildlife habitats and how to create full-cycle, soil-plant-animal-human support systems. Because it's so effective, permaculture workshops are held regularly at local Navajo Chapter Houses and Hopi villages. People get pretty excited when they see that by improving their lands, they can economically sustain small food production enterprises and sometimes avoid moving to distant cities in search of employment."

From listening to Roger, I was reminded of Jenny's comment about Navajo adeptness at importing new ideas into their culture. They had done this now with permaculture techniques, integrating them into their own agricultural practices. Roger also explained the importance of growing and consuming traditional crops as a method of disease prevention in people. Radical departures from centuries-old diets have left many Native People alarmingly susceptible to diabetes, obesity, and high blood cholesterol. Studies have shown that a return to their traditional foods can lead to dramatic health benefits as well as stimulating the local economy. Also, the switch from imported to regional products keeps money on the reservation that would otherwise be siphoned off to outsiders. By providing a plausible model of physical, economic, and spiritual self-sufficiency, the Village agricultural program aids personal self-esteem and reduces the need for social services. And—I was about to learn from Jenny—few things are more important to the tribes than essential social services.

"Hello, Tom!" Roger and I turned our heads to track the source of the greeting. It was Jenny, standing near a small building alongside an access road. "Time to catch the bus," she shouted, waving me over to her. I thanked Roger for his company and told him I had a meeting to catch. He nodded graciously and bid me a fruitful journey.

CHAPTER 11

HOLISTIC HEALING

"The tribes desperately need more social services," Jenny said as we waited at the shuttle stop. "And that's why our hospital and health care facilities are so important."

A twenty-passenger bus pulled up, colorfully painted with Anasazi, Hopi, and Navajo designs. Blue letters on its white metal sides informed us that the bus was powered by hydrogen fuel cells. Moreover, this hydrogen was produced locally with solar energy.

Upon entering the bus, I was struck by the unexpected mix of passengers—European tourists interspersed with local Navajo and Hopi. The Europeans, mostly German and French, chatted away in their own languages. Indian families, primarily of women and children, sat tightly clustered together, silently observing the boisterous foreigners. As I moved to the back of the bus, the children tracked my every move with wide, dark eyes.

"My cousin Francine is the director of the hospital," Jenny whispered as the bus gathered speed, its four electric wheel motors quietly surging to life. It took about fifteen minutes to reach the hospital complex. Jenny described how the hospital had already benefited the surrounding community by subsidizing health care with dollars from off-reservation patrons, and by providing many local jobs. The hospital supplies an array of auxiliary services, too, including free transportation to its main facility and mobile care units that travel to the most remote parts of the reservations. A sophisticated telemedicine capability assists with rural health care and allows direct interactive visual and audio links with physicians and medical facilities outside the reservations.

When we arrived, we found the hospital hosting a team of health care professionals from twenty developing countries who were touring the facility. They were particularly interested in the unique blend of Western, Eastern, Native traditional, and holistic medicine that the hospital practiced. The facility is the only one of its kind in the United States that offers such a broad range of treatment methodologies. Not surprisingly, North Americans and Europeans flocked here in droves.

Inside, we had to push through a collection of frenzied reporters attempting to gain information from the director, a smartly dressed woman in her forties who exuded great self-confidence. Her brown eyes burned with resolve, and her voice was strong and vigorous, as she described the facility's philosophy and methods. After detailing the institution's stellar record of performance, she cautioned the visitors about certain perceived shortcomings of traditional Western medicine.

"The Diné are a sovereign nation, and therefore we have the right to determine the best treatment methodologies for our patients. We respect and use the Western model of technological and chemical intervention, but our approach also includes the energies of the Earth and the powers of Spirit. We find allopathic medicine indispensable for many cases, but we hold equally valuable other methods, such as Eastern medicine and our own healing traditions. We consider our medicine men and women to be legitimate, professional medical practitioners, equal in skill and importance to our radiologists and surgeons. We know of native herbs that promote recovery from illness as well as or better than manufactured synthetic substances. We've observed the therapeutic power of human touch, lovingly administered through massage, chiropractic, and the potency of more energetic, noncontact techniques such as chanting and ritual. If you seek proof of our effectiveness, I encourage you to interview our patients. They are the ones who should judge the success or failure of our methods."

Holistic Healing

Jenny stood beside me, her arms proudly folded across her chest. "That's Francine. She's a true warrior." Jenny waved to her cousin as the director led a group of reporters down the hall to her office.

Jenny then gave me a short tour of the facility. As we explored the complex, I saw plenty of typical hospital gear, but the atmosphere was very different. Here the rooms were beautifully adorned with murals depicting southwestern landscapes—sunsets over towering mesas, coyotes howling in silver moonlight, and spirit figures emerging from within trees, sandstone cliffs, mountains, cloud formations, and double rainbows. Soft pastels throughout contributed to a calming ambiance. The recovery rooms were spacious and relatively free of ubiquitous chrome-edged furnishings. Instead, each room was unique and filled with original artwork from the community.

I noticed acupuncture charts and diagrams of body pressure points hanging on several walls. Most rooms smelled of aromatic cedar-juniper and sage incense; and in quiet corners, small altars stood adorned with feathers or a woven basket containing a leather pouch full of corn pollen or crystals, or turquoise necklaces.

But I'll always remember what I saw in the hallways—a diverse assortment of healers. Name tags identified them and their healing specialties. I met Chinese and U.S. acupuncturists, homeopathic doctors, East Indian Ayurvedic experts, and other alternative medical practitioners. Most interesting to me were the local medicine men and women who tended to remain quiet and inconspicuous. They could be recognized by the items they carried—fat medicine pouches, elaborately beaded eagle-feather wands, and tightly bound packets of sage.

Everyone kept stressing to me that the treatment of disease should not be viewed solely in terms of either Western or Eastern, traditional or modern. Rather, all healing paths can offer value, with each form of medicine a possible tool, including methods that are primarily psychological or spiritual.

"The whole person is important here," an herbalist in

residence told me, "and that means body, mind, and spirit. We use a variety of treatment approaches. We might call for an x-ray to diagnose an area where there is pain, then an acupuncturist to treat that pain. If surgery is required, we may choose anesthesia. But we prefer a noninvasive approach if it will work just as well and with less risk. We avoid prescribing synthetic medicines whenever possible because we know there are often better options . . . a major one being herbal treatment. Herbs might work more slowly, but there are usually fewer side effects. And psychological and spiritual counseling accompanies everything we do, depending on a person's needs and spiritual beliefs. We look beyond symptoms to identify underlying causes and begin there. And we know that full recovery usually requires a major shift in lifestyle. That's where counseling can be most helpful. A positive, healthy attitude is everything."

"I'm really impressed," I said. "I don't know of a hospital anywhere that offers such a broad range of services. You're really fortunate."

"Yes, we are," Jenny nodded approvingly. "But you know, the Diné have always known that for balance, a person must have a healthy body and engage in good work. We call this *Hózhó*, which translates in English into 'walking in beauty' or the 'Beauty Way.' We strive for peace, joy, and harmony in all aspects of our daily life. Our traditions also strongly encourage self-sufficiency and dignified work to support life's ethical, social, and environmental dimensions."

Jenny informed me that the Southwest Intercultural Collaborative had already helped to empower people and strengthen community by eliminating the need to travel off the reservations to deal with most medical needs. On-reservation health care facilities also provided a valuable opportunity for gifted young men and women to work with each other, and with experienced healers, while ministering to their own people. This arrangement allowed health practitioners to explore ways to balance traditional and contemporary healing methods.

"But I'd like to show you how we're preserving our tra-

HOLISTIC HEALING 117

ditional teachings. Let's go over this way."

Jenny then led me to a building that adjoined the Native People's University. The complex was part of the university's library, audiovisual, and multimedia archive. Jenny explained to me how indigenous knowledge is compiled from around the world and useful educational materials are prepared for the tribes. About a hundred people are employed in this task alone. High capacity data and video links provided interactive access with the outside world. Once the teams do their work of cataloging and synthesizing information and transferring it to CD-ROMs and videotapes, the material is then made available to the appropriate users worldwide.

As we entered a room full of people and computer monitors, one screen in particular attracted my attention. A woman noticed my interest, beckoned me closer with a friendly wave of her hand. "This is our multimedia botanical project," she said, glancing back and forth between the screen and me, her keyboard clicking while she spoke. "We're working to increase our database of native plant classifications with their Diné, Latin, and English names. It will provide our people ready access to this information." She then confided, "Plants are very important to the Diné. We believe they are gifts from the *diyin diné* or Holy People. Some plants are used as medicine, some as dyes, and others for spiritual purposes. Unfortunately, much of this knowledge is disappearing with the passing of our elders. We hope our young people will be encouraged by this work to educate themselves about its value. Most of this is not for the public," she cautioned me.

"Over a thousand different species of plant life can be found on our 25,000-square-mile reservation," she went on. "Perhaps seven hundred Diné *Hataalii,* or herbalists, still practice this sacred art which has been carefully handed down through oral tradition and personal training. Unfortunately, the presence of synthetic chemical-based medicine has undermined our traditional methods of treatment. So we've taken action to preserve the knowledge while respecting its sacred nature. For this reason, we've limited our public database to perhaps only one hundred plants while we carefully protect other information that relates to ceremonial and spiritual use. Those who choose to become practitioners must undergo an extensive apprenticeship before they can know more. That's the way it must be learned."

"Are there many young people that take up the study?" I asked.

"Not so many anymore," she responded, her voice betraying a note of sadness. "Practically speaking, few young people are willing to spend the long hours in the field necessary to attain herbal expertise in the traditional way. Not many have the patience when they're tempted by television, video, sports, and the other distractions of contemporary life on the reservation."

It seemed alarmingly clear to me that—worldwide—vast stores of medicinal and ritual wisdom are being lost daily due to the passing of key individuals and even entire cultures. Although such losses cannot be accurately quantified—as with the extinction of plant and animal species—the collective quality of human existence nevertheless is tragically diminished. Learning from electronic databases or books and videos is fine, I thought to myself, but such media fail miserably to approach the profound direct personal experience.

I do know the difference. I traveled to the Hopi mesas when I first came to New Mexico, and I had the opportunity to view some of the fabled Hopi ceremonial dances when they were still open to outsiders. I've been there at dawn, perched high on yellow sandstone block rooftops in the ancient villages, to witness the entrance of a phalanx of fifty masked kachina dancers. I've felt the rush of excitement as primal emotions welled up within me, as I shifted my attention to those otherworldly beings suddenly appearing before me. As the drums commenced and the low-frequency chanting of the men charged the dry desert air, and the rattles cried in unison, I would find myself catapulted into realms beyond words, where no technological replication, however sophisti-

Holistic Healing

cated, could compare. In contrast, the finest rendering of virtual reality would pass into simplistic oblivion.

There, in those old villages of stone, I dropped into cellular memory. My body became a living sensor, connecting me to the totality of the past. The Tibetan monklike drone of the dancer's voice-rattle drove us all forward, then backward in time; the dancing kachinas never dropped the count, never missed a critical pause no matter how asymmetrically inserted. Then we journeyed together into the rhythmic straightaway, into the crack between worlds, and on and on and on until the unexpected and breathtaking climax. All the while, the miracle and mystery of existence was invoked, the divine explicitly summoned. As the fabric of the universe parts, man and woman are made whole and unquestionably connected to god and goddess, Earth and infinite cosmos. And in this ephemeral union of form and spirit, I would remember to remember.

CHAPTER 12

LIFE OUT OF BALANCE

"Can you tell me about the mining?" I asked Jenny as we relaxed in her simply decorated living room in her home near the Village. "I understand it's long been a source of tension for both tribes."

Rising from her seat, she silently removed a large file folder from a nearby shelf and placed it on the well-worn dark pine coffee table in front of me. She returned to the fat lounge chair opposite me and slowly closed her eyes. I could see she was working hard to release the tension of the day. I honored her need for silence, and so did not intrude with speech. Instead, I sat back and enjoyed her presence. I doubted if I would ever find anyone else who would touch me as deeply as she had. At the moment, I couldn't imagine Jenny as not part of my life in some way.

"Please excuse me if I'm not responsive," she apologized, briefly opening her eyes. "I need a little time to collect my thoughts."

"I understand."

"I have some papers in the file. You're welcome to look through them."

I leaned forward from my seat on the couch and opened the file folder. In twenty minutes of careful study, I learned much about the history of mining on the reservations. Apparently, in the late 1990s the Hopi and the Navajo had reached a critical turning point regarding natural resource use and economic development on their lands. A major point of conflict concerned coal and water. The tribes had lots of coal, about five billion tons, enough for two hundred years of mining at present extraction rates. Several international mineral development corporations and certain western and southwestern electric utilities had poured billions of dollars into building four mammoth coal-fired power plants on and near the reservations during the 1960s. The coal and water leasing agreements between the utilities and the tribes were arranged under highly questionable circumstances. And after forty years of operation, the plants themselves remained the source of considerable controversy due to numerous adverse cultural and environmental impacts.

The Hopi were most concerned about impacts on their water supplies, as both tribes shared the same underground aquifer. This single source of pure water was being mined at the rate of 1.5 billion gallons per year to supply a coal slurry line, which transported pulverized coal 273 miles to the Mohave Generating Station in southern Nevada. According to Hopi-hired hydrologists, the aquifer could become bone dry by 2010 or 2015. For nine hundred years the Hopi had depended on this precious, pristine source for drinking and bathing and crop irrigation. For the Hopi, water is sacred, "like a bloodline to the heart."

"It's a sad, tragic story, isn't it?" Jenny remarked, without warning.

I looked up, surprised by her sudden animation. "I'd certainly say so. I'm especially disturbed by the large scale of everything . . . and the effects of water extraction. Four massive strip mining operations and four giant power plants—all within a hundred and fifty miles or so of here!"

"Yes. But the worst effect so far, at least from a human point of view, has been the relocation of Diné people. Over a period of three decades, ten thousand Diné living near the coal-rich Black Mesa/Big Mountain area—the residence of our 'Female Deity'—were required to move from their traditional lands to substandard government-built housing. This housing is often located in distant border towns, many of which are notorious for their racist attitudes. It's considered to have been the largest forced-relocation program in the history of the United States. But you need to hear from those

Life Out of Balance

who are personally involved. Tomorrow we'll take a drive out to Black Mesa."

For hours, it seemed, we pounded along lonely dirt roads in Jenny's mud-splattered sport utility vehicle. Every few miles a well-worn dirt road would spin off to a small homestead several miles in the distance. The typical Navajo homesite usually consisted of a one-story frame-style tract house, a hogan, a large pile of juniper wood neatly stacked nearby, a corral, a pickup truck, and several dogs and children staring at us as we drove by. An outsider might understandably ask why anyone would want to live here in such extreme remoteness. All I could see was flat desert land without trees. Homes lacked telephones or electricity, and residents had to deal with intense heat in the summer, crushing cold and isolation in the winter, and immobilizing mud in the spring. According to Jenny, most families here regularly haul their water and undertake day-long expeditions to remote towns to buy food and supplies.

Yet, I couldn't help but admire these amazing, rugged people who cling so tenaciously to the land, who consciously reject the mindless and devastating Earth-consuming lifestyle that most people in the world seem bent on acquiring. Here in these vast open spaces of the Arizona desert, I sensed the profound quietness, the ambiance of purity, and relished the opportunity to experience a closeness to the heartbeat of Mother Earth.

"We'll be visiting a friend of my grandmother's," Jenny informed me as the car made a hard left turn onto a barely discernible feeder road. She slowed the vehicle to accommodate a low wash and then accelerated up a short sandy hill. I was thankful our vehicle had high clearance as the tracks were so deeply worn. Patches of thin, brown desert grass sprouted a foot or so above the center strip.

As we negotiated the short driveway, several young children and three rather forlorn-looking dogs rushed toward us. Swerving quickly to avoid the animals, Jenny parked alongside an old faded blue Chevy pickup missing its rear bumper.

The truck's bed was half filled with several fifty-five-gallon drums. Hose attachments dangled over the truck's side, leading me to conclude that it served as the water supply truck.

The children excitedly led us to a nearby outdoor arbor that was supported by huge posts of well-weathered juniper wood and covered in a latticework of cottonwood and cedar branches. The shade it provided was cooling, and the breezes that filtered through, sensual. We were greeted warmly by two Diné women—one in a dark velvet dress and turquoise necklace and the other wearing jeans and a tan sweatshirt. An elderly Hopi man sat nearby wearing a pair of worn khaki pants and a simple shirt. Jenny introduced me to her grandmother's friend Donna Mae and to the younger woman named Laura, a second generation Diné activist whose family had lived in an area that was eventually strip-mined. I was also introduced to Manuel, who resided in a nearby Hopi village. Jenny spoke in Navajo to the women and in English to Manuel. Jenny and I were asked to be seated. An older girl brought us two large steaming bowls of mutton stew mixed with posole. I felt truly welcomed and at home.

After we finished eating, Laura described her family's experiences. "I've lived here all my life and watched how the process to remove us from our land affected us. I saw my mother change from being a gentle, loving, and happy person into a hard woman. I watched her cry whenever she thought about what was happening to us. I saw young men in my family turn to alcohol to escape their reality, and often these men abused their wives and young children. I watched broken families neglect their children and turn to suicide. I saw people do what they do because they didn't know where to turn their anger. Many young men I know are still full of anger, like time bombs waiting to explode. Even the very young ones feel the grief—and it will be with them all their lives. I've even watched myself become racist, become angry against our neighbors—the Hopi—the tribal governments, and the U.S. government for causing us to suffer so much. When we tried to speak up about this, we were ignored and abandoned."

Laura's voice caught in her throat and she lowered her head. Everyone fell silent as she struggled to hold back the tears. I felt a dagger of pain run through my body, my own eyes moistening in empathy.

Laura continued in a halting voice. "That's the human side of it, but there's the land part too. What's going to happen to the land? We can't just continue to tear it apart! And what we do to the land affects the whole Earth. It affects everyone."

Donna Mae then spoke about land impacts. Jenny translated into English for me. "There will come a time when there will be no future," she warned. "When we finish destroying everything, who will know how to survive? Who will teach the children how to live in balance with the Earth? Who will be able to remember the old ways? We can't replenish these things—the clean air and water, the undisturbed land. Our land, Big Mountain, is a sacred shrine. Our children, our animals, hold the balance. We beg the Earth to help us continue. No matter how poor we are, we will continue to fight to preserve the land."

She paused to take a deep breath, and then spoke bluntly. "The mining companies are taking out the insides of Mother Earth. They are ripping out her guts for profit, for greed. She is in great pain. You see, coal is like the liver, and uranium is the heart and lungs of Mother Earth. They take these things out and only put back dust and ashes. We know that everything is one whole. You can't take parts away and not give anything back."

Donna Mae sighed and wiped the tears from her eyes. "Our leader is nature—the Earth, the sun, the air, and water. This is who we talk to. When resources are taken, the Earth will lose its balance with the moon. And the moon controls the balance with water. We see this is already happening. Now there is a haze. The sunlight is meaner. This is what happens when you put dust and poisons in the air every day."

Manuel, obviously a shy man, stared at the ground and spoke very slowly. He said that, although he did not live near the mining operations, he had seen the effects. As a Hopi farmer, he had for years been visiting the ancient springs that, for a millennium at least, had supplied mesa top villages and neatly terraced gardens with year-round water. "I've noticed that many springs have dried up. Others no longer provide water year round," he said in a raspy voice. "Our people depend on this water. We live in a desert. Without water, our culture will die. But Hopi springs have more than merely physical value," he added. "Important ceremonies are performed at the springs, and special offerings are given. These springs are sacred and are considered as blessings to the Hopi. Every ceremony asks to continue this blessing of water. Water is our life."

I gazed at these amazing people before me. They're the canaries in the mine, these Diné and Hopi people. These remarkable survivors, still attempting to live in a harsh, unforgiving, yet stunningly beautiful and strangely magical land, are bellwethers, lightning rods, for all of us. Here, miles from the decision makers of the industrial world, these simple-living, gentle stewards of the land must confront the full onslaught of industrial society's unending appetite for electrical, atomic, and fossil power. That is, they and the quiet Earth on which they pray and live out their lives.

Power. It's about power, of course.

"Why does the white man always want to take the power from the land?" Donna Mae asked, reading my mind. "Why not keep it in the ground so it can benefit all people, all generations?"

Jenny added, "Over many generations, our land has been consciously invested with power by our ceremonies, prayers, and rituals. I'm not surprised that valuable minerals exist here in places that we consider sacred. Is this a coincidence? Is there a connection between the minerals and the spiritual energies? Many Native legends warn of dire consequences for people should these minerals be disturbed—as is happening today."

Donna Mae looked down and stared intensely at her hands, folded on her lap. "The Holy People have charged us to protect our sacred lands and honor the spirits that live

Life Out of Balance

here. In return, we draw upon the land for our food and livelihood, our visions, and for healing and preserving our families. Many traditions and legends refer to this ancient bond and what will happen if we fail. When people no longer honor their sacred trust with the land, great negative forces will be released by nature. Winds, waters, and atmospheric cycles will fall out of delicate equilibrium, causing earthquakes, volcanic eruptions, floods, and plagues. I think we are seeing this happening right now with 200-mile-per-hour hurricanes and all the floods, droughts, and forest fires, and melting glaciers."

As our meeting ended, I found myself profoundly moved by the dedication and sincerity of these gentle guardians of the land. It was, though, indeed painful to be reminded of the terrible fact that we are, in effect, "ripping out the guts of Mother Earth" for money and to support our technological conveniences and our material addictions. The Diné and many other indigenous people in the world have sounded the alarm, but will anyone respond? If the Hopi and Diné traditionalists are right, that the Earth's vital circulatory and respiratory systems are threatened by continued mining, the future of humanity on Planet Earth may well be decided in these remote, silent lands of the U.S. Southwest. I found this realization disturbing and ominous. And I needed to know if there was something . . . anything I could do to help restore the delicate balance.

CHAPTER 13

THE BEAUTY WAY

The dry heat of the afternoon finally became tempered by the approaching dusk. I welcomed the coolness after a day of high emotional as well as physical temperatures. After dinner, Jenny, Laura, and I lounged outside Donna Mae's house, under the arbor, sipping cups of lemonade.

I stared into the distance, my sight traveling perhaps a hundred miles unimpeded. Against the still, bright horizon, I could detect the faint outlines of large power line towers marching across the desert. That image made it all too easy for me to conjure up scenes of distant cities sucking dry the vital fluids of these southwestern sacred lands.

Everything seemed out of balance. I felt out of balance. And the day's conversation had seemed out of balance. I realized I needed to gain a larger perspective. So, in my mind I questioned what I had heard: Yes, it was true, many Diné and some Hopi had suffered from having to move, but involuntary relocation is a common occurrence everywhere. Each year in the United States, hundreds of farms are lost and thousands of mortgages are foreclosed, forcing families to abandon homes sometimes handed down over many generations. Daily, millions of people worldwide are forced to flee their homesteads and homelands, due to war, pestilence, or environmental destruction. The world is full of involuntary, homeless refugees.

Nevertheless, a great injustice has occurred here. It's the old story of money, greed, and power, pursued in ways that reek of dishonesty and exploitation of others with less political power. All these things have conspired to create yet another tragic human drama, perpetuated by members of my own culture. What action could I or should I take? And how much was I driven by my own "white man's guilt?"

I found no answers but my attention was drawn to Laura's mention of a Solar Energy Conversion Plan. I asked her to explain it to me.

"Well," she said, her enthusiasm building, "it became clear to everyone that despite the tragedy we found ourselves experiencing, life had to go on. We had to adapt to changing circumstances. And I think we brought attention to the fact that the tribes could not depend forever on their income from the coal and water mining. Everyone could see how terribly dependent we were and how far our tribe was from any possibility of economic self-reliance. The SunSpirit Village concept, though, opened a lot of peoples' minds to other possibilities, a major one being the idea of developing our renewable energies like solar. So those of us who were most affected personally by the mining asked Diné and Hopi students who had recently returned from college to help us draft a plan to harness our solar energy potential."

"And what will it do?" I asked.

"The plan, which has been adopted by both tribes, places a special tax on all coal mined on the reservations and burned in the power plants. The money raised from this tax will be used by the tribes to repower the coal-fired power plants with natural gas and solar energy and to build new renewable energy generation facilities—like at SunSpirit Village. We'll greatly expand our solar equipment manufacturing plants. That'll mean jobs, jobs, jobs—for Diné and Hopi people."

"So the tribes could become major regional power producers and distributors themselves, rather than mainly recipients of coal and water royalty fees?"

"Exactly," responded Jenny. "We believe it's time to begin controlling our own destinies. We know we have valuable natural resources such as land and sunlight. If we can utilize these resources in ways that don't compromise our contract of stewardship with the land, then we can serve our own pressing needs and those of others as well. And such models are really important as demonstrations—especially for Indian people."

We finally called it quits when it became hard to see. Manuel had left late in the afternoon, and Laura departed in the darkness. I went to bed early that night, crawling into the small tent Jenny had brought for me. I was exhausted from the long drive and the emotional roller-coaster discussions. Jenny slept in the house with Donna Mae, and I was quite content to sleep out under the stars, sparkling vividly against an inky black sky, undiluted by the presence of electric lights. I savored the amazing quiet and pristine darkness.

Gazing out of my tent at the night, I recalled my evenings on the mountain in my hermitage at the PsyEarth Institute. But here the landscape is uninterrupted by trees and feels very different. I sense something unfathomable in this land. Perhaps it's the imprint of the human-invested prayer power mixed with the mineral energies that the women spoke of. When I try to quantify what I feel, the image that comes to me is of a landscape inhabited by multitudes of mysterious spirit beings and forces, flitting about, taking care of business, and observing, always observing, what the humans might be up to now.

I'm usually a deep sleeper, but this night something else took control of my unconscious mind. Whatever it was, it continued to flash an image, the same one, repeated many times. I studied it. It resembled a rock pinnacle, about three-hundred-feet tall, sloped enough to climb if you were careful and large enough on top to permit a person to recline. It reminded me of a similar geological formation I had noticed a mile or two from my hermitage cabin. I was drawn to it at the time, but never undertook the journey. But here it was again. What did it mean? Was it drawing me somewhere?

I mentioned the dream to Jenny and Donna Mae the next morning. All three of us were sitting at the breakfast table, but Jenny remained quiet, mulling over the matter.

"I think it's a message," she finally said, staring at her cup of Navajo tea. "It may be that you're supposed to go somewhere to be given some information. Perhaps Donna Mae will recognize it."

Jenny spoke to Donna Mae in Navajo, describing my vision. The elder thought for a moment, and then her eyes widened with excitement, and she began to speak rapidly.

"What did she say?" I asked Jenny.

"She says there's a rock formation not far from here, just over the mountain. It's called Tower Rock. Local people go there sometimes to seek visions. It's on national forest land and there's a campground there, too. Not many people know about it because it's pretty far away from any main roads."

"And it looks like what I described?"

"Yes, that's what she says."

"So, what does this mean?" I asked.

"What do you think it means?" Jenny responded.

I stopped thinking and closed my eyes and tried to call the image back. Nothing happened. I looked at Jenny. She was waiting for my answer. I got up from the table and walked outside. Beyond lay the vast expanse of Navajo land, silent, bright in the early morning sun. I could feel it. Something was waiting out there for me. On the mountain.

I heard Jenny behind me and turned to face her.

"Well?" she asked with a quizzical look.

"I need to go there," I said, surprised at my conviction.

"Good," she said. "I agree."

We spent the rest of the morning dealing with logistics—how much food and supplies we'd need and how to transport our gear. Donna Mae suggested we use her horse. We wouldn't need much anyway, Jenny said. This was not a major group expedition, just an individual search for vision. I'd be fasting anyway. According to Donna Mae, we should reach Tower Rock in about five hours of moderate speed hiking. I figured we'd spend one night in the campground and I'd spend one night on the rock. We'd both be back here in about forty-eight hours.

At first the trail wound uphill though a labyrinth of sandy and eroded arroyos. It was hardly wide enough for the horse in some places. A wide-brimmed brown felt hat protected my head from the sun. Jenny wore jeans, a sleeveless shirt, and her moccasins, and of course her turquoise necklace. On her head was a green baseball cap with a logo that read "Diné Power Company." Her braided hair was carefully threaded through the back of the cap, and attached to the braid was her eagle feather, which turned in the wind as we walked. Her presence gave me considerable confidence, and for the first time I understood why the Diné were considered fierce and powerful warriors.

It felt great to be on the trail with Jenny. Last time we had hiked together, I barely knew her, and she went one way and I went another. This time we had a common destination. When I mentioned this to Jenny though, she disagreed.

"We'll only travel part of the way together," she corrected me. "Then you'll need to go on by yourself. I'll tend the fire and hold the center, but you must climb the mountain. And you'll be doing that alone."

"And what do you think I'll find there?"

"I can't say. The mountain summons you, not me."

The way she put it sounded so serious, but then, she knew much more about these things than I did. Still, I had the good sense to realize that if I was going to be successful, I needed to get up to speed. I recalled what Arin had said in class weeks ago, about information, knowledge, and wisdom. First, gather the necessary information and data, place it in a context, and add intuition, reason, and conscience. Then you have knowledge. Mix knowledge with experience and see what works and what doesn't, and "cook" for countless hours. Eventually, you have the beginnings of wisdom. I didn't have the time for a lengthy cooking process, but I sensed this exercise had something to do with at least developing my own personal base of knowledge. So, step one was obtaining information, and I believed Jenny was a good source. I would ask her.

"I'd like to know more about what you call the 'Beauty Way.' Is it just an exemplary ideal, or can it actually be integrated into daily life?"

"It's like this," Jenny answered, glancing back and forth

between the trail and me. "We understand that knowledge comes from the four cardinal directions. The balancing and wise use of this knowledge help us make the decisions for ourselves, our families, and our communities."

"So, it's knowledge then?"

"Well, more than that. It's not just a head thing. It involves the mind and heart, body and spirit. It's a kind of total experience of life, a knowing, an acceptance—a recognition of the divine power within and without. If we can feel this power flow through us, then we are Hózhó—beauty, balance, and harmony. Once this awareness is attained, we can then walk the path of balance, walk in beauty."

"And somehow the information given by the four directions helps you do this?"

"Yes. It involves understanding and practicing certain principles. The directions are 'anchored' by mountains that guide and protect us. The East represents dawn and spring to us; it's Mt. Blanca in southern Colorado. The East gives direction to life, 'the first knowledge inherent in the dawn,' we say. We look to the East for clarity, intelligence, character growth, excellence of heart and mind, respect for nature. Otherwise, there would be greed, confusion, and chaos.

"The South is the blue horizon and summer—Mt. Taylor in New Mexico and travel. It's about making a living with self-sufficiency and dignity. The South teaches us that work has an impact on the environment. Moderation is important, too . . . really central to the Diné philosophy. Our own internal balance depends on the proper relationship with our environment and with the power and strength of our people and community.

"The North is darkness and winter—La Plata Range in Colorado and the purpose of hope. This is about understanding how all life is interdependent. If we destroy the natural balance, our overall well-being is threatened."

"And the West?"

"The West is about twilight and autumn—San Francisco Peaks in Arizona and family cohesiveness. This direction emphasizes positive human relations. That's why our clan connections mean so much to us."

"Yes, I notice when the Diné meet someone for the first time, the questions asked are usually about family ties and last names, not about professional titles or academic achievement. You seem more concerned about relationships between people than about the professional labels given by society."

"That's because we feel that where you come from is more important than what you do or where you work."

Could I someday learn to walk in beauty? I asked myself this as we continued silently up the trail. Perhaps first I needed to rediscover, redefine what beauty means to me: Harmony? Balance? Perfection? Sustaining such a pure state of mind seemed improbable. Unattainable. Hard even to conceive of. What is beauty anyway? My culture tries to tell me that it's an attractive person in a glamour magazine, a new sports car, or an unspoiled tropical beach. No. I think it's more like a child's happy face, a lover's longing embrace, a lilac bush in bloom, moonrise over a still lake, pure silence, parents who really listen, a workplace filled with supportive friends, a future filled with opportunity. Perhaps it's just living simply, getting by with minimal material possessions. Or having plenty of time to think or not to think, to write, or to share daily tea with friends and ponder the changing of the seasons.

Out here, even in the pale shadow of white man's high-tech world, people have found a comfortable balance. Plenty of work gets done. This is a place where human rhythms are tied to the natural rhythms of time, flow, space, and spirit. The pace of life is so different here. I can feel it in the air and see it in the faces. None of that clenched forehead stuff—tight bodies, tight dresses, tight shoes; and neck-choking, head-and-heart-separating ties are nowhere to be seen. Instead, as I walked through the Village, I could feel a relaxed but highly present man or woman pass by me—moving naturally into work, into relationship with others, into loving, creative encounters, into artful, spiritual living and, I'm sure, also into disappointment, surprise, error, and not-knowing.

"We treat time and process differently than does the non-Indian world," said Jenny without taking her eyes off the trail. We make time for each other, for family, for friends, for art, and for our spiritual work. We call it 'living on Indian Time.' Indian time has its own rhythms, forms of understanding, and sets of priorities."

Gradually we ascended into the tree line and junipers gave way to ponderosa pine and oak. I welcomed the cool shade of the tall trees. Finally, the trail widened as we descended into a beautiful hidden valley. A clear stream zigzagged along its bottom, bordered on both sides by a broad, green meadow. We stopped to admire the surprising green in the midst of an otherwise dry terrain. Then I gasped—there at the top of the valley—was Tower Rock. Just as I had seen in my dream. Abrupt, imposing, a sandstone pillar rising high out of the ground, unlike anything around it—treeless, striped with red and orange bands, steep but climbable with good shoes and sure footing. In the forest, along the side of the valley, perhaps a half mile from the rock, I could discern a small clearing in the trees. Probably the campground, I thought. After hiking for another forty-five minutes, we approached an opening in the trees that led us into a cleared area. There was a flat space suitable for pitching a tent, and a small fire circle surrounded by logs and stumps for sitting. Next to the camping area was a four-foot-high rack of sticks from which hung several feathers, colored ribbons, and fabric. Clearly we had come to a place that held special meaning.

We unloaded our gear from the horse, and Jenny let it out to graze on the meadow's lush grasses. I started a fire and arranged our water containers for easy access, then pulled together two large log ends to serve as chairs. Then we discussed the agenda.

"It's too late to climb the mountain today," I said.

"Yes," agreed Jenny. "Anyway, you need time to fast and prepare yourself. But we'll begin our work tonight."

As the afternoon light faded, we drew ourselves closer to

the fire. Jenny's face looked radiant in the golden fire light. She had changed some of her clothes and was now wearing a purple velvet blouse and a silver concho belt. She unbraided her hair, and allowed it to cascade luxuriously down her back. My heartbeat quickened with anticipation. As the sky darkened, I watched her begin a ritual which she initiated by casting a circle of cornmeal wide enough for me to stand in.

"Stand there," she said. "I'll smoke you with sage for strength and protection. Call upon your spirit guides to help make your journey a success. Tonight I'll offer prayers, too, to guide you on your way."

I closed my eyes and inhaled as Jenny used a beaded eagle feather wand to fan the sweet-smelling smoke around me. She started at my chest, then worked her way up and down my body. She circled me, praying in Navajo. Just as she finished, though, I saw out of the corner of my eye a large object hurtling rapidly and soundlessly through the air, skirting our campsite and disappearing into the trees above us.

"Did you see that?" I asked.

"Yes."

"What was it?"

"An owl."

"An owl? Aren't owls considered bad luck by the Diné?"

"Some say the owl symbolizes evil, that its appearance portends a death."

"Not mine, I hope," I said, trying to hide a twinge of fear.

Jenny smiled understandingly. "I consider Owl a messenger. Owl brings warnings because Owl can see things others cannot. The death that Owl speaks to is likely metaphoric—the imminent death of old outmoded ways of thinking and being."

"So you think he has a message for me?"

"Yes, I think so. But tomorrow you'll know more specifically just what that message is. I think you should sleep now. I've got work to do tonight, and you have work to do tomorrow."

I snuggled deep into my sleeping bag, feeling both great excitement and a gnawing fear. The visit from the owl was portentous, to be sure. But my prior experience with animal energies had given me the knowledge that when such unexpected encounters occurred, magic was afoot and allies were likely present. Just before I fell asleep, I glanced back toward the fire. I could see Jenny's dark silhouette casting long, dancing shadows into the forest. Yes indeed, I thought, magic was afoot and allies were present.

CHAPTER 14

THE VISION

I rose early. Dawn arrived late to the valley as the sun's rays were blocked by a mesa's eastern walls. In the foggy light I could see Jenny slumped on the ground near the cold fire circle. She must have fallen asleep while guarding the fire. I pulled myself out of my sleeping bag and walked over to her. Sensing my presence, she slowly opened her eyes and straightened herself into a sitting position.

"The morning brings good energies," she said. "You need to be on your way. But first, did you have any more dream images?"

"Yes, the tower kept appearing, and I saw myself on top of it."

"That's a good sign," she replied approvingly.

I packed very little, just three quarts of water, some fruit, a plastic tarp, a pair of shorts, and a light jacket. And a six-inch knife in my belt. That was it. I planned to spend the night there, but the whole idea, Jenny said, was to surrender to the elements, become one with the earth, rock, and sky, and take only the minimum necessary for physical survival. This, she said, is a kind of ritual statement to the spirit world—an offering of my willingness to expose myself to whatever. The idea is to become totally vulnerable, to act in full trust, casting one's fate to the wind in the hope that the spirits will treat the petitioner kindly.

And truly, that's how I felt as I prepared to depart—that I was indeed casting my fate to the wind. As I stood there in my hiking boots, T-shirt, and brown felt hat, with a small backpack on my shoulders, Jenny administered a final blessing, using her feather wand to wash me in the sweet-smelling sage smoke from head to toes and all around.

"We use sage to bless a person who is about to begin a journey. It will rid your body of undesirable things."

When she had finished, she looked me straight in the eye, her mind probing into the depths of my soul. She said nothing for long seconds. Still silent, she reached into her pocket and removed a small suede braided medicine pouch with a long leather thong attached to it. She lifted the pouch and placed the thong over my head, resting the pouch carefully on my chest. "This is for you to use," she said. "It contains corn pollen, a very sacred substance. Offer a pinch of it to each of the four directions and give thanks to the spirits. It will also bring you protection."

She smiled, leaned forward, and gently hugged me. I closed my eyes, and inhaled deeply and slowly, focusing all my attention on the moment.

"Your journey begins now," Jenny said, her voice playful, yet full of import. "Go. The spirits are waiting for you."

I placed my hat on my head to protect me from the sun and moved swiftly down the trail, Jenny's medicine pouch bouncing on my chest in synchrony with my rapid and purposeful stride. In the distance Tower Rock rose at the top edge of the valley. The imposing rock formation was guarded by a shadowy canyon, so the access to the pinnacle was not immediately obvious. I trusted the gateway point would reveal itself to me in due time.

By noon, I had reached the canyon edge. The afternoon sun was beginning to scorch the treeless area so I changed into my shorts and continued on.

My attention shifted rapidly between the constant flood of sensations transmitted by my skin and the myriad calculations being run by my mind. I moved catlike through the strange and beautiful canyon. Seeking to remain in the shade, I walked a path of tree and rock wall shadows. The sinuous nature of the narrow canyon forced me to climb over large vertical slabs of gray stone.

As the canyon twisted and broadened, the white stone wash that was its bottom widened too, inviting me into its dry belly. I moved up the soft slopes, drawn into the yielding sand

The Vision

of its ascending flanks. The sun's hot touch on my bare skin triggered my sensuality sensors. As I moved forward, I pressed against the "female" summer heat of the afternoon. I longed to relieve myself of the isolating barriers of protective clothing required by my fair-skinned race. I had to be careful, though, knowing my safe sun time was limited. Still, I felt the sun's seductive, sweet heat relentlessly intoxicating me..

Moving silently and smoothly, as a skillful warrior of old might travel, I was alert, adrenaline-charged, and always at the ready. I scanned and sensed the canyon's walls and studied its every mode and mood. I carefully navigated through pinched crevices and rocky chutes where great torrents of water would smash through without warning when the monsoon rains came. In gullies, I walked below giant juniper trees that sent arching roots into this alien place like long-armed tentacles of some giant land squid cleverly hiding just beneath the surface of the ground.

I was now well within the canyon proper. Inexplicable forces pulled me forward. I was astonished at the hidden beauty that surrounded me—remnants of a strange primitive drama worked by the relentless forces of time, water, and erosion. And I sensed a subtle tone of knowledge, intended for me only.

I climbed a nearby sandstone ridge to obtain direction. I was confronted by an eerie spire of contorted rock that stretched exuberantly toward the sky. I immediately knew this pillar of fantastic stone as my intended destination.

My heart beat faster. Every inch of my skin came alive with expectation. What unknown challenges lay ahead? As I prepared to begin my climb, I fingered Jenny's medicine pouch and whispered a prayer for protection. Instinctively, I knew this was the place where vision is known. This is what I had sought.

I calculated my route to the top. It would not be easy. I needed to ascend a steep slope strewn with broken shale, scrub juniper, and small oak brush, with full sun exposure all the way. One slip and the sharp, loose rocks would tear my skin mercilessly. No matter, I was being summoned. I headed up, adrenaline pumping in my veins, all muscles straining, all resources deployed. As careful footstep followed careful footstep, my weight often forced the unstable surface to its limits of physical adhesion. The steep hillside somehow held, or my foot lifted off just as it gave way, sending rocks clattering down the hard slopes, sound slicing through the rarely disturbed silence of the canyon labyrinth.

Breathing heavily, sweating from every pore, my practiced muscles lifted me ever upward to the summit. Obedient to some yet unacknowledged force, I rested on a flat, sand-covered shelf.

Now triumphant, I surveyed my new kingdom. Waves of low mountains rolled from horizon to horizon. The valley from which I had come lay silent and nurturing with its simple stream winding through the protective meadow. I thought of Jenny back at the campsite. I wished she were here to help me celebrate the success of the climb, but then, maybe she was.

I was transfixed, but I had work to do.

The first order of business was the corn pollen offering to the spirits of place. I extracted the pollen from the medicine bag and placed a pinch of it in a small hollow in the surface of the rock which seemed intended for such tributes. Next, I faced each of the four directions, honoring in turn the spirit of each and also acknowledging Mother Earth, Father Sky, and all the various walking, crawling, flying, and swimming creatures. A pinch of pollen for each accompanied the prayer. The ancestors and the Creator himself, herself, were finally honored.

As I prepared to invoke vision, I removed my boots, socks, and shirt to assure myself the most intimate physical contact with the golden sandstone ledge on which I stood, and to provide direct contact with the air around me. I was now alone, physically vulnerable, and psychically surrendering myself to the elements. High above on my eagle's perch, I offered myself to the spirits. They could strike me down or lift me up. It was up to them. I had entered their domain. I could not hide. So be it.

I began my prayer, a call to the spirit world. I asked for

The Vision

knowledge, how I might serve myself, my planet, my fellow creatures and humans, in a better, more effective way. I raised my voice with chants of ancient word sounds, unintelligible to my mind but recalled from some distant time, and truly heartfelt. I awaited the spirit's presence, its acknowledgment

Then, as if on cue, gliding across the slick undulating surface of the sun-heated air, a skillful flyer—a hawk—nodded greetings to me. An ally perhaps? Together we shared the common space of altitude, and gazed on forest vastness below. And to my left another hawk pilot, maybe a partner, swept down from a still higher mesa across the canyon.

Tuning into my body, I felt tremendous energy surging upward, charging my legs, loins, and chest, coalescing in my head, solidifying my entire frame into a stonelike sculpture. A vibration began within me, communicating the awareness that I had become an extension of the rock itself. A powerful earthly force was possessing me, taking me into itself, bonding with me. My flesh became a wonderfully receptive surface as the wind brushed down upon me, wrapping me in its sensual dance, seeking and caressing every crevice and curve of my entire being. "My brother, the wind," I thought to myself. He answers. The spirits are pleased with my sacrifice.

Gradually I experienced an energy pulsing through me like a concentrated laser emanating from the rock base beneath my feet. I found erotic the thrusting of the wind and the hot kiss of the sun on my skin. Together these surreal forces challenged my ability to maintain full consciousness. But I was no match for their combined strengths, and I slipped rapidly into an altered state. Images swam before my mind's eye. A seeing came forth.

That seeing, like a formless cloud, took shape as my mind worked to define it.

That seeing revealed itself in a panoply of images: a group of elder Diné women with hands outstretched looking up and pleading for help; an aerial view of yawning coal strip mines; the tan earth torn open, raw, to expose dark veins of black gold, remnants of ancient rain forests, secretly cached away by the Earth for hundreds of millions of years. I watched in horror as outsized machines with jaws the size of houses devoured the precious treasure. As I turned around I saw multitudes of belching power plants rendering the compressed carbon into yellow-brown smoke and toxic chemicals.

I looked up, and I discerned the shape of distant cities and the adhesive pall of pollution that encapsulated them. And then I felt a rush of wind surround me, and I lost all contact with the ground. I instinctively reached down with my hand to reassure myself of my position on the rock, but I touched only space. Instead, I felt myself supported by eagle wings. The wind velocity increased, and I realized I was moving rapidly.

More images: Alaskan Indians watched with dismay as ice shelves the size of cities slid into the ocean. Square miles of permafrost melted into unnavigable mud. Island communities stood by helplessly as ocean waters rose, consuming whole villages and large chunks of formerly dry land. Birds fell from the air, confused by absent food sources, dead lakes, and dying forests along their migration routes. Plankton populations crashed and fish and whale populations plummeted in response. Many species of trees, plants, and animals succumbed to rapid extinction as temperature changes fatally disrupted their habitats. Coral reefs began dying off as ocean water warmed excessively, UV-B radiation increased, and predator numbers mounted. Millions of square miles of the boreal forests in North America and Europe turned into gray skeletons as massive insect infestations took their toll, no longer checked by killing frosts. Agricultural yields dropped as hybrid grain crops failed due to destruction by new strains of blight and longer-lasting droughts. In Africa, millions of wild animals died of thirst as monsoon rains failed to materialize at the proper time. The seasons shifted and exotic plant species invaded new lands, wiping out whole continents of native plants.

In the Atlantic and Pacific oceans, I observed vast menacing storms gathering and twisting into great shapes, fed by winds in excess of three hundred mph, dashing themselves furiously against coastlines, obliterating everything in their path. And most ominously, I saw mile upon mile of black

The Vision

clouds of deadly insects and pathogenic organisms moving northward to wreak havoc in environments previously impenetrable, now rendered vulnerable by warmer weather. Yellow fever and malaria had now become commonplace in most of the U.S. and Europe. Food quality decreased and soil toxicity increased as a drier climate weakened soil, concentrated heavy metals, and accelerated erosion.

Such destructive synergisms quickly outstripped the ability of technology and human ingenuity to keep pace, and whole nations began to panic. With the natural diversity of plant and animal life now significantly reduced, local ecosystems were unable to mount any effective defenses. The planetary environment was now changing so rapidly that tens of millions of people became refugees, flooding into inland cities, collapsing essential infrastructure, and pushing governments beyond their ability to cope. Chaos reigned. Wars intensified. Atomic blackmail became a more frequent occurrence.

I began to panic as the images accelerated beyond my ability to assimilate them. I experienced an increasing intensity that threatened to plunge me into a state of lethal disequilibrium. I resisted the dark tractor beam and instinctively moved my hands to Jenny's medicine pouch that still hung upon my chest. I touched it and squeezed my eyes tight, trying to recall her face and the power of her presence. And, amazingly, she answered my summons by appearing in my mind and extending her hand. Now joined in spirit, I merged her energy with mine, as I had been taught at the PsyEarth Institute. Almost immediately, I felt the spinning cease and my physical body began to stabilize.

The chaos of images faded as I sensed the presence of a new force surrounding me. It took the form of an understanding within me that I had, in fact, glimpsed a possible future for humankind—if mid-course corrections were not forthcoming, and soon! I searched my memory for a means to define a context. I remembered that Owl had visited the previous night, as messenger. Just now, I'd been given a preview of a world undergoing major change brought about by an impending climate shift, a global warming. But perhaps, in fact, it was a global warning—a wake-up call to world leaders and the people of all nations to rally, to change the way we use our technologies and resources. And I saw that inaction would, as surely as the sun rises each day, result in planetary disasters of biblical proportions.

I asked the force that held me in its thrall, What errors has humanity committed to have drawn such potential disaster to itself? The answer was quickly forthcoming. "The scourge of which you speak need not have visited the planet Earth at this time. It could easily have passed over but for an invitation from humankind so obvious it could not be ignored. Your species has chosen to dramatically expand its numbers and pursue unrestrained material growth while disregarding the limits of its physical support system. Thus, the judgment is humanity's own, invoked not by heartless, malevolent, external forces, but instead initiated by itself."

And then I saw the loving aspect of the force, strangely beautiful, remarkably peaceful, and deeply compassionate. I would describe it as a universal force called to Earth to help humankind deal with its unfinished business. I knew this business to be our task to prepare the Earth so men, women, and children can once again dwell in healthy lands, forests, and waters, rich with diverse and abundant bird, animal, and aquatic life. This will be a world inhabited by beings who've learned to love each other and the Earth—without expectations, without conditions—fully experiencing Life while joyfully discovering Truth.

"But," I incredulously asked my cosmic oracle, "how could such an extraordinary shift take place? Is there a possible action that would turn the tide and prepare the ground for a vision as beautiful and as wonderful as you suggest?"

I soon received my answer. "It requires the reconstitution of the human molecular and atomic structure, a change that extends to the very core of the human operating system itself. A thorough renovation. A total transformation. Those who humbly and in love apply themselves to this prodigious effort will someday, once again, gain the ability to recraft matter, eventually restoring and refurbishing the integrity of Creation itself."

This message was not original. I had heard it before. But to me it rang with great immediacy and urgency—that the appointed time was pressing sharply. It was a message that if we ignored, we did so at the risk of the continuity of life itself.

The vision sank away into the background light. I was reaching the limits of my ability to absorb any further input, and I plunged into a deep state of unconsciousness. Hours passed, and my mind was filled with images of Earth in ruin alternating with Earth in renaissance. The trance, it seemed, continued all night long. I woke fitfully from time to time, to drink some water and admire a first crescent moon dodging ephemeral night clouds. Several times I experienced scenes of Jenny's face merging with Owl, warning and comforting me.

I awoke to the brightness of dawn light. I knew it was time to leave my tower in the sky. I thanked the spirits for my vision, and left as tribute a small polished obsidian stone I had carried with me.

Now hungry, but strangely rejuvenated internally, I descended the flanks of the sandstone pillar, which seemed to me steeper than during my ascent. I moved stealthily through the canyon, acutely conscious that my body felt very different.

By late afternoon I arrived back at the campsite. I was hot, sweaty, exhausted, thirsty, and hungry. Jenny was there to welcome me, but forbade me to speak of my experience just yet.

"It's important to take some time to cleanse yourself, rest, and regenerate," she said, handing me a clean towel and pointing toward the valley stream.

Casting off my few clothes, I immersed myself in the cool running waters. As the healing liquid enveloped me, I felt born again and almost ready to return to civilization. I had essential information now, I said to myself. And I'd been given knowledge that was intended to be shared with many others, as I possessed the power of effective communication. I had a job to do, and I was determined to get on with it.

Later that afternoon, after a long nap and a gentle massage, I sat with Jenny under the trees near the campsite. Carefully, I recounted my experiences of the previous day. As I repeated the details, I observed the light fading from Jenny's eyes. A pale shroud seemed to envelope her face. She stared vacantly into the distance, and as her eyes began to moisten, she blinked rapidly and looked down toward the ground. Tears crept slowly down her cheeks.

"Are you all right?" I asked, halting in my description. She sniffled but remained motionless, as if paralyzed.

"Donna Mae is right," she muttered in a somber voice. "Donna Mae keeps telling me the Earth is in so much pain. That there's too much killing and death. That the fragile beauty nature has worked so hard to build for so many millions of years is now being destroyed. Spider Woman's web of life is being shredded beyond repair. I am so sad."

Jenny paused and wiped her face with the back of her hand. "Mother Earth is trying to tell us to stop abusing her, that she is a living being. She is our Mother. All life comes from her. If we cause her living systems to die, then we'll die too. Why can't people understand this simple fact?"

We sat together for a long time, silent, not knowing how to relate to what was happening to us or to the potent vision I had received. Finally she spoke again, her face brightening a bit. "I'm not really surprised that you received this vision. I've had an intuition that you've been called to do special work, to help inform people of the urgent problems and issues that confront us. I also have a feeling you'll play a major role in a global drama yet to reveal itself."

"Can't you tell me more?" I pleaded with her, highly curious.

"Nothing else has been revealed to me. I just know my job has been to help you on your way."

"So . . . will you come along with me?" I asked impetuously, and as quickly regretting my words. My heart raced. I sensed I was pushing her too hard. I knew my request was inappropriate. And to my dismay, Jenny did pull back. I watched her rise and walk slowly toward the valley, apparently deep in thought. I feared her impending answer. After a time, she returned and sat cross-legged directly in front of me. She looked into my eyes and grasped my hands in hers. Her eyes were red and swollen.

"I can't leave, Tom. I need to work with my people. There's too much to do here. We have so many problems. I've tried to give my full attention to our process together and be open to its needs, but the truth of the matter is that we are of different cultures and have different histories and different destinies. Let's be thankful our paths have crossed for a time. Let's be thankful our experience together has enabled both of us to learn so much about ourselves and each other. But I believe our respective destinations require separate paths. I'm sorry. I truly am."

It was a hard trip back for both of us. The excitement of immanent discovery was lacking, our little adventure had ended, and neither of us really wanted to confront the immensity of the tasks that lay before us. I had plenty of time to express my disappointment to Jenny while we returned to Donna Mae's house and then drove back to SunSpirit Village. I tried to change her mind about coming with me, but she was unyielding. I drew strength, though, from her personal focus and determination. I knew I had my work cut out for me. In this regard, my own determination to go forward served as the trigger to help me shift my attention away from my own feelings of sadness and loss. I decided that as soon as I reached a phone, I would call Jack to check in with him.

And, in fact, he was most pleased to hear from me and lost no time in alerting me to the latest developments at the World Stewardship Council.

"The PAPA's just demanded that the industrial nations donate ten billion dollars worth of renewable energy and water purification technologies to developing countries. WSC officials have agreed to meet with the PAPA to discuss what's available and most appropriate."

"Jack," I said. "I've learned a bit about renewable energy power systems and other environmental technologies. It's only a start, but perhaps I can be helpful."

"Yes, indeed, I think you can, Thomas. That's my plan, but on your drive back to Albuquerque, I want you to swing by the

International Center for Appropriate Technology. It's on your way. There you'll learn a lot more about the state of the art of these emerging technologies. Then you'll be able to better understand the PAPA's needs and perhaps help them."

I froze on the spot. "Help Them? I'm not quite ready for that yet," I told Jack.

"Well, Thomas," he replied, clearly desiring to challenge me, "you better learn quick because this is fast becoming the number one crisis item on everybody's plate."

After I hung up, I recalled Jenny's prediction about my future involvement in a global drama. I could feel the energy taking form, and I could sense myself being drawn toward its hot, turbulent core. And too, the calamitous climate change scenes hung vividly in my mind's eye. Perhaps I have something important to offer that is needed immediately, not ten years from now. I could feel the pieces coming together. My part in the drama was not fully evident, but certainly I needed to step forward. With the information I might gather at ICAT, combined with what I had just learned at Tower Rock, perhaps I could help avert large-scale bloodshed or further painful dislocation of Native people and continued destruction of Mother Earth's life-support systems.

PART III

THE INTERNATIONAL CENTER FOR APPROPRIATE TECHNOLOGY

Where there is contradiction there can be no creativity. Creation is only possible where there is love.

—J. Krishnamurti at Los Alamos, 1995

CHAPTER 15

MAKING A BETTER CHOICE

Koyaanisqatsi. Life out of balance. The phrase continued to haunt me as mile after mile of interstate passed under the car. I was now on my way to the International Center for Appropriate Technology, or ICAT as it was commonly called. I felt out of balance emotionally since I'd said goodbye to Jenny. And I had no idea when I'd see her again. Fortunately, Jenny's good friend Laura had joined me for the ride to ICAT, having recently enrolled in several of its science and technology training programs.

Laura easily sensed my not-so-skillfully hidden heartbreak. "I think Jenny was very drawn to you," she said, choosing her words carefully. "But you have to remember that her mother married a non-Indian man who left her soon after Jenny was born. She grew up without a father around, and she saw the stress that caused her mother. I don't think Jenny wants to go through the same experience."

"I hadn't thought of that," I said. "Are relationships and marriages common between Indians and non-Indians?"

"Not exactly common, but they do happen. Love knows no cultural or racial boundaries. People are going to fall in love whether they're Indian or not. It's a fact of life. Relationships by themselves are hard enough, but when you add in cultural factors, they can become really difficult. I know women who've sacrificed their one true love for duty to family, tribe, and community. They carry around the weight of that painful decision for the rest of their lives, wondering if they really made the right choice. Tradition, family, and tribe are powerful things."

"So I guess I'll just have to accept Jenny's decision."

"Yeah, that's about all you can do, Tom."

We drove along in silence as I contemplated Laura's words. It seemed a bitter pill to swallow, but my options were limited. For now I had to put Jenny out of my mind. Changing the subject, I asked Laura, "What takes you to ICAT?"

"I've known about ICAT since it started up, but what really caught my attention was an apprenticeship program where they train students to do technology transfer with villages in developing countries. That's what I'd really like to do, work with other indigenous people. Help them install renewable energy equipment, set up water purification systems, and establish educational programs."

"How long is the program?"

"I've enrolled in their two-year science and technology program. After that I do a six-month apprenticeship at their model Third World Village. Then I'll spend a year or two in the field somewhere. Eventually, I might want to get a degree in environmental law. But we'll see how it goes."

"Will you return to the reservation?"

"Someday. But, at this point in my life, I feel I need to go out into the world and learn as much as I can, so I'll have real skills to offer when I return."

I glanced toward Laura. "I think you have a destiny to impact people in many places."

She turned away. I hoped I hadn't offended her. Staring through the windshield, she responded in a serious tone, "My uncle, who's a medicine man, said he saw me 'traveling on the wind like the seeds of summer grasses, carrying ideas and knowledge to the four directions.' I know I just can't stay home and help my grandmother with the sheep. That's not the way for me. I like science and I want to learn ways to blend appropriate technologies with spiritual and sustainable ways of living."

Laura's goals encouraged me to examine my own personal commitment toward making a better world. I realized there were many things that I could do right now. I could stop watching television, live more simply, learn about energy efficiency, reduce my resource consumption to the minimum, recycle as best I could, buy products that will last, and educate myself more about critical environmental issues. Yes, and emulate the traditional Diné and make nature my teacher. By rethinking how I live my own life and by questioning the subtle ways I become addicted to "Media/Consumer Culture," I could minimize my participation in such a destructive way of life.

The car gained altitude rapidly, straining against the steep, winding grade. We had driven off the interstate and were now climbing toward the hidden mesa-top fortress, which was formerly one of the world's premier nuclear weapons laboratories. It was there at Los Alamos, during the closing days of World War II, that the West's best and brightest young physicists produced the world's first atomic bomb.

Soon the entrance gate appeared. A large archway painted in rainbow colors rose above it, its sides flanked by poles exhibiting flags from perhaps a hundred different countries. A blue and white sign invited incoming drivers to stop at the adobe-style Visitor Center located just inside the entrance.

Laura and I decided to check it out. After parking the car we walked up the stone steps of the center. Upon entering the lobby, we were greeted by an older bespectacled gentleman with a great mane of white hair.

"Welcome to the International Center for Appropriate Technology," he said proudly. "My name is Ted Grollier." We introduced ourselves and Ted then asked if we had any questions about the ICAT. I asked right off how a weapons laboratory could so radically shift its design and purpose.

"I'd be glad to explain it to you," Ted said, ushering us toward a lounge area with a spectacular view of the multi-striped canyon, a thousand feet deep, that dissolved into the broad and historic Rio Grande valley. "I was working here as a chemist at the time, so I remember well the original debate. As deteriorating ecosystems around the world began to draw national and international attention, a diverse collection of environmental, military-conversion, and youth and religious groups came together to try to define a means to address the problem technologically. They called themselves the Coalition for Critical Environmental Technologies. It didn't take them long to make a pretty good case to the President and the press that rapidly worsening global environmental conditions demanded a Manhattan Projectlike crash program. The coalition noted the technical nature of many environmental problems, and argued that such problems would likely yield to a major research and development effort. The world didn't need more bombs, planes, or exotic weapons test facilities, they said. Instead, they contended that the planet's population would be far better served with improved cook stoves, cleaner cars, more pollution clean-up technologies, inexpensive water purification systems, and renewable energy power plants."

"Did the government think the idea was practical?"

"Not at first. But the coalition kept harping that if only ten percent of the world's annual $800 billion military budget were redirected toward meeting critical global social and environmental needs, we could solve many of our most pressing needs within a decade. They also cited numerous studies that said U.S. national security would be strengthened by working vigorously to reduce international political and social stresses stemming from rapidly degrading natural environments."

"Then there was that secret document," Laura added.

"What was that?" I asked.

Ted continued, "Under pressure from several senators, the Pentagon was forced to release a classified document that underscored the urgency of reversing trends of environmental deterioration before eventual political instability threatened national security and economic progress. The conversion advocates immediately tried to leverage this admission into insisting that the cold war was history; and what more fitting place to design the next generation of appropriate technologies than the birthplace of the nuclear arms race itself? Why not turn atomic swords into pollution-prevention plowshares? Invent technologies that would benefit rather than harm people?

"What about the personnel here?" I questioned. "How did the scientists react?"

"At first I was highly skeptical of the proposal as was most of the lab staff. To some, like myself, it was risking the loss of high salaries, to others it was loss of major corporate profits, and for the government bureaucrats it was the future of the country's premier nuclear weapons laboratory. Groups lobbying for conversion insisted the most important consideration was the health of the planet and the future of civilization. Certain factions within the U.S. government and the military/industrial complex were truly appalled to think that the most advanced war-tool design factory on the planet might be dismantled and reduced to the demeaning status of prototyping better cook stoves for Tibetan peasants. Some of my physicist friends found this prospect totally inconceivable and branded it a 'treasonous heresy.'"

"I'm sure they raised a ruckus."

"You bet. When the guardians of the status quo suddenly realized the lab might actually be converted to nonweapons activities, they immediately unleashed an army of public relations experts to counter what they depicted as a dangerously misguided assault against our national security.

"And so it went: verbal exchanges on TV, impassioned oratory in Congress, and countless articles in newspapers and magazines debating the pros and cons. But in the end, a compromise was struck—national security would be preserved, while global technology transfer needs would be addressed. The proposed deal called for the Department of Energy to lease a substantial portion of the land and facilities to a non-profit, internationally staffed, research and development group for ninety-nine years at a dollar a year. The group would operate independent of the lab and take responsibility for its own funding, equipment, management, goals, and operational style. Its basic mission would be to serve as an incubator for the development of a new generation of appropriate, efficient, and cost-effective environmental technologies. The new tenant would draw upon existing expertise and resources at Los Alamos while assisting the lab to reenvision how it might better relate to real-world environmental problems."

"But Ted, I can't understand why the choice was made to use Los Alamos as a practical site for such an undertaking. Why select a military facility, one saddled with a long and highly controversial history of health and safety problems?"

"Well, as it turned out, the site selection committee could read the handwriting on the wall. They knew it was time for a change here, and I and others who were advising them could see that the world really needed our expertise. I was instrumental in persuading the committee that our technical human resources and raw computing power were without peer, and that our laboratories were the best in the world at making one-of-a-kind items that could be exhaustively tested. Plus, I stressed that northern New Mexico—an area of small, rural, traditional agricultural communities—closely mirrored Third World nations where many of the new technologies developed and refined here would be deployed."

"And there's another factor that's important, too," Laura interjected. "The local Pueblo Indian people have long used this land for spiritual purposes. I heard that representatives from the pueblos testified that the laboratory rested within the folds of a sacred mountain covered with sacred pueblo ruins and shrines—many still ritually attended to this day. They reminded the site committee that the area is full of spiritual power, and that that power had been tapped in the making of the first bomb, for better or for worse. Perhaps it could be called upon again—hopefully this time with greater humility and respect—to heal humanity and the Earth."

"So how did it all come out?" I asked, a little impatient and ready to move on.

"The youthful millions rallied forth," bellowed Ted melodramatically while sweeping his right arm toward the center of the room. "They organized huge gatherings and swamped the White House and Congress with millions of

Making a Better Choice

letters, faxes, and e-mail messages. Schools, teen magazines, college newspapers, and computer networks were abuzz with the debate. Their platform was simple: They said there was no future in a world awash in deadly weapons, bereft of natural resources, and universally hazardous to their health. They demanded the right to clean water and air, healthy forests, biological and cultural diversity, and nontoxic food. They insisted that they be afforded the opportunity to realize their own dreams, as had their forebears. The decisions made now by those in power, they warned, would irrevocably determine the future for world youth—whether it would be one of grim struggle for basic survival or one of broad opportunity in an environment of natural beauty. The young would have their say in this momentous decision, and they raised their voice in unison. They called for life!"

"And apparently their voice was heard," I said, anticipating Ted's next statement.

"Heard and heeded. When all was said and done and the final congressional vote was taken, the President announced our country's decision to the world. He began by emphasizing the new role of the United States as a responsible leader for environmental restoration. He encouraged everyone to take up the challenge to build a better world, and he promised to direct the full force of the U.S. scientific community toward this end. 'Swords into plowshares—this time it's for real,' he said. 'Let us begin the Campaign to Restore the Earth. It is a noble, necessary pursuit; we must wait no longer—as all of life is now at risk.'

"With that grand statement, the President signed the document acknowledging the formation of the new partnership. As one of the early converts to the International Center for Appropriate Technology, I was, of course, extremely pleased. I knew one major hurdle had been eliminated—the funding and securing of facilities. But all of us here know that the greatest challenge lies still ahead—to pull the planet back from the brink. And there's no guarantee we'll succeed. I'm optimistic because I believe we've got plenty of quality people here and mighty powerful tools to work with."

Laura and I then thanked Ted for his history lesson and took our leave. As we departed, Ted suggested we next explore the Peace Garden, located just behind the Visitor Center. It was important to visit, he insisted, because it embodied the nonmaterial aspects of the ICAT. And such aspects, he said, were just as important as the technical or scientific ones. Laura heartily agreed, and we exited the side door and walked together toward the ICAT Peace Garden.

CHAPTER 16

A HARD TRUTH

Laura and I were immediately drawn toward the series of organic constructions which contained colorful herb arrangements and rustic ponds. Intrigued by the attractive parklike setting, we walked along a simple woodchip path bounded by carefully chosen round river stones.

The serpentine path directed us toward a large stone circle. In the center rose a six-foot wooden pole, carved like a totem pole with faces from different cultures. Behind the wooden monument, set in a skillfully mortared rock wall, was a mosaic rainbow of tiles depicting the planet Earth from space. Below the globe, I noticed a bronze plaque announcing the founding date of the International Center for Appropriate Technology. The word "Peace" was rendered in several languages. A kind of shrine had also been constructed and its nonverbal statement was self-evident. I could feel the palpable presence of a deeply desired human expression for a new, more harmonious world order. It manifested itself in the artifacts of prayerful expression—artfully bound feathers, offerings of animal fetishes, and miscellaneous unique tokens—and also, simply, as just a kind of sacred feeling in the air.

We spent long, silent minutes at the shrine, adding our own prayers and intentions for world peace. We then returned to the car and proceeded up Bengal Tiger Boulevard—the old Trinity Drive—the town's main street, and across several blocks to the ICAT science college where Laura would be taking her courses. I helped her unload her suitcase and bid her farewell and good luck. Next, I drove to the public transportation center, parked my car, and boarded the waiting blue and white electric shuttle bus. Inhaling slowly, I relished the rare mountain air while scanning steeply sloping hillsides of green ponderosa pine that marched up to the 11,250-foot summit above. A truly spectacular setting, I thought. At the same time, I called to mind J. Robert Oppenheimer and his crew of brilliant young physicists working here on the Manhattan Project during the mid 1940s—so absorbed in the urgency and excitement of those heady times. None of them could fully imagine the impacts their momentous achievements would have on future generations. And, too, I felt the loss of innocence as humanity crossed that fateful threshold into the Atomic Age. The world would never be the same.

I pondered this place of contrasts, where nuclear reactors and high-tech military research facilities shared grounds once occupied by thriving, peaceful Indian villages. Occasionally those remaining pueblo ruins not bulldozed for lab space, parking lots, or chemical and radioactive waste disposal pits, surprised the visitor with their incongruous presence—sometimes appearing mere feet from the busy roadside.

I looked about the landscape at the bland, monolithic, windowless metal and concrete buildings. They still spoke loudly of their original purpose—better weapons design. They struck me as reminders of a nation's deepest fears, of political paranoia and power addiction unrestrained. And I thought of the land surrounding those buildings, forced to serve as an eternal repository of poisonous radioactive fury. I asked myself: How will future generations judge this place? As being necessary at the time to save United States citizens and to preserve a democracy? Inevitable, from a human evolutionary standpoint? An effective fifty-year deterrent to an all-out global nuclear war? Or an incalculable human, financial, and natural resource waste without equal in all of history, one that will burden humanity for millennia to come? Certainly the world has paid an enormous price for its nuclear obsession. The U.S. alone has spent four trillion dollars on its nuclear weapons program since the beginning of the Manhattan Project in 1943.

Conceivably, with the redirection of the laboratory away from weapons design and toward global environmental restoration, an opportunity for national psychological and political transformation might exist. Certainly the past cannot be changed. The contaminated land here will never fully heal in human lifetimes, but human intentions can change, and with that shift can come healing and revelations to ensure a future beneficial to all. These thoughts filtered through my mind, translating into silent prayers. Somehow, I hoped, humanity would finally understand that it needs to serve the interests of all life on the planet.

My reverie ended as the bus stopped directly in front of a three-story building labeled "Real-Time Planetary Diagnostic Center" in four languages. Disembarking, I followed an African man dressed in colorful flowing robes. Together we entered the building.

Inside I was met by a guide, an older, energetic woman named Michelle who was smartly dressed in a pantsuit. I immediately noticed her French accent. She led me into the main operations complex, a kind of "Earth Situation Room," which housed a twenty- by thirty-five-foot curved electronic map of the world. The initial impression was breathtaking. I scanned the pulsating screen. The continents were easily identifiable, with different colors representing a variety of geographic features such as forest cover, deserts, mountains, and oceans. A sophisticated and highly detailed, almost 3-D, graphic depiction enabled the viewer to quickly sense the topographical makeup of any particular region of the globe.

I noticed a curious variety of illuminated symbols scattered across the big map, some of which were blinking. Certain ones seemed obvious. A cluster of small black skulls and crossbones no doubt indicated the presence of toxic waste. The international radiation symbol likely marked a site of high radioactivity. A fish skeleton, I surmised, indicated polluted water. But I had no explanation for the yellow, orange, and red blinking spots and dots. I suspected, though, that they meant trouble. Adding to the mystery, they appeared everywhere across the map, including on the oceans. Looking for a telltale pattern, I determined that the highest concentration was in tropical rain forests.

"The blinking areas denote at-risk, endangered, and protected species as well as projected extinctions," Michelle informed me, observing my careful scrutiny of the map. "We, of course, can't be absolutely sure which species where will become extinct when, but our model is pretty accurate."

"How do you track these things?" I asked.

"Through a process known as pixel analysis. Our computer software calculates the biodiversity of a landscape directly from remotely sensed, aerial-acquired data. The individual pixels, or elements of the photographic or electronically sensed image, are analyzed digitally and compared over a given time period. We know from our baseline studies what each element or color wavelength means, what element of biodiversity it represents. If and when the pixel information changes, we know an associated change in the biodiversity has also occurred. We can therefore measure the change and relate it to a particular species of fauna or flora."

"It's disturbing to think those blinking items are actually species disappearing before our very eyes," I said. A wave of sadness surged unexpectedly through my body. "It makes the loss so real. And there are so many of them."

"Yes, about three or four an hour now."

She lowered her eyes. Neither of us spoke. The Australian Dodo, the Alaskan Sea Cow, the Black Rhino, the Siberian Tiger, the Snow Leopard, hundreds of species of frogs and thousands of species of plants and insects going, going, gone. I knew many already existed only as photographs or drawings in books, cataloging what humanity has squandered due to its rapacious appetite for land and salable product. My eyes moistened, my heart beat faster. I swallowed hard to quell the anger that began to rise precipitously in my throat.

"I'm sorry," I said, embarrassed by my unexpected rise of emotion. "I feel an affinity with animals. Sometimes I sense them communicating with me. When I see their extinction so graphically described, I find it a bit overwhelming."

Sensing my discomfort, Michelle paused, and then walked toward me. "Yes," she said in her second language, while standing next to me in a way that would protect our privacy. "It is hard for me, too . . . to understand these things and why they are happening. You see, I'm now just learning about this science of biodiversity. I'm a student in environmental biology with a specialization in toxicology. I want to understand how toxic chemicals move through the environment and how they affect people . . . and of course animals too."

Michelle's presence began to temper my emotions, and I became curious about her. Why would a person in her fifties decide to undertake the study of such a complex and rigorous field as toxicology?

"Why toxicology?" I asked. "Isn't that a difficult area of study?"

"Well yes, it is," she answered quickly, "but you see I have already some substantial experience, which I have learned the hard way."

"Really?" I said, unsure of what I was inviting upon myself.

"Yes," she replied. I watched her face shift from friendly openness to private pain. "For most of my life I lived in a small industrial city in France. Everything was fine. I got married and had two children, and then both of my children—one was nine and one was fifteen then—became very sick. At first the doctors said it was nothing, but after more tests, I learned my children had rare bone cancers. Soon we discovered that other children in the area had developed the same disease. The mothers tried to get the government to investigate, but they kept giving us excuses. Finally, a French environmental health organization conducted tests that showed that our drinking water was polluted with chemicals from a nearby factory that manufactured paint for military aircraft.

"We asked the French authorities to close the wells, clean up the area, and provide us with money for health costs. They wouldn't admit that the chemicals were coming from the factory. Eventually, my children died, and my husband got ill from the stress. So, I'm here learning all I can about chemicals and how they move through the environment. I want to help others avoid the kind of suffering that I've experienced."

I was stunned by Michelle's story. Here was another person who had decided to dedicate herself and her energies to grappling with a very serious global problem. And apparently she was not put off by the technical nature of the subject. Also, she seemed to be approaching her task with a great deal of caring and love.

"Are you working at ICAT now?"

"Yes. I decided to use the settlement money to pay for my scientific education. Soon, I'll have my Masters degree and will serve as a toxicology advisor to ICAT. My present assignment is to learn the operation of the Planetary Diagnostic System. Would you like to see more?"

"Sure," I responded.

"Let's go over to the control area then."

I followed her a dozen feet or so to a nearby raised table upon which several computer keyboards and monitors resided. She invited me to sit down next to her. "Inside the blinking area you'll see a number. When I select a numbered area, the computer will display a detailed description and history of the species indicated. Yellow means at-risk, orange endangered, and red extinct. Like this." She typed in the number 1025. The monitors played a short video clip of a stunningly beautiful Siberian Tiger in the top part of the screen. Below the photo was a map of its former and present range, a bar graph depicting a dramatic drop in population numbers, and a brief description of its species' history. A highlighted note at the far bottom of the screen discussed the reasons for its decline and the grim prognosis: extinction considered inevitable within two or three years.

I struggled to absorb these facts in a detached manner, but my heart breached my mind's defenses, betraying me to raw feelings. A world without tigers? I knew I would probably never view a tiger in the wild, but some part of me wanted to know they were still out there, doing what they do best—

being wild, representing the wildness in all of us. The world would be diminished by their departure, as it would and will be by the loss of so many other wonderful biological and botanical beings.

"Officially this is termed a Real-Time Planetary Diagnostic System," Michelle informed me, "but we call it our 'Earth-Watch Map.' It uses a very powerful GIS, or Geographic Information System program that we've customized. It's the only one of its kind in the world and requires the combined power of several super computers. That's why it's located here. The scientists at Los Alamos were working on a similar system—prior to ICAT's arrival on the scene—for the tracking and analysis of air, water, and soil pollution in the state of New Mexico."

She went on to explain that the computers receive a constant data flow from many sources, including other scientific laboratories and universities around the world, public and private research stations, ships, aircraft and satellites, and high-speed land lines. Also, a steady data stream is delivered from a multitude of remote sensors located on ocean bottoms, mountain tops, in deserts and rain forests, as well as from field agents with portable computers. Highly sophisticated computer programs at ICAT sort through the data according to type and intended application. Eventually, the data will appear in graphic or text format depending on the needs of system users.

"The system can model all kinds of possible environmental scenarios. Some common ones are climate change, ozone layer depletion, population growth impacts on ecosystems, migration of chemicals through the air, soil, or ground water, variations in species, and the spread of infectious diseases. My particular interest is in learning how pollution patterns travel and how they impact the environment. Here, I'll run a globalwarming scenario for you."

In a matter of seconds the map changed dramatically. The clear shapes of continents in greens and browns vanished beneath an angry pattern of orange, yellow, and red swirls. Large numbers at the bottom of the screen depicted a series of ascending dates in five-year increments: 1996-2000, 2001-2005, 2006-2010, 2011-2015. Yellow turned to orange, orange became red. The planet appeared to be suffering a major case of sunburn. At the top of the screen the title read: "Global Warming Scenario—2000 to 2100."

Just then the door opened and two young men wearing ICAT badges on their shirts entered the room. They walked rapidly forward, their faces expressing strong concern. The man with blond hair spoke first and forcefully, "Michelle! We have a problem, a mystery to solve. Can you run the Diagnostic Program for us?"

"Of course," Michelle answered confidently. "What do you need?"

The two men moved quickly past me and sat at the control panel for the EarthWatch Map. Michelle straightened up, her hands poised over the keyboard. Noticing me, they introduced themselves as Eric and Miguel, both agricultural research scientists.

Eric told Michelle, "We're receiving reports of massive insect infestations in certain agricultural and forest areas of Southeast Asia. The size of the infestation is bad enough, but the plants and trees don't appear to be able to cope with the onslaught as well as they usually do. Consequently, agricultural yields have dropped radically and trees are dying faster. We need you to profile these areas for us to see if we can discover the cause or the source of these problems."

Eric then handed a sheet of geographic coordinates to Michelle, and she entered them into the computer. Immediately the colors and images on the large map shifted, first blanking out entirely; then the computer began to assemble each designated area one at time, into a tilelike pattern for side-by-side comparison. Once the general geographical area was depicted along with its associated topography, the computer drew in cities, rural villages, pipelines, factories, power lines, landfills, power plants, and other major human-made physical elements. Our group then stared silently at the collection of visual data.

"Can you show us the air-flow patterns over the affected

areas?" I asked Michelle, suddenly experiencing a strong sense of déjà-vu.

"For what time of the year?" she asked.

"Last few years," I said, "and annual predominance, if possible." Michelle entered instructions into the computer and multicolored lines appeared over the images indicating the information I had requested.

"I bet air pollution's a major cause," I said, mildly confident. "I see lots of fossil fuel power plants and some industrial areas near the affected sites. It's possible the carbon and sulfur dioxide emissions from those plants are causing a local climate change."

Eric noted, "Our meteorological data shows that the affected areas have experienced a reduction in rainfall and increased drought conditions during the past few years."

"And I can see that the prevailing winds would carry the SO_2 from the power plants right into the forests and over the fields. The SO_2 deposition would acidify the soils, weaken them and concentrate trace metals in the soils." Everyone looked at me, surprised by my knowledge of soil chemistry.

"And acid soils lower the plant's resistance to insect predators," added Eric.

Miguel then interrupted, "Yes, and warmer climatic conditions speed up insect metabolism development times, dramatically increasing their numbers. Unfortunately, hoards of insects are poised to move into many areas of the world as soon as the temperature barriers are removed."

"We clearly have a problem here," Eric agreed. "It does seem we're looking at one of those destructive synergisms of environmental change: local warming, prolonging of drought conditions, increased acidification, and weakening of soil and plants. Then we factor in the explosion of predators and we can expect eventual collapse of agricultural and forest ecosystems. Not a pretty picture!"

"And it spells disaster for local populations," added Miguel morosely.

"And eventually all of us," I added.

"Well," Miguel concluded, "air pollution does seem to

be a logical cause here . . . at least it could be one major contributor to the problem. I'll call for some soil tests for verification. Thanks for your help."

I shook hands with both men, and then they left the room. I turned toward Michelle. "I've never seen such a dramatic way to visualize on a global scale the subtle interaction of so many complicated, invisible processes. It's fascinating, but it's also scary. You need to get heads of state in here to see this for themselves."

"We try. But most of them just don't want to know. It would mean drastically changing their way of operating and doing business. You have to remember there are many people in the world who profit well, both politically and financially, from exploiting the environment. I've experienced it personally."

"I know you have," I said to her gently, sensing the rising discomfort triggered by her memories. "But what you have here is a way to teach a kind of ecological literacy. You can help people visualize how everything is linked together. The EarthWatch Map makes it easy to understand that when a critical link is broken or disturbed, it could lead to disaster."

We had lunch together in the facility's busy cafeteria. I found the setting afforded a wonderful opportunity for people watching—with all the different faces and modes of attire that an international staff presents. At the same time, I could sense a war-roomlike intensity hanging like a dense shroud over the facility. Yes, people took time to eat, but a definitive aura of urgency was apparent.

I asked Michelle about the scientific and public reaction to the EarthWatch Map's projected future scenarios. She explained that scientists and researchers have found the system a highly useful tool for environmental research because of its huge, up-to-the-minute database and outstanding graphics. Even nonscientists can get the big picture quickly. She also noted that responses differ depending on gender and age—men often leave the room with faces screwed into sober scowls, whereas women frequently depart awash in tears. Children and young people require special attention when they visit as they often become quite disturbed by what they see.

"Michelle," I said, "I need to learn about the technologies you're working on here that relate to water purification and renewable energy. Those technologies seem really key to addressing basic quality of life issues in developing countries. Can you help me?"

"Those are not my areas of expertise. I suggest you visit the Northwind Design Center. I have a good friend there, Dr. Frantz Saskitz. I'm sure he can help you find what you're looking for."

CHAPTER 17

APPROPRIATE TECHNOLOGIES

The shuttle paused at the entrance to the Northwind Design Center, a two-story metal, hangarlike structure nestled protectively in an extensive grove of middle-aged ponderosa pines. I suspected that a six- by ten-foot lighter-toned area in the asphalt driveway betrayed the former location of the old guard building. Just beyond the phantom structure's edge, I noticed a narrow line in the ground, a likely indicator of a chain link or barbed-wire security fence. I wondered if the ghosts of decades past watched with bewilderment and consternation as men and women of many nationalities and languages intently went about their business—as they once had, sixty plus years ago—but now with very different goals and intentions.

The shuttle halted at the building's entrance. I stepped out into the clear, crisp air. It was rich with the thick fragrance of a high-altitude pine forest. Overhead, a serene cobalt sky provided a powerful feeling of well-being. I could sense that things had changed here "on the hill." Nuclear scientists were no longer opening dark doors daily to reveal nature's most deadly secrets, releasing unspeakable horrors to prey on present and future generations. Instead, these old post-war facilities now housed caring, intelligent, and imaginative minds brought to bear on solving the real-world day-to-day survival problems facing humanity.

As I entered into the spacious building's interior, I found myself thrust into a dizzying assortment of people and their projects. My eyes leapt from one kind of odd-looking device to another. Some were recognizable as to their apparent function, but many were not. However, I easily identified small models of bamboo housing structures, a large variety of solar cookers, and an assortment of electrically powered cars, bicycles, and rickshaws. One whole section of the building, near a huge south-facing glass wall, was devoted to a display of voluminous plastic tanks filled with water, plants, and fish.

A high-pressure excitement filled the air. An ethnically diverse body of workers moved about rapidly, most dressed casually in typical U.S. clothes, but others wore brightly colored native costumes. As I scanned the room, observing personnel hustle between offices and assembly areas, I became aware of the wide variety of ages. Young, middle-aged, and older men and women scurried around, over, and under their strange, sometimes spectacular, and often disarmingly simple-looking projects, with the intensity of a mother preparing her child for the first day of school.

A young Asian woman, noticing my presence, walked over and offered her assistance. "Can I help you?" she asked charmingly.

"I hope so. I'm looking for Dr. Frantz Saskitz. I was told he worked around here."

"I'll page him for you."

She retrieved a small black communicator from her belt. Her nimble hands entered a code, and then returned the device to her belt. "He should be here in a few minutes. There's a lounge behind you."

"Thanks," I said. She smiled and continued on her way.

I had little time to collect my thoughts before an older man of possibly East-European descent approached me. Dressed in khaki pants and a multicolored, open collar, short-sleeved shirt, he stepped up and introduced himself with unexpected gusto, requesting that I address him as Frantz.

"Ah . . . so Michelle sent you over. Fine woman. Very smart. What can I do for you?"

I explained my interest in some basic water purification and energy technologies that might be of interest to rural communities in developing countries. "Of course, of course," he responded, then looked away to think. During the silence, I became aware of an intermittent welding torch crackling in the distance. Underlying its characteristic zzzztttt, a general motor hum, the echoing clank of metal rods and tools dropping on concrete and the babble of worker's voices swirled around me in a thick sound soup.

"But first you need to consider the whole picture," Frantz began. "Food, water, energy. We have serious problems with all three. And everyone is affected, not just rural people in the developing world." As he spoke, I noticed a pronounced tension in Frantz's voice. "We've just passed perhaps the most important critical resource threshold in modern human history."

"What's that?" I asked.

"The peak point of our oil and gas supplies."

"You mean the world's production of oil and gas is now declining?"

"No, no. We don't produce any oil or gas. We never did and never will. We don't produce them. We extract fossil fuels from the ground. Do you understand the difference?"

"Of course, you're right. It's an old way of thinking . . . and clearly erroneous."

"That's been the idea all along. To make people think man can actually make or generate fossil fuels. It's a very misleading way to describe the process because it hides the fact that fossil fuels are nonrenewable on a human time scale. Only nature can produce fossil fuels. And nature requires lots of sunlight and photosynthesis and many millions of years to do the job. Consider that in a couple of hundred years we'll be using up a precious, finite resource that took seventy million years to make and is three hundred million years old!

"You might say we're engaged in a wealth depletion economy. Instead of burning up our oil, giving us only a one time use of energy, we should be converting it to plastic and building solar panels. That way it could continue to give us energy for twenty or thirty years. Our oil would then be producing long-term value for us. We would, in effect, be putting our capital into an energy bank. Solar panels, wind generators, hydrogen production—all represent ways current oil can be used as an investment rather than as an expenditure. This is what I call a wealth addition economy."

"It certainly does make a lot of sense," I said, amazed at Frantz's persuasive logic.

"Most people don't understand how the entire foundation of our present world economy rests on an ancient, finite, diminishing quantity of stored sunlight. Our food, transportation, manufacturing, and energy systems all depend on fossil fuels. The world gets eighty percent of its energy from burning fossil fuels. But now the critical curves have crossed. Oil and gas supplies have peaked and extraction has leveled out while world demand is increasing. It now requires more energy to find and extract a barrel of oil than is contained in that barrel. If we take into account projected population growth and increasing industrialization in developing companies, the well will be dry, so to speak, around 2050. That's only about a generation away. ICAT, therefore, has taken it on as a major technical challenge—to help move civilization away from its fossil fuel dependency that is rapidly altering the planet's biosphere in highly destructive ways. We need to move toward an economy that keeps excess carbon out of the atmosphere and still provides people with the basic necessities and conveniences of life."

"That's a big job. Can you do it?"

"Certainly not alone. A transition of this scale is comparable to the switch from wood to coal and coal to oil. We're needing to undertake the Third Energy Revolution. It'll never be cheaper or easier to make the changeover than right now. Everyone needs to work together to make it happen soon, because we need the plastics and inexpensive energy that fossil fuels provide to make the transition to renewable energies. The longer we wait, the more difficult and expensive the transition will be. That's why we've created a powerful cooperative international working environment here with sophisticated tools and resources. And we work closely with both the private and public sectors."

"I can feel the urgency."

"Most of us work six days a week. It's stressful, but it's very exciting. Come. I want to give you a closer look."

Frantz first led me through a nearby office where I picked up the requisite visitor's badge. Along the way, he continued to explain the breadth of the operations there. "It's the Big Three we're concerned with. Or maybe I should call it the Big Four."

"What's the fourth?" I asked.

"Shelter . . . food, water, energy, and shelter. But shelter's not so dependent on utilization of nonrenewable resources. Shelter can be made from many abundant local resources such as stone, earth, and various kinds of biomass like straw, bamboo, wood, and common waste materials like tires, bottles, cans, cardboard, metal, plastic, and so on. We've got a whole crew of people working on inexpensive and simple shelter systems."

"But back to food, water, and energy," Frantz said, gesturing for me to follow him toward the series of large clear-plastic tanks that covered maybe five thousand square feet of space. "The building you're in right now is our demo area. It's where we display the current state-of-the-art design, prototype, and production models. Elsewhere are located many separate design and workshop facilities. But here you can get a good view of our progress."

I gazed across at what appeared to be large circular tanks filled with various kinds of plants and fish. "This looks like it might be for food production," I guessed.

"It depends on who's doing the eating. There's lots of consuming going on by microorganisms, so it really belongs in the water category."

"So it's a water purification system?"

"Yes. Even though the world has plenty of water, ninety-eight percent of it either isn't drinkable or accessible. Of course, the oceans are full of water, but full of salt too. Unfortunately, we're using up and contaminating our fresh water supplies at an incredible pace. At least a billion and a half people have no access to clean water. And polluted water is a primary corridor for transmission of disease. It's estimated that nearly eighty percent of all diseases can be traced to contaminated water. But there are numerous ways to purify polluted water. One particularly useful one, already very popular, involves using nature's own cleanup agents in a technique called biological remediation. Sometimes, such systems are known as 'constructed wetlands.'"

Frantz then led me over to the tall cylindrical fiberglass water tanks. The tanks stood in front of a huge glass window, exposing the organisms inside to copious amounts of New Mexico sunlight. As I studied the series of wall tanks more closely, I noticed the water's color progressed from murky brown to crystal clear from the first to last tank.

"These systems use nature as their design matrix because nature usually finds the most efficient way to process waste. This sewage processing system is a good example. As the contaminated liquid flows through each tank, it's acted upon by specially selected plants and organisms. Through natural biological action, harmful metals and dangerous pathogens are removed. We let the bugs do the work. Our waste is their lunch. You see, in nature, there's no such thing as waste. Everything is a resource to be utilized as food by some organism. All you need to make a system like this run is sewage and sunlight. And there's plenty of both around the world."

My guide then described the remarkable pioneering work in such systems undertaken by John Todd of the Center for the Restoration of Waters in Massachusetts. I was informed that over the past decade, Todd and his associates had developed the concept of "Living Machines," self-contained human-made networks of biological purification systems powered by the sun. Each living machine is an ecological system designed to accomplish a specific purpose. Todd's Living Machines are usually housed inside a greenhouse or "bioshelter" to maximize solar energy and minimize the use of land. Fish tanks inside the bioshelter serve not only to process a contaminated waste stream—be it water, sewage, or septic—but store solar thermal energy as well. The fish

Appropriate Technologies

grown in the tanks can later be utilized for compost, and combustible gases can be derived from the waste stream. These gases can, in turn, provide energy for vehicle operation or home cooking and heating. Excess solar heat captured by the bioshelter itself can be used to warm adjacent buildings.

Frantz went on to explain how some Living Machines mounted on rafts use wind and solar powered pumps to draw heavily contaminated lake sediment through floating biological purification systems. Results from such applications have been dramatic, transforming dead lakes into live ones. Other Living Machines have been constructed on 18-wheel trailers to provide portability.

"But this is a pretty elaborate setup," I remarked. "Do you have any home-sized systems?"

"Yes, and the household systems will prevent almost any kind of dangerous bacteria or pathogen from leaving the home and entering into the environment."

"Really! How?"

"It's rather elegant, in fact. You start with a composting toilet, preferably a solar one which you can build yourself from wood and plastic. The heat in the solar composting toilet destroys all the dangerous pathogens, yielding an ashlike compost material clean enough to use as fertilizer. Liquid wastes from your shower or sink are directed into either a small constructed wetlands like you see in the tanks here, or through a biofilter device that contains biological organisms that consume and remove the contaminants. The outflow can then be used for irrigation. Choice number three is a solar pasteurization system that can be constructed from copper tubing and commonly available wood and glazing materials. It produces an output that is very clean."

"Do these systems replace the standard septic system?"

"Completely. And they usually cost less too. And, of course, you get the extra benefits of water for irrigation and good compost material. Best of all, no nasty nitrates or other harmful chemicals are introduced into the groundwater or surface waterways. These systems can be used almost anywhere, and would go far toward protecting vital water supplies and aquifers."

Frantz now led me over to another part of the demo area. "All of our devices are designed to be low maintenance and inexpensive; many can be manufactured from local materials. Now that we're moving into energy, let's start with the basic stuff—how to cook without cutting down forests and loading the atmosphere with more carbon dioxide."

He introduced me to an Oriental woman, Dr. Osahi Komura, the senior scientist for cookstove research as well as primary mentor for a team of international engineering students. Her "family" of students, as she devotedly referred to them, was doggedly pursuing innovative ways to reduce or eliminate wood and dung use for cooking fuels. She pointed in the direction of several types of glass- and plastic-covered metal and wood boxes currently under construction. "These are solar cookers. We test them for durability, performance, and cost. And here," she said, walking about twenty feet toward an assortment of black iron devices, "are the stoves."

I learned from Dr. Komura that since wood and dung currently provide the only practical heating or cooking fuels for most of the world's population, the use of these increasingly scarce fuels by local populations ensures that the local ecosystem would eventually collapse. The need for wood for purposes of cooking and heating causes rapid deforestation, and increases erosion and destruction of watersheds. Hours of backbreaking labor and miles of foot travel are required each day—usually by women—to secure even a small supply. Use of dung, although not threatening the forests, robs the land of much-needed natural fertilizer. "If you can only use dung or wood—you should have a stove that uses these fuels most efficiently. The stove must be inexpensive, able to be locally manufactured, and acceptable to the women who do the cooking."

"I guess the long-range goal would be to find energy sources and fuels to replace wood and dung entirely," I said.

"Yes," Frantz responded. "That's where we're going next."

He thanked Dr. Komura politely. She tipped her head

slightly while her bevy of fledgling design scientists eagerly awaited her attention. This youthful group was bound by a palpable excitement. They knew they were working against the clock. Each day their new stoves remained unavailable for use, more thousands of acres of precious trees would fall to provide wood for cooking fires, and millions of tons of carbon dioxide would be released into the atmosphere. Indeed, I was told that the need for household wood fuel accounts for over half the global timber harvest.

"We'll visit the outdoor lab," Frantz said excitedly. As we exited through a large side door, I was surprised to see a sizable collection of model solar homes and an impressive array of solar ovens, photovoltaic panels, large reflective parabolic dishes, and curved troughs aimed at the brilliant New Mexican sun. There, in a wide yellow field of perhaps ten acres or more, were also bulbous gas and water storage tanks flanking a complex of metal buildings. At the far edge of the field, I noticed mounds of dirt and organic matter. A dozen or more types of wind generators were set up nearby. Workers seemed to be everywhere, making adjustments to equipment, engaging in discussions, analyzing blueprints, and assembling or disassembling various devices. In the background I could hear music emanating from a portable radio—probably solar powered, I imagined.

"This is our renewable energy research center. The wind- and solar-power generators, of which we have many different kinds, are obvious. You'll also see displayed here numerous examples of passive and active solar architecture, all heavily instrumented. And over there is our biomass and biogas or sewage-to-energy facility. Inside the complex we just left is a data receiving room where we perform detailed, comparative analyses of the various prototypes and processes employed out here."

We began our investigation by examining a group of photovoltaic panels. "As you probably know, photovoltaic or PV panels generate electricity directly from sunlight. It's a rather simple and extremely elegant technology. It has no moving parts and the panels are virtually maintenance free. PV systems are in great demand around the world, particularly for rural villages, as forty percent of the world's population is without electricity. That's 2.5 billion people! Most villages will likely never receive power from grid systems because of the high expense of grid extension."

"What do people do for light and electricity?"

"They generally use kerosene, gasoline, or diesel generators or do without. These fuels are expensive and they pollute the indoor and outdoor environments. One of the major women's diseases in rural Third World villages is respiratory illness caused by exposure to indoor pollution resulting from the combustion of wood, dung, coal, and kerosene. If we can remove these toxic elements from the indoor environment, women's health will improve dramatically. Solar cookers, PV electricity for lighting, and hydrogen fuel can do the trick.

"The PV systems we have here are less expensive than previous models, use nontoxic solar cell material, and are designed so they can be upgraded with more efficient cell material or new photoconversion devices. One of the new technologies we're working on is a plastic polymer/electrode system similar to polarizing lenses. The major structural elements used in the panel's manufacturing—the glass and metal—can be made locally, thus providing an economic development opportunity for the community or country as well."

Franz next led me toward a large parabolic-dish solar concentrator system that was coupled to a small Stirling motor and generator. "This solar dish system or 'genset' can generate about seven kilowatts of electrical power per hour. It holds the world's record of twenty-nine percent efficiency for converting sunlight to electricity! The engine can be mass-produced just like a car motor. We can also make hydrogen from its electricity. The hydrogen can then be used for cooking or heating or to make more electricity with a fuel cell. In a rural village setting, this single power system could provide electrical power, hot water, and refrigeration, and process drinking water for perhaps eight to fifteen homes.

Appropriate Technologies

And speaking about refrigeration, we've developed several types of efficient, inexpensive units that use only ozone friendly refrigerants."

"But what do you do when the sun isn't shining? Use batteries?"

"You could, but batteries have their problems. Most use toxic chemicals. They lose efficiency, wear out, need to be replaced frequently, and they often end up in landfills. Actually, they're no longer necessary, now that we have inexpensive fuel cells. Hydrogen-powered fuel cells can do just about anything batteries can do, but in a much cleaner and better way."

"Fuel cells are great! The rental car I drove up here is a new Ford fuel-cell model. It's so quiet and smooth and has plenty of acceleration."

"We're very excited about fuel cells, too, especially those that use hydrogen directly. We're working hard to accelerate the transition to the hydrogen economy where fuel cells will replace most battery applications and internal combustion engines, especially the hydrocarbon burning kind. Just imagine how much quieter, cleaner, and people-friendly our world will be when noisy internal combustion engines are largely eliminated. And no more hundreds of millions of gallons of used motor oil spilling into waterways and noxious fumes polluting our atmosphere. The only 'emission' of a hydrogen fuel cell is potable water. And hydrogen is non-toxic and a common by-product of plant and animal waste. Thus it can be recovered from sewage, plant material and animal waste. Hydrogen is a renewable, inexhaustible, natural substance. It's the base element of the stars and the universe."

"But what about all the gasoline and diesel internal combustion vehicles, boat motors, and lawnmowers that are already in use? Can we do anything about them?"

"The six hundred million fossil-fueled vehicles presently on the road? We recommend converting as many as possible to run on hydrogen or landfill gas. And there's a major benefit when you do this. An ICE (internal combustion engine) that burns hydrogen actually cleans the air that passes through it. It does this by ingesting airborne contaminants such as hydrocarbons, tire particles, diesel soot, and carbon monoxide and more completely burning them as it operates. The result is cleaner air. Thus we can turn an ordinary vehicle into a Minus Emission Vehicle or MEV. Look over here."

Frantz led me into an adjacent room filled with all kinds of vehicles and engines. An assortment of men and women in coveralls appeared totally preoccupied with their work. Every few seconds an engine would start up, then quit and workers would huddle around laptop computers that apparently monitored engine performance. Frantz paused in front of an elegant test stand-mounted eight-cylinder radial engine. It looked very unusual. "Here's an engine that's three times more efficient than your standard gasoline internal combustion engine. Its direct injection system and sophisticated electronics allow it to burn hydrogen, landfill gas, methane, or turpines. It's optimized for hydrogen so we call it our 'world hydrogen engine.' And of course, it's an MEV. It's not as quiet or as simple as a fuel cell engine, but it lends itself well to mass production."

"If millions of cars are going to run on hydrogen, we'll need to make lots of it," I remarked. "How are we going to do that?"

Frantz pointed to a rack of ribbed metal devices connected by thick hoses to a series of tubelike tanks. "Remember that water—H_2O—is made up of hydrogen and oxygen. Those banks of electrolyzers over there use an electric current to break apart the molecular bond in water, releasing the hydrogen and oxygen. The resulting hydrogen gas can then be stored and later used in a fuel cell to make electricity, or directly combusted to cook with, heat homes, or run vehicles. Units like these can be purchased for the home, and can run on any kind of electricity. So, all you really need to make all your own energy is sunlight and water, plus some equipment, of course."

"But how practical is making hydrogen on a large scale? How much sunlight, land, and water would it take to signifi-

Appropriate Technologies

cantly impact our consumption of fossil fuels?"

"If we'd place solar electric generators with a solar-to-electric conversion efficiency of twenty percent on about one-fifth of New Mexico's land base, we could make enough hydrogen fuel to completely replace all the natural gas, oil, and coal used annually by the United States. And average New Mexico rainfall would be sufficient to supply all the water we would need for the electrolysis. Impressive, eh?"

"I should say so!"

As Frantz recounted all the wonderful breakthroughs the teams were producing on a weekly basis, we suddenly found ourselves surrounded by an enthusiastic group of young workers who had come to investigate our presence.

"You should see our new hydrogen fuel cell electric buses, bicycles, wheelchairs, rickshaws, and boat engines," one insisted.

"And the train. We've converted a diesel locomotive to hydrogen power, too," remarked another.

A Hispanic-looking woman with an air of confidence stepped forward to address me directly. She spoke, her voice rich with an accent. "I encourage you to visit our urban design modeling room. There you'll see small-scale examples of our all-renewable energy-powered mass transit systems. We've also made good progress toward finding ways to limit private vehicle use in urban areas. Our clean energy mass transit designs would help many of the most congested cities of the world. We're exploring ways to make hydrogen from sunlight in the desert and then ship that hydrogen by pipeline to places like Los Angeles, Phoenix, or Mexico City. All that's needed is money and political will. We have the technology and the know-how."

The woman brushed her long, lustrous black hair from her face. I could easily sense her quiet excitement. As she spoke, I listened attentively to her tales of the group's successes and failures. They shared with me their visions, too—of cities with humane and comfortable housing, of people working and living in safe environments where jobs paid a good wage, work was meaningful, and people had time to socialize, laugh, sing, dance, and make music together. Life would become something to enjoy rather than a never-ending struggle to survive at a minimal level of physical comfort. Where technology served people rather than dooming them to a fast-forward, productivity-based existence fatally severed from nature.

During the rest of the afternoon Frantz expertly guided me through many work areas to meet with the personnel and study their projects. I met with biologists working for simpler and better birth control methods and with botanists probing the inner secrets of soon-to-be extinct plants. I gazed over the shoulders of urban planners who would sit for hours at a clip, skillfully modeling city designs on computers. I watched them rearrange cars, transportation systems, garbage and waste products, basic infrastructure, parks, and factories—rethinking Mexico City, São Paulo, Calcutta, Rio de Janeiro, Los Angeles—trying to find better ways to manage people and their cities.

I also observed economists, anthropologists, sociologists, and architects, a whole building full of them poring over tabletops piled high with studies. They hovered over city models complete with mockups of food production and waste recycling systems. I saw walls covered with charts filled with energy statistics. It seemed they were reenvisioning everything—the whole assemblage of human civilization. Nothing was considered sacrosanct—not the market place, not politics as usual, not contemporary patterns of development, not embedded governments and institutions and their precious ideologies, and particularly not status-quo relationships to gender, ethnicity, and class. Everything was up for reconsideration. All was judged potentially re-designable.

I could see that some of the most creative minds and best tools had been brought together at ICAT with one primary mission: to insure that applications of science and technology would become truly a part of the solution rather than the source of so many of the world's chronic problems. To underscore this point, Frantz invited me to visit the full-size models of community-based appropriate technologies located nearby. "And tomorrow I hope you will join us at the Village Technology Center?"

"Sure," I said. "I'd like to see how your technologies are

applied in a village setting."

"Good, Tom. Your timing is excellent. It will be an interesting day, as we happen to have a special delegation arriving from Central America. They call themselves the Pan American Peoples Alliance or the PAPA."

My jaw dropped immediately as I absorbed the surprising news. Frantz noticed my shocked expression. "Have you heard of them?"

CHAPTER 18

THE EAGLE'S CRY

There it was, just up ahead. The hand-carved wooden sign painted blue and white read "Village Technology Support Center." The shuttle bus rounded the curve and headed up the single lane that looped around the front of the building. A covered walkway welcomed me as I disembarked. Several three-dimensional signs provided an easy way of locating the various facilities.

The weather had changed dramatically. No longer did the familiar cobalt blue sky provide a comforting canopy over the forest of pines. Instead, a gray fog crouched menacingly upon the mountain, depressing temperatures into the chill zone and amplifying my uncertainty of what to expect from my first personal encounter with the PAPA. The day, it seemed, carried a kind of foreboding, a warning of the unexpected. I felt both excited and anxious.

I found the village models neatly nestled inside a six-acre parklike landscape. The setting could have been Africa, Central America, or Asia. Gravel pathways strung together several tight clusters of single-story buildings made from native materials. I walked toward the first complex, labeled "Simulated Central and South American Rural Village." A large central building was flanked by three adjacent smaller ones, and all were interspersed with ample open space. Next to the central building was an intricate arrangement of various solar devices. I recognized an array of photovoltaic panels, several types of solar thermal heating systems, and numerous water and gas storage tanks. An outdoor shower and washing facility adjoined an area of tall green plants, a constructed wetlands, which, no doubt, served to provide a biological system of water purification.

Upon first inspection, the area seemed deserted. This was strange, I thought, as Frantz inferred he'd be here to meet me. A mystery, indeed. All was quiet, except for muffled traffic sounds in the distance and occasional raven cries echoing through the tall pines.

I continued down the path toward the main cluster of buildings; some were made of concrete block and others had bulging wide walls, likely straw bale constructions. As I turned a corner, a group of four women became visible, talking excitedly together in an open plaza. As I approached closer, their voices stilled. They glanced toward me, cautious and curious. All wore ankle-length dark skirts embroidered with various geometric designs. Three of the women wore thick wool sweaters that incorporated subtle woven images, while the fourth wore a brightly colored patterned blouse. All four were of short stature. One appeared Hispanic and the other three were clearly of pure Central American Indian descent.

I felt very self-conscious as the only male, and as a male of a different culture. I walked over toward the women, acutely conscious of the stares directed back at me.

"Hello," I said cheerfully.

"¡Hola!" responded the Indian woman dressed in the colorful blouse.

Spanish, of course! I thought. That's their native language. I hope somebody here speaks English. Even though I had lived five years in New Mexico, my Spanish was minimal.

Stepping forward, I introduced myself to the speaker. She nodded graciously, and I trusted she understood me. To my relief she replied in heavily accented English.

"Welcome to the Village Technology Support Center, Señor Tom. I am pleased to have you meet las señoritas Eva Luisa, Isabella, and Zenaida. My name is Juana. I am from Guatemala."

Each of the women shook my hand gently. "Eva Luisa, Isabella, and Zenaida are official representatives from a group called the Pan American Peoples Alliance or the PAPA. Some people think they are . . . *peligroso* . . . or dangerous, so we have given the staff the day off so we will not be disturbed." Juana laughed. "Señor Tom, do these women look dangerous to you?"

"No, but then I don't really know them. Should I be afraid?"

"Perhaps you should," said Eva Luisa, smiling cryptically. "At least until we get to know you better."

"Oh . . . and they have been accompanied here by a gentleman from the World Stewardship Council," Juana added, turning to point toward the interior of a building from which a tall, middle-aged man emerged. He was silhouetted in the light from a window, so I was unable to recognize him.

"This is Señor Xavier Gonzales. He has officially arranged for the PAPA representatives to come here."

Another surprise! I was speechless.

"Hello, Tom," Mr. G announced from a distance. "How nice that we meet again."

I had last remembered Mr. G looking impressive in a smart business suit. But his pressed jeans, casual flannel shirt, and full head of carefully trimmed, thick black hair lent him an air of European aristocracy.

Mr. G explained his presence. "I'm glad to see you here, Tom. Your editor told me you'd be touring the facility. As you can see, I have arranged for the PAPA delegation to travel to ICAT and see if any of the technologies might be useful to them. But I will let them explain their needs."

"I am the PAPA's technical advisor," said Eva Luisa in a confident, no-nonsense way. "And these are my two assistants—both indigenous women. They do not speak any English, only their native language and Spanish, so I will need to translate for them. I am from Mexico, and Isabella is from Guatemala. Zenaida is from Peru. Our lives are very difficult, so we have come to see if ICAT technologies can help us."

Eva Luisa continued, sweeping her arm in front of her and looking toward the building units and plaza, "These buildings are beautiful and you have all these wonderful devices, but you must try to understand the problems of our life in the rural areas. You do not have so much rain here. In our communities, it rains and rains, sometimes for days without stopping. When you try to walk from here to there, the mud reaches almost up to the knees. But then, droughts can also destroy our corn harvests, and we are left with only wild vegetables to eat. It is not unusual for people to go for days without eating. We have no modern medicines and we suffer from many illnesses and diseases. Mosquitoes and fleas are everywhere. The women become undernourished and are unable to breast-feed their babies. Some women have many children, but frequently the children die from diarrhea. Fertility education is unknown and unavailable. Our schools are very inadequate. Most of the women cannot read or write. These are some of the things that we want to change."

"Eva Luisa has told you only part of the story," Mr. G said, a tension rising in his voice. "In the rural areas of southern Mexico, for example, twelve thousand villages have no roads. Forty-five to ninety percent of the people suffer from malnutrition, thirty percent are illiterate. Health services are abysmal—two clinics and five doctors per ten thousand people and only one operating room per one hundred thousand people. One-third of the homes have no electricity, despite the fact that the area provides large amounts of hydropower to Mexican cities and the region is a major location of oil, gas, and timber extraction. This is very wrong!"

"I can understand your dilemma," I said. "I recently visited an Indian reservation in Arizona where the people also suffer from the exploitation of local natural resources by outside companies. Self-sufficient ways of living are being destroyed by mining operations and the pressures of population growth and changing lifestyles, and the people who live there, too, are denied access to their own resources."

"That is why we must fight back," Eva Luisa said forcefully, "and we cannot continue to live under such conditions."

"And you shouldn't!" I said. "It's truly unnecessary. From what I've learned, there are many technologies here that could help improve your lives. And if people in the developed countries would get serious about using renewable energy and implementing energy conservation initiatives, there would not need to be oil and gas extraction taking place on your lands. Also, if your governments helped you to develop your own local sustainable logging operations, you could reduce or eliminate the damage to your forest resources."

Eva Luisa frowned in frustration. "But these changes are beyond our power. We have little influence at governmental and international levels."

"Yes, I understand," I admitted. "But ICAT can show you and the world what's possible—here and now."

Eva Luisa seemed unimpressed and unconvinced. Perhaps I needed to understand her needs better. "Could you tell me, then, what are your most pressing needs?"

"We need clean water, electricity, and information on health care and family planning," she added, speaking emotionally. "Adequate education must be provided and women's equality issues must be addressed. You see, all these things are a necessary part of creating a healthy standard of living."

"Those are the kinds of the issues we've tried to address here at the Village Technology Support Center," offered Juana in a polite but assertive voice. "Come, follow me."

Juana led us into the building complex, which provided several simple rooms that were used for meetings and classes, and a multimedia library and teleconferencing facility.

"Education can be given here for the things you mentioned. Our programs include information on ecology, sustainable farming, recycling, pollution prevention, business management, land rights issues, and other subjects of importance. We can also provide basic literacy classes and math science skills."

"So, this facility serves as a kind of all-purpose education and communication center." I said. Juana nodded her head.

"And in the field," Mr. G added, "these technology centers would be connected to the WSC GlobeNet telecommunication system."

"Through a satellite network?"

"Yes. With a dish antenna like the one over there." Mr. G gestured through the window to a gray satellite dish that pointed at the southern sky.

"The World Stewardship Council Distance Learning Center sends education programs, and provides audio and video connections to the technology centers by satellite," continued Juana, "because most rural villages are not connected to power or telephone lines. The remote technology centers and the WSC can communicate directly with each other, even make teleconferences together. This makes it possible to gather important information and solve problems easier."

It became obvious to me that the Village Technology Center was the WSC link to the field, that these technology centers represented a grassroots delivery system of enormous power and potential. It was an ideal means to further the education and environmental literacy of Third World communities around the world. Moreover, each center could serve as a point of contact between the WSC and local organizations and village leaders in a given bioregion. The system also linked like-minded individuals and groups to each other. It was an ingenious and eminently practical approach that balanced critical centralized functions with necessary decentralized operations and applications. Ideally, once people established viable regional networks, they could begin to pressure governments to address their problems. Over time, long-lasting economic, social, and political empowerment of a region could then occur.

"Outside we have technologies to make life easier and healthier, especially for the women," Juana said, leading us into an open plaza area filled with various types of portable and stationary solar ovens. "These solar cookers are used to prepare meals for community gatherings. In this way, people can be introduced to the concept of cooking without using wood. Portable units can be loaned or rented to families for use at home. Regular workshops are held in the villages to teach people how to make their own solar cookers from simple materials."

Juana then guided us through a display of solar troughs, parabolic dishlike devices, and flat plate collectors that provided hot water to a series of sinks and stone-lined pools for general use. A large solar evaporator/distilling unit was linked to a row of faucets and plastic one and five-gallon containers. A holding tank ensured that plenty of clean water would remain available to the community. Next, she explained how the artificial wetlands or model biological sewage system processed waste material from the toilet and washing facilities while the newly purified outflow irrigated a small orchard. "The sewage treatment system is very important," she explained, "because it will protect the groundwater from becoming polluted. And polluted groundwater is a primary way that disease is transmitted."

I learned that the array of photovoltaic panels was the main generator of electricity for the tech center. The electricity was stored in batteries and used with an electrolyzer to make hydrogen for use as a cooking fuel. The hydrogen might also be used as a transportation fuel or with a fuel cell pack to make more electricity. A wind generator mounted nearby on an eighty-foot tower provided an alternate source of electrical power.

I watched as the PAPA women carefully followed Juana around as she explained the various devices. They intently scrutinized each technology and its method of use. Unfortunately, all of the discussion between Juana and the PAPA women was conducted in either Spanish or the indigenous language, so I had no way of knowing exactly what was said. When we paused at the solar electric equipment, Eva Luisa seemed to have many questions, and she became very physically demonstrative, moving her arms back and forth, squatting down and hunching over as if she were undertaking some kind of strenuous physical activity. Clearly, though, the women were fully engaged in the tour and discussion, and seemed powerfully impressed, judging by the positive nodding of their heads and the frequent use of words such as si, si, maraviloso, and fantastico.

As I continued to observe their interaction, I became aware of the sun slipping behind the shadowed mountain to the southwest and a deeper chill beginning to envelop the forest. Truly, I thought to myself, humanity's major challenge is to find humane ways to deal with a growing population without further destroying the planet's natural resource base. In this respect, technology could play an important, indeed, a crucial role, I was certain. Better antipollution technologies and construction of mass transit systems and renewable energy power plants would conserve existing natural resources while cleaning up our environment and reducing development pressures on rural communities.

Obviously, I thought to myself, more efficient technologies can reduce energy use, but a note of caution is warranted: No technology should be accepted without consideration of its true environmental cost relative to its benefits. We must always ask the hard questions: Does the technology harm the Earth; and does it help us meet our needs in a sustainable way? And as corollaries: Can we find wiser uses for our technologies? Can we do more with less? Or, better, do without? Can we learn to live more simply? When we do, costs usually go down along with stress levels. Resources are then freed up for distribution to others, who may have much greater need.

Ideally, it seemed apparent that ICAT and the Village Technology Support Center could provide people and their communities with certain technological benefits. But other potentials exist. As individuals become exposed to new ways of thinking and doing, the process of human social, political, and economic innovation would be amplified. Fresh solutions to global problems would likely emerge and, in turn, trigger others to offer additional solutions and refinements. Eventually, those ideas with special merit would converge at places like ICAT and the WSC to subsequently undergo further evolution and be redistributed back out into the field. And over time, humanity might begin to realize a new symbiotic relationship with itself, and everyone and the environment would reap the benefits.

Mr. G now turned toward me. "The world must be changed. We are living in a tragedy when fifty thousand people die each day from starvation and over a billion suffer in abject poverty. A new way must be found. A new politics, a new social, moral, ethical, and economic reality must be created. And I think you can help us, Tom."

I blinked as Mr. G's eyes stared laserlike into my face. A shiver ran up my back. "What do you mean?" I asked.

"You're the journalist. You have the attention of the public. You can carry the message of change to the people."

"In theory, maybe, but my media efforts will reach only a small audience. What you're talking about is finding a way to reach millions or billions of people."

"Yes, that will be necessary."

"And more than reaching them, we will need to find some way to inspire and engage people to take action."

"Yes?" Mr. G said, seemingly awaiting my next thought with strong anticipation. I paused and reflected on my PsyEarth training. I asked myself what would be effective in such a situation? The answer came quickly—access the group mind, plumb the collective unconscious, summon the spirit forces.

I inhaled a deep breath. "I would like to propose that we undertake a special group process." All eyes were now upon me and Eva Luisa was translating to her associates while I spoke. "I think we need to join our hearts and minds together to find answers . . . Juana, is there a facility around here we could use for a private ritual? Just a small meeting space—ideally in the woods?"

"We have a circular adobe building, which the local Pueblo people built for staff and visitors to use for special occasions. Will that work?"

"Nicely," I said. "Can we all meet there at sunset tonight?"

Mr. G and Eva Luisa looked at each other, silently debating my proposal. After apparently neither one of them desired to object, they nodded "yes," and following the translation, the other women concurred with my plan.

I returned to my apartment to retrieve a certain important tool—my eagle feather. I wasn't at all sure what I would do once everyone had assembled together. But this was one of those moments of truth when one simply has to trust that he or she is doing the right thing at the right time and will receive the necessary support at the critical moment. I would depend on my eagle feather to assist me to summon whatever forces needed to be evoked for the upcoming ceremony. In my mind I prayed I would not be disappointed, or terribly embarrassed.

The sun was beginning to set behind the mountain, and the daylight was fading rapidly. Our small group had gathered in front of the brown adobe building. To me, the building looked like a *kiva*, the traditional ceremonial structure used by the Anasazi and Pueblo people. The structure was perfectly round, about twenty feet in diameter and ten feet in height, and partly bermed into the hillside. A solid pine door provided the only entrance. Juana produced a key from her embroidered bag and unlocked the door. All I could see inside was blackness. Juana reached into the doorway and extracted a second key that was apparently mounted on the interior door frame. She asked me to take the second key, go around to the back, climb onto the roof of the structure and unlock the top opening. I did so and swung the three-foot-square hatchlike device back on its hinges. What light remained from the departing sun flooded the small room below.

When I rejoined the group, they were milling about the circular room, admiring its simplicity—adobe block walls with a *viga* and *latilla*—log-beam and cedar-stick—ceiling. Other than the firepit, located in the center of the floor, and the square opening on top, the room was devoid of features—except that is, for a pile of pillows stacked against the wall.

I then directed everyone to each take a pillow and find a place around the central firepit. The pit was already filled with small pieces of wood, stacked in a vertical teepeelike fashion. Balls of newspaper were stuffed inside the pieces of kindling. The fire was ready to go.

My companions had all brought something special to wear. Mr. G had fastened a wide colorful woven belt around his waist, and the women all wore brightly patterned shawls over their blouses, each decorated with a distinctive design. A necklace of small colored stones and silver coins hung down Eva Luisa's chest.

I chose to sit at the south end of our circle. Mr. G positioned himself to my left in the western sector, and the women spread themselves out in an arc opposite Mr. G, filling in the east side of the circle. The north end remained open. Somehow, without any verbal communication, we seemed to be intuitively acting as if the whole event had been previously choreographed. I found this effect most curious.

When we were fully seated around the central firepit, I became aware of a new group consciousness that had spontaneously emerged. Mr. G looked toward me, his gaze penetrating and intense. I had the distinct feeling that there was much about him that I didn't know. That there was a story, lurking in the ethers, that I hadn't yet been told.

Juana now asked if she could light some copal incense to initiate our ritual. I agreed. She withdrew a small hollowed-out clay animal figurine from her bag, set it near the firepit, and placed within the receptacle several pieces of the incense. Upon igniting, the dried sappy material began to fill the room with a strong sweet-smelling odor. The smoke would serve to purify the room and the people. I withdrew my eagle feather from my pack and placed it in front of me. All attention focused on it. Mr. G smiled knowingly, apparently resonating with or at least approving of my actions and intentions.

"I invoke the Eagle," I said slowly and consciously, "to guide us to a place of broad vision—to help us find answers and solutions to the urgent problems the world now confronts." I paused to allow Eva Luisa to translate my remarks. As she did, the Indian women nodded in agreement, eyes downcast toward the floor.

"I have something that I think might assist us with our vision," Mr. G intoned after allowing a pause to follow my invocation. He reached into his pocket and removed a colored piece of cloth. Laying the cloth on the ground, he unwrapped it, and a half dozen pieces of a brownish green, spongy substance were revealed. "This is a technology of a different kind—a sacred technology. It's a medicine that is used by shàmans when they need to make important decisions for their communities. I think it will help us tonight. I offer it to you. Just take a piece, chew on it for awhile, and allow it to dissolve in your mouth."

There followed a short pause but no discussion among the group. Everyone reached forward unhesitatingly and willing hands reverently retrieved pieces of the mysterious material. And so did I.

"I will light the fire now," I said. Everyone nodded in concurrence. As the flames began to build, Mr. G ingested his portion of the vision medicine. Everyone else did the same. Quickly, the interior of the small chamber began to fill with the heat of the fire, and its walls began to glow orange in the firelight. The blue smoke wove its way upward and out through the roof hatch, which appeared to us as a jet black door to another dimension. No one spoke, but I noticed the Indian women had closed their eyes and were swaying back and forth every so slightly. A low humming noise filled the room, its source impossible to ascertain because of the building's circular nature.

My attention remained fixed on the dancing flames. I stared into the fire, allowing myself to be drawn into its essence. We all sat in silence, waiting for something to happen. After about fifteen minutes, I felt myself losing contact with my normal state of consciousness. As my comfortable connection with the known world began to recede into the distance, an initial fear arose. I sent it on its way, thanking it for its reminder of caution. I allowed myself to slip into another reality, where time and space took on wholly new qualities, and my senses began to inform me in different ways. My body sensations became minimal, and my awareness of information and realms beyond the normal heightened. And then, something called out to me to look deeper into the flames. Much to my surprise, they began to assume the shape of eagle wings, and abruptly coalesced into a full-grown eagle, which gloriously ascended from the flames, flapping its powerful wings noiselessly. I blinked several times to confirm what I was seeing. But there it was—an eagle that had suspended itself over the fire. As I watched, spellbound, it moved into position above Mr. G, and rotated its razor beak back and forth menacingly. I blinked again in astonishment and quickly glanced at my companions' faces. No one else seemed to notice the extraordinary apparition.

I returned my attention to the great bird of prey. It stared at the women and released a loud, ear-splitting shriek. Instantly, I noticed all heads raising and eyes scanning the room for the source of the outrageous sound. I watched the women closely, expecting them to stare wide-eyed at the eagle. But instead, their shoulders merely swayed dreamily in unison, their faces lost in trance, an intense sensuality exuding from their collective presence. Suddenly a hazy red glow enveloped them. I next observed their images shimmering like a wind-disturbed, still lake surface, while above them materialized a huge anacondalike serpent figure. I gasped as it, too, appeared to hang in midair, its gleaming, silvery spotted body undulating slowly, imitating the women, its fierce triangular head twisting right and then left in slow motion.

Eva Luisa whispered in an audible but distant voice, "La serpiente esta aqui. The serpent is here." Mr. G smiled comfortably, as he too could see the great reptile swim through the rippling waves of light cast by the crackling fire.

This was an amazing display of illusions, I said to myself. But it couldn't be real. Immediately, Jenny's face inserted itself into my mind, cautioning me. "These things are real—if you allow them to be."

Okay, Jenny, I replied mentally. You're right. I will believe. I will pay attention.

The Eagle, now satisfied that its companion, the Serpent, had fully materialized, leapt forward. Both creatures began a circular dance in the air above us, spiraling around and around as if there was no ceiling. In fact, I could not discern any roof, only dark sky above me. As their rotational movements increased, I found it harder and harder to separate the two forms. And then they became one—a feathered serpent—which having reached an apex point in the sky about forty feet overhead, suddenly plunged into the fire and disappeared. The fire, in response, exploded in brightness and sparks and then dimmed dramatically.

The walls of the circular room began to glow with a golden luminescence. A multitude of faces appeared—dark-skinned men and women, a collage of children's faces. Visages of men and women struggling to make a living.

And other faces began to take form on the opposite, west side of the wall, but of people living in a very different set of circumstances. Men and women of wealth, endowed with ample resources. Healthy children, well-fed and materially secure.

The Feathered Serpent then rose from the flames and hovered in space above the fire. Directly across the wall from me, images of the WSC began to appear. The female president of the WSC stood behind her podium speaking and gesturing dramatically, but in silence. Her image faded slowly, to be replaced by a male figure, the spokesperson for the PAPA—El Aguilar. He stood alone at first, attired in his jungle dress, arms folded across his chest. Somehow, I knew these two people were key to the necessary transformation that we sought.

The fire crackled and sputtered. The Feathered Serpent had disappeared, and the walls of the round room became blank but still throbbed with the singular golden fireglow. Everything appeared normal once again.

I glanced around me. My companions opened and closed their eyes slowly and breathed deeply, broad smiles covering their faces. We remained in silence for perhaps a half hour, an hour . . . I really didn't know for sure. It was impossible to judge time under these circumstances.

Mr. G was the first to break the silence. "Quetzalcoatl, the Feathered Serpent, has returned. Now anything is possible."

CHAPTER 19

A DIFFERENCE OF OPINION

We had all agreed to meet the following morning at the Village Technology Support Center in order to assess the events of the previous night and to plan future strategies. As I awoke, though, I soon realized I was still reeling from the effects of the previous night's extraordinary events. I still wasn't sure just what happened to me, and us. The vividness of the images remained burned in my mind while the heat of my sensory experiences clung fast to my body. Inside, I felt like a changed person—like I had seen the world anew, and understood that I had an important part to play in the creation of that new world. I knew now, with certainty, that there was no turning back. I was on board, on line, going forward—to wherever I might be headed. This fresh realization felt both scary and exhilarating. I would need time to sort it all out. But I had a meeting to make in ninety minutes.

With a struggle, I showered, got dressed, grabbed a quick breakfast of orange juice and french toast at a local restaurant, then caught the shuttle bus to the Tech Center. The morning air was cool and overcast, like the day before, and once again flush with the unknown. I was the first to arrive at the center. The gate was open so I walked slowly toward the cluster of buildings. We would convene inside the teleconference/classroom.

It was a cheery space—white walls and large windows that could be opened to admit the breath of trees and the chatter of animals. The room contained several large chalkboards and working tables. This is how a classroom should look, I thought.

One third of the room space was carpeted and full of pillows. This seemed a much more inviting space in which to meet, so I promptly arranged six pillows in a small circle. Hardly had I finished when the group arrived, conversing happily in Spanish. "Buenos días," I said, bumping up against the limits of my Spanish.

"Buenos días, Señor Tom," Juana replied, smiling broadly.

Mr. G then approached me, his back to the women, apparently attempting to create an opportunity for a private conversation with me. He stood close and addressed me directly and seriously. "You've come a long way, Tom, since we first met on the flight to Earthhope Village during that rainstorm. What's happened since then? Your personal confidence and mastery of the elements is impressive. You handled last night's events quite well."

I smiled, appreciating the compliment. "Well, you might say I underwent a rather accelerated period of personal education during the past year. I attended a program at the PsyEarth Institute which enabled me to undertake some serious mental and physical renovation. The process allowed me to familiarize myself a bit with, shall we say, 'other kinds of realities,' and focus on how I want to live my life."

"It seems to have worked. I can hardly believe you're that same naive young man I met back in Belize on the plane."

I felt my face flush with self-consciousness. "But Mr. G, I have a question for you. Was the crossing of our paths entirely random, or was there some intentionality associated with it?"

Mr. G adopted that now familiar-to-me secretive look, like he wasn't telling me everything, but that he was being as truthful as present circumstances would allow. "To be honest, Tom, I sensed we had a destiny together. I knew that the moment we sat down in the adjoining seats. At the time, I could not foresee where it would take us, but I knew it was important that I establish a connection with you."

At that moment, the women approached the circle of pillows I had created. "We need to begin our discussion," said Juana, always the good host, moving things along. "We have only a few hours before the technical crews and students will arrive. We need to get to work!"

A Difference of Opinion

"Yes," Mr. G agreed.

We made ourselves comfortable, sitting cross-legged on the cushions. During the pause while everyone settled themselves, I became aware of a major shift in our group energy. It was as if we were now newly bound together in a more familiar, more intimate way. I sensed a collective feeling of trust and respect pervading the group. The invisible walls between us seemed thinner now, replaced by a fresh openness. I suspected the change was a result of the previous night's common experience. The ritual had transported us to a distant land together, and we experienced otherworldly events, images, and emotions—as one mind, one heart. The spirits had revealed themselves, gifted us with knowledge, spoken to us of vision, and consequently charged us with a responsibility to act. But what should that action be?

"Quetzalcoatl, the Feathered Serpent was there," recalled Eva Luisa. "We all saw him." She glanced at the Indian women, who expressed their collective agreement.

"Who is Quetzalcoatl?" I asked.

"Quetzalcoatl," said Mr. G, "is a mythical, religious, and physical symbol in Mexican cosmology of supreme importance—to history, and perhaps our future as well. The feathered serpent, the marriage of the bird and the snake, represents the dual nature of the unconscious—the above and the below, heaven and earth, light and dark. The transformation of man and woman into god and goddess."

"So Quetzalcoatl is a kind of archetypal figure?"

"Yes," Mr. G responded. "Quetzalcoatl is the supreme magician. He represents the good, the light, the ability to enter into the flames to be sacrificed so that life might continue in a better way. He is death and rebirth. He travels into the underworld and is burned, frozen, decapitated, and humiliated, and is tested time and time again. But he perseveres, finds enlightenment, and returns a completely reconstituted being. The Indians of Mexico considered the planet Venus an embodiment of Quetzalcoatl, as it becomes both the evening and morning star. For this reason, Quetzalcoatl is often called the

'Lord of the Dawn.'"

"It is prophesied that Quetzalcoatl will return someday to initiate a new era, the Sixth World," added Eva Luisa. "And I see the symbology of the feathered serpent as representing human balance. Let me explain. I see la serpiente—the serpent—as representing the female energy and el aguilar—the eagle—as representing the male energy. In the feathered serpent, these two essential energies are joined together with equal strength and power. The serpent grows by shedding its skin and making a new one. It transforms itself often. Women experience this same process of death and rebirth every month with the passing of their blood—and, also, they give birth to new life. So women naturally experience change on a regular basis. And women carry the transforming energy of the serpent in their sexuality. For me, the message of last night, of the visit of the feathered serpent, is that we must encourage the whole world to embrace a more correct balance of the male and the female—in order to create a more equitable life, especially for the women."

All the women's heads nodded in agreement as Juana continued to translate while we spoke.

"But how do we do this?" I asked.

"The poor must rise up," said Eva Luisa sharply. "We must make our case to the governments. We cannot bear such desperate conditions any longer. The PAPA has fifty thousand soldiers ready in ten countries. We must say to the world, ¡Ya basta!, enough! "

"Eva Luisa is right," Mr. G said.

"Let's examine this more carefully," I said, desperately searching my mind for another persuasive alternative. "The message I received last night did not include the use of violence. I saw masculine and feminine energies being united as a key to the global change process which you mention is necessary. I saw El Aguilar and Sari Singh, the president of the WSC, working together to find a peaceful solution to the issues you raise."

Eva Luisa and the Indian women shook their heads, unconvinced. I had to continue. "Do you know of Mohandas Gandhi? He was able to mobilize the common people of India to defeat the most powerful nation on Earth at the time—the British Empire. And he did it without violence, with something he called 'truth force.'"

"But that was almost sixty years ago," Mr. G commented, "and he was not dealing with a unified global alliance of governments, transnational corporations, and their armies."

"Certainly," I said. "the world is quite different now. But your message is similar. You, too, speak of the power of truth."

"Yes, but the dispossessed people of the Third World cannot and will not sacrifice their dignity any longer," said Eva Luisa.

"You can't prevail against the military technologies of the industrial countries," I said, my emotions rising. "You will be crushed, and your people hunted down mercilessly and killed. I don't think you want to suffer like Guatemala did—a thirty-six-year war that left behind eighty thousand dead, forty thousand widows, and one hundred thousand orphans. It's too high a price to pay."

"We might as well be dead, if we don't," said Eva Luisa angrily.

"Okay, what do you have to work with then?" I asked.

"Our truth, our dignity," said Eva Luisa, "our ability to imagine how life could be, and our ability to live in the 'not yet'—the promise of a better future."

"I think you'll need a lot of allies," I argued. "You'll need to enlist the aid of others who share your feelings, your frustrations, your ideas, and your ideals. And you'll need to translate this collective consciousness into action. Gandhi did this most effectively when he led a one-thousand-mile march to the sea to gather salt in defiance of oppressive British policies. But violence is not the new way. It's the old way. It leads only to more pain and suffering for everyone. And it only breeds additional violence."

"How do you suggest they do this?" Mr. G asked, looking directly into my eyes. In fact all eyes were now riveted on me. Another moment of truth had arrived. I summoned my PsyEarth Institute experience into my consciousness, searching for resolution. The group waited anxiously for my response.

"I don't have an answer right now," I said defensively. "But I suspect that much of the world's population would sympathize with you, that they've also had enough. Enough violence, enough separation from nature, enough of the rat race that barely allows most men and women to put food on the table and keep a roof over their heads, despite countless hours of grueling physical labor. They've had enough of the racism and mindlessness of everyday living. Enough of the suicidal destruction of the planet's life support systems, and enough of the growing inequities of power and wealth in our social and economic systems.

"This is not how human beings are meant to live. We have a far more noble collective destiny. I think, in essence, human beings are loving, compassionate creatures who desire to live in peace. To succeed in establishing a world that encourages our true humanity to emerge, we must find a way to release that collective desire for liberation, for freedom to get on with our true soul mission—which I suspect has more to do with experiencing ecstasy than drudgery. Clearly, we must find a way for everyone to express the enough, the ¡Ya basta!, and summon the will to change."

Silence filled the room as the group absorbed my words. "I think the PAPA will exercise its ultimatum," said Eva Luisa. "This will be the force that will bring about the change."

"No, I don't think so," I said, disagreeing sharply.

"It is two weeks before the PAPA will take action," Mr. G interjected. "Maybe with the help of the WSC, a new way of thinking or a new plan can be discovered. Come back to the WSC with me and explore what it has to offer."

"Two weeks is not much time," I said, discouraged.

"I don't think the PAPA will wait any longer," Mr. G responded, looking toward Eva Luisa for confirmation.

"No," she agreed, her eyes fixed on Mr. G. "We have already waited too long. The feathered serpent will rise from the flames to help us take back our dignity."

PART IV

THE WORLD STEWARDSHIP COUNCIL

One of the basic tenets of quantum physics is that we are not discovering reality, but participating in its co-creation.

—M. Talbot, *The Holographic Universe*

Nothing is possible without individuals, nothing is lasting without institutions.

—Jean Monnet

CHAPTER 20

A MEETING WITH THE PRESIDENT

Eva Luisa's statements continued to haunt me for the next several days. They seemed so final, so unyielding. Certainly, I could sympathize with her concerns, her pain, and certainly, she served as a powerful voice for the oppression that women throughout the world suffered on a daily basis. But I was unconvinced that her political approach would truly achieve the ends she so ardently desired. But what would? That was the question that motivated me now. And my intuition led me to believe that the WSC might provide a basis for at least some kind of resolution to the pressing matter of the PAPA ultimatum.

With the driving wind of time howling at my back, having only two weeks left before the PAPA would act, I felt I needed to move fast to alter the projected scenario. I had accepted Mr. G's offer to explore the resources at the WSC and therefore wasted no time in getting back to Belize. Friends in Albuquerque and relatives elsewhere were understandably disappointed that they would receive no more than a perfunctory debriefing on my adventures during the past eleven months. Within twenty-four hours I was on a plane back to Belize. The trip was smooth this time; there were no violent rainstorms. Once there, I quickly settled into my guest quarters—a simple studio located in a series of duplexes reserved for visiting media representatives. My first order of business was locating Mr. G. He was pleased to discover that I had arrived safely. But he already, to my great surprise, had scheduled me for a meeting with Ms. Sari Singh, the president of the WSC.

"I would prefer to explore the resources of the WSC before meeting with President Singh," I objected.

"No, Tom. You need to meet with her first because she sets the energetic tone for the WSC. Then you'll better understand the attitude of the people who work here. Trust me, you'll see."

"All right," I agreed reluctantly.

"Good. Your appointment is at 2:00 this afternoon in her office. You'll be on your own as I must leave for important meetings elsewhere. I have some considerable traveling to do. But you'll do fine. She's an open and friendly woman."

Mr. G shook my hand and I forced a smile, but my mind raced ahead, calculating what questions I might ask and how I should act with the distinguished president of the World Stewardship Council.

I had several hours to gather my confidence, sitting quietly under the sprawling gray ciba trees that surrounded the WSC administration building. I found myself easily distracted, though, by the psychedelic-colored parrots that raucously patrolled through the treetops and the small bands of monkeys that played hide-and-seek on the building's grounds. Had I not been so nervous, I would easily have succumbed to the thick humidity and heavy afternoon heat that worked relentlessly to dull my mind and senses.

At 2:00 pm I arrived at President Singh's office, dressed in neatly pressed white trousers and a tan shirt. The suite of windowed rooms that comprised her work area was alive with the sunlight that streamed through a wide opening in the jungle canopy. Elegantly carved stone and wooden statues, beautiful woven tapestries, painted three-foot-tall earthen jugs, papier-mache masks and other native artifacts from around the world were tastefully exhibited throughout the complex of rooms. Ms. Singh entered the room, welcoming me with a broad smile and an outstretched hand. I felt in the presence of a person totally confident of her personal power. Her ankle-length silk dress of burnt orange edged with purple and gold danced gracefully about her slim body as she walked. A simple necklace of pearls strung on a fine gold chain clasped her neck, and large blue lapis and gold earrings adorned her ears, which peeked out from her rich black hair when she moved her head. At fifty-four, she radiated an essence of calm, physical beauty, and a poise that can only result from an authentic maturity of mind, body, and spirit. Nevertheless, her deep dark eyes, gently arching eyebrows, and elegantly formed face projected a youthful vigor and pronounced energy of purpose that belied her chronological age.

"Welcome to the WSC, Mr. Westbrook. Perhaps we can speak outside on the terrace where we won't be interrupted."

"Of course," I said and followed my host, her dress flowing angel-like as she led me through a set of french doors onto a flagstone patio covered by a thatched roof arbor. After we sat across a glass table from each other in comfortable wicker chairs, Ms. Singh got directly down to business.

"I understand you're here to search for a nonviolent alternative to the PAPA's ultimatum, and that you've already spoken with the PAPA representatives regarding their intentions. Am I correct?"

"Yes, I'm hoping that with the resources of the WSC a way might be found to bridge the gap between the PAPA and the world governments."

"It is my ardent belief that we at the WSC can somehow help all the parties concerned to find a compromise that will not lead to violence, and I am willing to do whatever I can to assist in that process."

I took a long look at Ms. Singh and could easily sense her desire to seek a peaceful solution to the challenge the PAPA presented to her organization. It was also evident President Singh was skilled in hiding her feelings, an ability necessitated by the demands of global diplomacy. But her eyes, her forward-leaning stance, and the tightening of her hands betrayed an inner anxiety. Clearly, despite the powerful and formidable power the WSC possessed—with its human and technological resources—she seemed at a loss to formulate a definitive solution to the PAPA challenge.

I offered her my thoughts on the matter. "The PAPA

wants the governments and the international corporate community to respond positively to their demands. These demands include better living conditions, economic and technical assistance, land redistribution, women's rights, and self-determination. We need to find ways that the WSC can help each of the parties to appreciate the other's concerns, and bring others who share these concerns into the mediation process. Can you suggest how WSC resources might be directed toward accomplishing this goal?"

President Singh leaned back in her chair and a sparkle emanated from her eyes. "We have at the WSC a considerable wealth of technological and media resources. But technology is useless if it is not utilized imaginatively, sensitively, and wisely. This requires individuals who are capable of acting in a manner that truly benefits rather than diminishes the collective whole. I ardently feel we have a powerful concentration of such men and women at the WSC. In order for you to be effective in your mission, though, you'll need to get to know our people as well as our technical capabilities. But first, perhaps, I should describe the kinds of people who make up the WSC."

"That would be helpful. How do you select your members?"

"With great care and scrutiny. We look for men and women of uncommon intelligence, imagination, integrity, empathy, and wisdom—people gifted with a special blend of intelligence and deep compassion for the Earth and all its beings. You might characterize them as true 'planetary citizens'—those individuals with a strong sense of global civic duty.

"We look for men and women with that rare quality of quiet leadership, those who can enable others to think 'We're doing it ourselves.' Those who can instinctively empower others to do their best. We specifically solicit individuals who can approach a community in need and provide exactly that piece of critical observation, insight, logic, technical advice, element of technology, or bit of education, encouragement, or friendship that is warranted at that moment in time."

A Meeting with the President

"How did you find such people?"

"From our original solicitation for positions, 250,000 applicants were divided into different groups and committees. The WiseCouncil has 13 members; the Project Steering Committee, 20; the Global Policy Council has 64; and the All Peoples Council, 260. Most of our governing and voting members are representatives of NGOs, nongovernment organizations."

"What's the function of the WiseCouncil? It sounds intriguing."

"Each member of the WiseCouncil of 13 represents a specific complete geographical/biological region or 'bioregion'. A bioregion, as you may know, includes all plant and animal life in a given watershed area. The thirteenth member, the Presider, serves as mediator and also represents the human element. But not just the human element of present time; the presider must also speak for the ancestors and descendants as well—seven generations previous and seven generations to come. Thus, the presider's job can be a particularly challenging one. This chart shows the division of bioregions.

Wise Council Representation

1. Desert Bioregion	7. Plains Bioregion
2. Ocean Bioregion	8. Earth
3. Forest Bioregion	9. Air
4. Polar Bioregion	10. Fire
5. River Valley Bioregion	11. Water
6. Mountain Bioregion	12. Spirit

13. Human Element

"WiseCouncil members are chosen according to the breadth and depth of their intuitive abilities, and they hold forth from a round table reminiscent of Arthurian legend. The WiseCouncil serves in an all-encompassing advisory capacity. Each member's job is to seek and nurture an empathic connection with the natural world, and—when required—to retrieve relevant information to be shared with the larger body of WSC participants and official voting bodies.

"In contrast, the 20-member Project Steering Committee proposes, deliberates upon, and carries out specific projects, programs, and other significant courses of action. It must submit its major proposals to the Wise Council for intuitive reflection and to the Global Policy Council for ultimate approval and funding. Because the Project Steering Committee is small, this group can work quickly and efficiently, responding to crisis situations almost immediately.

"Formal project analysis and implementation plus public policy making is the charge of the larger Global Policy Council. These 64 individuals are representatives of groups who focus on specific problem areas, such as population growth, forest preservation, poverty, women's and children's issues, health care, technology, and educational media. The even larger All Peoples Council of 260 members comprises the full voting membership of the WSC. Here we find popularly elected representatives from the NGOs who provide us with vital connections with local, regional, and national membership bodies. The All Peoples Council in turn elects the members of the Global Policy Council. With all these creative thinkers in touch with what is really happening at the local community level, I think it's fair to say that we are unique in our ability to consistently represent and address the needs of the world's people at the grass roots level. And we can mobilize them quickly through our extensive media network.

"But, aside from the necessary organizational infrastructure, I think we, as an institution, are able to serve as an incubator for highly focused creative and original collective thinking and acting. The WSC is a place where latent human energy can come alive, become electric and joyful, even amidst the often contentious nature of the work. Although most of our members represent constituencies external to the WSC, these individuals remain effective because they hold as primary the collective good. And we take very seriously the assumption that the 'world community' includes the animal and plant kingdoms as well as the geologic, biologic, and atmospheric elements as co-equal stakeholders."

"How do you include the points of view of those not able to formally participate in the decision making process?"

"To guarantee inclusion of all relevant parties, our WSC research subcommittees frequently adjourn to the field. Investigatory sessions might convene deep in a Brazilian jungle, in a Saharan desert camp, or an endangered turtle refuge on the Yucatan Coast. While living for several weeks or months in a local community, task force members will undertake and record individual and group interviews. The sharing of tribal customs is also an integral part of the trust building process. On occasion, despite the often significant personal risk, WSC representatives have participated in important rituals with natives of the Amazon Basin and special ceremonies in the Sierra Madre Mountains with Tarahumara Indians."

"This is an impressive process of inquiry," I admitted. "It seems you leave no relevant stone unturned."

President Singh continued with emphasis, "I remain convinced that responsible policy makers must think holistically and selflessly, and, whenever possible, nature's voice must be heard at the table of talk, too."

"How does the WSC manage to stay in touch with its field ambassadors?"

"Electronics is the key. Mobile video equipment always accompanies the research teams. Once a satellite linkup is established, the field team shares its process of inquiry live with WSC headquarters. Simultaneously, the signal is sent over a global public network of broadcast stations, cable systems, and radio affiliates. Sometimes several remote teams link up for a two-, three-, or four-way teleconference, soliciting input from those similarly affected elsewhere in the world. In this way, commonalities between disparate groups become apparent, and powerful new alliances are often formed. I suggest you visit the Video Communication Center next. Our people there will explain the WSC outreach program to you. These programs are important because I believe we are already addressing some of the key issues that concern the PAPA."

"Is there anyone in particular I should contact?"

"Yes . . . Rashid. He's our resident communications wizard. He's in charge of making magic with our cameras, computers, satellite connections, and people resources."

CHAPTER 21

MAKING THE INVISIBLE VISIBLE

Cool power. That's the first impression I had upon entering the WSC communications complex. Once the heavy wooden door closed, vaultlike, behind me, I knew I had stepped into another dimension, a kind of airport for the senses. From here one could travel to the most remote destinations and be there now—electronically. From the balcony that overlooked the Video Communications Center or VCC, a wired hive of human and electronic activity, my eyes scanned row upon row of high resolution video monitors. Their vibrant images dazzled me: a camel caravan shuffling across the desert; the strobe lights and pounding guitars of a Russian disco; a council of Maori tribesmen, arms flailing, engaged in heated discussion; Japanese children lost in a Kabuki puppet show; and more.

Gazing down from the precisely arranged linear ranks of monitors and complex switching devices, I examined rows of computer screens bursting with multicolored data, graphics, and text. Some displayed geographic imagery of entire continents while others focused on specific river valleys, mountain ranges, and targeted bioregions. False-color aerial imagery, taken from satellite cameras, tracked rain forest vegetation and biodiversity changes caused by erosion, ranching, encroaching human development, and stratospheric ozone depletion. Computer-graphic images visualized deadly air-pollution plumes and their attendant land contamination patterns resulting from upwind industrial centers. Still more monitors depicted toxic contents in waterways and oceans.

As I stood transfixed by the collage of foreign and sometimes spectacular images, a youthful but serious-looking young man dressed in casual working clothes noticed my presence, interrupted his discussion with several staff members, and waved me down to the floor. I descended the dozen or so steps that led to a small, slightly raised platform below the entrance balcony. My vantage point provided a commanding overview of the room. The dark-complexioned man approached me. "Hello," I said. "I'm looking for Rashid."

"I'm Rashid Kassem," he said, confidently. "Is there something I can help you with?"

I explained my directive from President Singh and added that I wanted to learn more about the WSC communications system and its capabilities. But I said I was also a journalist and was interested in his personal background and how he became involved in this work. He thought for a minute and then began speaking with strong emotion, "I'm from Egypt. For years, I've observed the many communication problems people seem to have with each other. Yes, religious differences complicate things, but if people could communicate better with each other, then perhaps we might have more peace in the world."

"I think you're right," I said.

"But we live in an age where electronic communication is everywhere, so I completed a Masters degree in Telecommunications Psychology at the University of California. After graduation I accepted a position here. In time I became the director of the VCC."

"You seem to be in your element," I said, "right at home. Tell me what goes on here. What do you do with all this equipment?"

"Okay. The Video Communication Center's job is to perform traffic control on the many video, audio, and data channels that arrive here from different satellites and fiber-optic land lines. Data is relayed from laptop computers and cellular phones after it is transmitted to low-orbit satellites. We also receive live, interactive, or taped programs produced throughout the world, which we then rebroadcast to the billions who make up the WSC's electronic audience. We call

Making the Invisible Visible

our complete computer, video, and satellite system 'GlobeNet'. At any given moment, our network is in touch with hundreds of electronic information sources and millions and sometimes billions of receivers and interactors. Our VCC operators combine video images with audio and computer information into usable forms to meet the needs of the WSC committees, researchers, and communications networks outside the WSC. Since much of our material is broadcast live, the public is able to participate in a wide variety of cultural interactions occurring daily around the world."

"And I imagine that the interactive nature of the process enables the viewers to feel they're living in an electronic village."

"Yes, it often does give that impression."

"Do you include commercials in your programming?"

"No, unlike the standard media, our radio and video networks charge no access fees and show no paid ads for commercial products. Rather, our intention is to provide an open communication forum for the world's people to share with one another their hopes and joys, their talents and skills, their concerns and lives. To tell their individual stories, you might say. The GlobeNet electronic network is designed to help people reach out for creative connections with each other. No cigarettes, cars, drugs, washing machines, or paranoid ideologies are peddled here. No damaging violent or sexist images appear. Instead of sowing fear and inadequacy, the WSC audio and video network strives to encourage personal self-sufficiency and empowerment through entertainment, thoughtful inquiry, and intercultural sharing. Because it has its own revenue sources, it's able to provide the kind of programming that best serves the real world needs of the planetary community."

"What would a typical broadcast day look like to me, a viewer in the United States, if I were tuned into the WSC channel?"

"Well . . . it might begin with a Navajo sunrise ceremony originating from northern Arizona. Next, there might follow a series of educational children's programs, a student-produced violence avoidance clip from Rio de Janeiro, a multicultural teenage forum on sexuality, a community leadership class from Canada, a women's herbal healing seminar from Asia, a family planning soap opera from Kenya, build-it-yourself straw bale house instruction from Argentina, a variety of math, science, and technology courses from the United States, and a home-based small business seminar from Mexico. Something like that."

"And in the evening? What then?"

"Every night we produce a two-hour 'Real News Newscast' that highlights inspiring people and projects from around the world. Our programs focus on people helping people in creative ways and on projects that improve the quality of life and the environment. We follow up news shows with insightful, intelligent analysis of world events and the human condition. Late evening programming is usually world music and general entertainment. Much of the music is taped in our studios here and broadcast live. But all entertainment fare must pass rigorous standards prohibiting gratuitous violence, sexual exploitation, and cultural and age discrimination."

"So who can receive your programming?"

"It's available to almost anyone with a TV set and antenna, cable or Internet connection, or satellite dish. And anyone with access to video recording equipment can offer tapes or live programs as potential program input to the WSC mini-uplink studios located in most major cities throughout the world. We can also receive video and audio clips through the Internet. Low cost production workshops are made available at most studios, as are equipment rental and editing resources that are offered on a first-come, first-served basis. Roving teams in mobile units—usually specially equipped 4-wheel drive vans—provide taping, editing, and transmitting facilities in the field. Community-owned and -programmed low power radio stations abound in rural areas, especially in Third World countries."

"And what's the size of your potential audience?"

"Our dedicated satellite network, ancillary broadcast stations, translator relays, and cable and landline networks give us access to nearly three billion people twenty-four hours a day, seven days a week."

"And how does what you do here connect and integrate with rural communities?"

"We have interactive links with community centers in remote villages so we can provide them with medical and economic self-help programs. Because the system has teleconferencing capability, government spokespersons can be questioned and straw votes taken. People's views and votes can be conveyed to politicians and relevant economic interests as well as registered here at WSC headquarters. If the political and economic parties fail to respond appropriately in a timely manner, a global boycott might be activated against a corporation's product line or a recall election urged for an uncooperative politician or political body. Some call this feature, 'electronic democracy.'"

"Please correct me if I'm wrong," I said, "but one particularly potent feature of the WSC media system seems to be its potential to make the invisible visible."

"How so?"

"Well, having studied the media for some time, I've concluded that we give lip service to democracy, but in reality, hidden forces work to restrict and limit true public choice. It seems the choices we have are often confined to the politically expedient and that which supports a high-consumption lifestyle. I'm afraid the sad fact remains that hourly, many nonconventional ways of being and creating are becoming forgotten because they're not in sync with the global shopping-mall monoculture. Thus, they're in effect rendered out of existence. The result, then, is a slow and almost invisible destruction of a whole, valuable diversity of options, cultures, and ideas on this planet. Somehow, we need to resist or reverse this insidious process. Otherwise, we'll be severely diminishing our overall quality of life."

Rashid nodded his head. "Yes, yes, I see what you're saying. And I appreciate your passion regarding it. GlobeNet has, in fact, developed an archive project to help preserve endangered human knowledge. We recognize that every day valuable practical-living and nature-related human information is lost due to the failure of elders to transfer their knowledge to the younger generation. Our response has been to try to identify certain at-risk areas of traditional knowledge and record as much as we can on audio, video, and digital tape before it's lost forever."

"What kind of things do you work to save?"

"Folk medicine, arts and technical crafts, Native agricultural, biological, and architectural knowledge—ways of seeing and living in the world that people have painstakingly developed over many generations—the nontechnological kinds of information and methods of information gathering. I guess you might call them the 'intuitive arts and sciences.' The WSC also supports a worldwide network of Schools of Rare and Endangered Knowledge as part of an international effort to preserve this valuable informational legacy."

"Wow, that's great. That's just what's needed!" I scanned the room and all its living equipment, and I became quite excited with the potential I could foresee. "You know, Rashid, the thought occurs to me that through the linking of three billion plus human minds over an open system free of commercial seduction, the WSC has created a formidable planet-wide electronic nervous system. A human alliance of such unprecedented proportion has the potential to make radical choices about its collective future. If our collective intelligence could be appropriately informed and focused, global transformation on a scale never before imagined could occur."

Rashid smiled knowingly. "Nicely put. We do discuss such things at our regular meetings. And we really hope to make something like that happen someday. But I'd like to give you a closer look at what we do. Let's go over here, and I'll explain what happens when things get really intense."

He then invited me to get comfortable in one of the six high-back chairs that were arched around a wide, low conference table, affording optimum visibility of all the surrounding monitors and screens. As I seated myself, I noticed a sophisticated telephone and intercom system and several computer keyboards on the table. Just beyond the table, at eye level, was mounted a panel of small color monitors whose images duplicated those on the larger monitors around the room.

"What's 'really intense?'" I asked, intrigued by the suggestive term.

"Well, when we're in a full alert situation, like during a hurricane, typhoon, earthquake, insurrection, that sort of thing. Right now it's pretty quiet, except for a typhoon we're monitoring over the Pacific."

He went on to explain how they handled the receiving and sending functions of GlobeNet—the scheduling of satellite channels, incoming computer communications, and video from around the world, and the rebroadcasting of transmissions. "This is a 24-hour operation," he reminded me. "It's necessary to simultaneously track multiple time zones and languages; consequently, each of our staff members has to be fluent in at least three languages. Normally, when time permits, programs are translated into several languages, but during crisis situations this isn't always possible. That's when things get really intense.

"When a typhoon hits Bangladesh and people are in the water and a few hundred houses are floating away, we hustle to get our disaster experts on-line. They then assess the situation and we work with them to send as much physical help as we can to the affected area. We do a computer analysis of the projected path and impact of the storm, locate available relief services, and establish two-way video—or at least audio—communication links. At the same time, we're doing our own damage control. You know, Mother Nature can take out our equipment as well."

Rashid then showed me one of the most powerful features of the system—its ability to provide real-time assessments of physical conditions almost anywhere in the world. He continued, "Our computers can access information from satellite imaging, local weather sensors, on-site observers, and volunteer mobile video crews. Some ground teams even have helicopter capability so they can provide live video from a crisis location within hours. Once a satellite connection is established, the VCC has its own interactive eyes and ears. Teleconference links then connect ground crews with distant advisors to assist the locals in dealing effectively with the situation."

I asked what it's like when circumstances are "normal."

"Then it's a wonderful experience of cross-cultural interaction—music, dialog, discussion, education, humor . . . like a global village festival and marketplace with lots of chance meetings, strange faces, exciting goings-on, and amazing personal exchanges."

Rashid explained how the VCC's task of managing incoming and outgoing visual and audio data sources while overseeing the smooth functioning of the networks is a major challenge. But the real trick, he said, is to weave the myriad inputs into something that has continuity and makes sense to a wide variety of people with real-world needs.

"How do you decide what information to rebroadcast and what to reject?"

"Live transmissions of inspiring events and productions of instructional programs are the primary responsibilities of the VCC; performing geographic and data analysis is not. For that kind of information you should visit the International Center for Appropriate Technology, or ICAT, in the United States. The ICAT people have their Real Time Planetary Diagnostic System."

"Yes, I know. I've spent some time there. It's very impressive."

"ICAT is critical to our operations as it provides the bulk of our technical data for our in-house program production and environmental analyses. We use a lot of their data resources, but our expertise is really in educational programming."

"What kind of programs?"

"Well, we try to cover the territory. We focus on the basics—such as writing, math, history, arts and sciences, computers—but we also offer a variety of specialized programs you'd only find at certain schools and universities that focus on global concerns. Right now we're working up a course on sustainable economies."

"You mean 'sustainable economic development?'"

"That remains a controversial subject around here. And perhaps it's an oxymoron. The question we ask is 'sustainable for whom'? And what does one actually mean by sustainability and development?" He quickly lowered his voice, flicked his eyes left and right as if checking if anyone was within earshot. Then he smiled, indicating to me he wasn't excessively worried about being overheard. But I got the point. "In theory, the concept of sustainable development sounds great," he said, "but in reality, does it really preserve the environment and provide people with long-term economic and environmental security?"

"Most development that I've seen doesn't," I said, "but realistically speaking, most people require some kind of economic undertaking to survive. Basic needs must be covered before most people can even think about protecting their environment."

"People here realize that. But they would strongly oppose the concept of growth for growth's sake—that, as they say, 'is the mentality of a cancer cell.'"

I thought for a minute about his comment.

Rashid continued, "But it's the mindset from which the industrial world presently operates. It's all about bottom-line economics. And the transnational corporations are always cooking up some new way to undermine important global checks and balances such as national sovereignty, local and regional economic self-sufficiency, and environmental protection laws."

"I guess what really worries me is this powerful tendency to reduce life to a common value system measured in monetary terms alone, one that has little or nothing to do with a sustainable future that will support a reasonable level of human civilization that's filled with rich, cultural diversity."

"How do you think we can avoid this trap?" Rashid asked.

"I think we have to question the concept of unlimited economic growth as so-called 'progress.' Instead, we must include social and environmental factors and the issue of intergenerational equity as economic priorities."

"This is, in fact, what we are trying to get at with the concept of sustainability."

"Yes. I know that in theory, sustainability seeks to assure a satisfactory quality of life for those in the present without compromising the needs of future generations. It's living off the interest of, rather than consuming, our natural resource capital. And further, our activities should not overwhelm the integrity of the natural system."

"But achieving such balance will not be easy, Tom."

"Do we have a choice?" I asked. "The alternative is not so comforting."

"No, indeed it is not. I believe education is the key, if we are to avoid a potential planetary meltdown. Our GlobeNet information system can make a difference. Let me show you just what it can do."

CHAPTER 22

GLOBAL ALLIES

"We think in terms of bioregions," Rashid said, his excitement about the concept patently evident. "In the simplest terms, a bioregion is an area defined by its natural watershed. Its boundaries are biologic and geologic rather than political. An area might be identified as a coastal, forest, or valley bioregion instead of as village X in Y province. Bioregional classification enables people to think in terms of integrated, contiguous physical environments and helps relate social, political, and economic problems back to their environmental origins.

"I can see the common sense in it," I said, "because it aids people in understanding how local goods, services, and resources are used, and how dependent they might be on the importation of essential goods, services, and resources from outside their bioregion."

"Yes. And that kind of calculation enables a community to determine how sustainably or nonsustainably they are living. In developed nations, most communities' worst fears are quickly confirmed. They'll discover that they import one hundred percent of their energy, one hundred percent of their clothing and other manufactured goods and probably ninety to ninety-nine percent of their food from somewhere else. And manufactured goods and food require transportation—most of which is still dependent on oil. But as oil supplies diminish, transportation costs will increase, thus raising all costs associated with the use of oil. Any sudden interruptions in oil supplies can really send the global economy into a tailspin. So you see, the level of vulnerability here is significant."

"This analysis also leads us into the concept of carrying capacity," I added. "We need to consider how many people a certain bioregion can support with its own native resources."

"I think every community, every city, should undertake these exercises to see where they stand. We find more and more communities are asking these questions: Could we become more self-sufficient? How vulnerable are we willing to become by permitting greater and greater dependency on outside resources? Would we like to move toward a more sustainable economy?"

"And then there's the overarching issue of *global* carrying capacity. I imagine you discuss this issue frequently here, and have some way to use GlobeNet to foster bioregional thinking?"

"We do try," Rashid replied, exhaling slowly and communicating to me a sense of being overwhelmed with the size of the problem. "Since a bioregion is a product of nature's design, we've attempted to incorporate natural design into our communications systems. Like nature, GlobeNet is a multilevel communication system that is structured in layers, cycles, and interrelated units. Information is entered at different levels in this interactive web—WSC headquarters, associate regions, community centers, and individual sites. The major difference between levels is usually the type of information each level is likely to contain. For example, electronic libraries in tropical areas deal mostly with social, political, environmental, and scientific knowledge of interest to tropical regions, and generally do not contain information about particular climatic, demographic, or economic interests found elsewhere."

"And can that information be accessed elsewhere?"

"Oh yes. For example, this morning we received an inquiry from a member of the Yanomama tribe in Venezuela who was looking for some information on anti-parasite protection and new forest preservation strategies. Our data files showed that rain forest dwellers in Malaysia and the Philippines had such knowledge on file or in their heads. So we sent an information request to Malaysia. A response was then transmitted directly to Caracas from the Malaysian village community center via portable laptop computer and WSC satellite link. In many instances, a request like this might take a few hours to complete, or it might take a few days or even weeks if the information is known only by one particular individual. But it's fast. Much faster and less expensive than could be accomplished by any other common means of communication.

"We also try to respond to people's needs for technical information. Some community might need an instructional videotape documenting a process of water purification that can operate on renewable energy using local materials and biological processes. Once our producers are notified of the need, researchers and script writers go to work. Soon our video programs are available in several languages for use around the world."

"Is there an issue here of cultural appropriateness?" I asked, remembering my conversations with Jenny.

"Definitely. Our programmers pay particular attention to how different cultures store, process, and convey information. Sometimes pictorial imagery, song, or dance might serve better than written text to communicate with certain cultures. Fortunately, our graphic specialists can construct just about anything in visual and auditory form that can be imagined. Cultural appropriateness, however, is a more challenging matter and requires that the production team work very closely with individuals from the culture or cultures that request the program."

"I'm curious about your communication nodes in the field. How many do you have and how do they operate? I know a major portion of the world's population lacks electricity."

"Within the last two years, since the WSC was founded, we've been able to site about five hundred technology support centers in the field—a mere drop in the bucket considering there are hundreds of thousands of rural villages in Mexico and Central America alone. You probably saw samples of them at ICAT."

"Yes, I did."

"Then you probably know that an important feature of the GlobeNet system is its distributed or decentralized nature. If one sub-network is temporarily disabled, identical information can often be obtained from other regional branches or from master databases. Because we try to install multiple datalinks—coaxial cables, fiber-optic land lines, microwave, cellular, and low power transmitters, and direct satellite links—the GlobeNet system can maintain its integrity despite local revolutions, equipment failures, or natural disasters. But you're right—at least one-third of the people living in rural areas of the world are without access to electricity, so we need to make sure most support centers are independent of local power grids. They're powered by renewable energy sources such as solar, water power, or wind, as are our regional networks and WSC central."

"And how do you use the support centers for local empowerment?"

"This is what's really amazing. It's an area where the WSC is beginning to have a major impact. We've learned a lot from teleconferenced discussions with communities around the globe. From these experiences our sustainable economic development specialists have been able to define new pathways for local economic assistance. We've worked hard to set up Distributed Economic Co-ops or DECs, composed of indigenous people, rural farmers, urban entrepreneurs, artisans, and community merchants who join together in regional and international marketing associations. These organizations can provide alternatives to the economic hegemony of transnational corporations. We use our distant learning programs to train interested men and women in basic communication skills and the use of the communications technologies. Consequently, electronically literate people staff the co-op centers, now equipped with fax machines and telecommunications hardware. WSC funding has also provided DECs with self-esteem, business management, organizational training, and microloan assistance, so each co-op is able to successfully undertake and sustain its own projects."

"Do these programs ever encounter resistance? I'd think they would tend to challenge the status quo."

"Vigorous resistance, which generally comes from entrenched special interests, that are often large international entities, working in collusion with national and regional governments."

"What can you do about that?"

"In many such cases, international legal and human rights organizations acting in solidarity with well-organized local populations seeking change have served to successfully break the stranglehold of those resisting positive change. But such groups must be able to rally the majority of the population behind them. Sometimes it works and sometimes it doesn't. It depends mainly on the creativity and political savvy of the local grassroots organizations."

"What kind of projects have worked?"

"Usually small-scale economic development that respects local traditions and lifestyles, preserves old-growth forests, water and air quality, and regional biodiversity. Most people have no interest in massive logging and power projects, large grazing operations, and major industrial developments. Top-down hierarchies and foreign-based finance strategies are consistently rejected out of hand in favor of cooperative management and community ownership. Most communities are aware of the kind of social/cultural damage those kinds of development projects create."

"So a type of learning is taking place about what communities want and what they don't want."

"Yes, but many communities don't have much political or economic control over their future. The larger global forces still dominate. But that's changing."

"How so?"

"Through our work and our creative use of communications technology, we've enabled local groups to acquire critical practical skills and become better informed politically. They now scrutinize the promises made to them, especially those originating from their own national governments. Consequently, their thinking has become quite innovative. For example, many forest communities now understand that the cutting edge of technology is shifting away from electronics and is moving toward biologic-based industry. And biology, lots of it, is what the nations of the Southern Hemisphere have, especially those with portions of still intact forest ecosystems. Not only do these rural communities still possess abundant physical resources, but they have plenty of biological knowledge as well, painstakingly developed and evolved over eons.

"These forest communities have seen that their unique traditional knowledge and physical resource base is becoming increasingly valuable in the global marketplace. They know now that such resources can translate into specialized cures for disease, life extension aids, and applications not yet known. The challenge, though, for traditional indigenous people, is to reestablish ownership and control of these assets."

"What can be done to give local people more control over their resources?"

"Well, after much discussion, we've come up with the notion of 'biodiversity futures.' The Distributed Co-ops pioneered this concept by forming legal entities solely owned by the founders themselves, with holdings consisting of their own biological and informational assets. The future market value of these assets is of course speculative—not unlike that of an undeveloped underground mineral resource. However, the co-ops recognize that the value of these unique and irreplaceable substances can potentially dwarf the worth of all other physical resources in the area. The marketing of biodiversity futures can be used by communities to raise money in a fashion consistent with their particular spiritual and social values. It also gives them control over their indigenous resources. And because they will inherit the long-term impact of any action taken, the local people will likely subscribe to the idea of sustainability."

"Has this happened?"

Global Allies

"Interestingly, even given the lure of potentially huge profits from control of local biological resources, most groups have opted for slow and cautious development. Instead of proposing maximum financial gain as the ultimate objective, many communities have asserted the philosophy of compassionate sharing and sacred stewardship. When we ask about their motives, we're often told by certain individuals that they've been charged by their ancestors and the spirit world with the task of ensuring that future generations will inherit a healthy environment. They say it's a spiritual as well as an economic issue. And this is good economics, too. They know that trees in an intact ecosystem are worth more alive than dead."

"That's wonderful, indeed. Hearing such things certainly bolsters my hope for the future."

"I have some videotapes that demonstrate our WSC-assisted rural economic development projects. Look up there on the screen."

Rashid entered numbers into a nearby computer and one of the largest display units came alive. "This videotape was produced by a group of Bolivian Indians to document a series of recently completed small-scale ecotourism operations that they started. The buildings are constructed of native materials and carefully sited within close range of nearby virgin forests."

The images of giant trees and misty waterfalls that came to life on the screen enabled me to easily appreciate the powerful presence of the centuries-old trees in their natural settings. A colorful graphic map informed the viewer that no roads penetrate the wilderness preserve; only small walking paths and electric tram routes provide access. The camera observed Native guides counseling visitors on how best to appreciate the special energies of this spectacular natural environment, and how to open to the majesty and richness of the subtleties of the forest. I learned from the tape narrative that the income generated from tourism and the sustainable harvesting of forest products generates many times the income for the local people than would accrue to them from a one-time logging operation. And, better yet, the severely negative impact of large-scale extraction is avoided as well.

Slowly, I began to perceive a pattern in all of this. Electronic communications have now become an essential component for social, economic, and political empowerment. Likewise, the notion of working associations has been freed from traditional limitations of place, time, and distance. Electronic networking makes possible virtual partnerships and associations. By providing powerful educational and informational tools and human resources to those normally outside the global decision-making loop—in particular the economically and politically disenfranchised—the WSC has introduced a tremendous leveling force.

Rashid explained that the WSC has facilitated a method of economic democratization by enabling organizations to come together with others who share common values, problems, and visions. In this way, timely linkages are preserved without regard to distance, travel cost, or limitations of personal mobility. Interested change makers are thereby able to achieve a critical mass of influence. With the option for easy, inexpensive electronic connections, a compelling new form of global solidarity and grassroots activism is manifesting. No doubt even greater changes are in store.

CHAPTER 23

SAVING THE TREE OF LIFE

"So what can you do about the trees?" I asked Rashid, as we walked along the long corridor and through a large wooden door that opened into an adjacent control room, apparently one of many. It was similar to the Video Communications Center where we had been talking earlier, but somewhat smaller. This room also contained a variety of monitors, but it seemed designed for highly focused specific work. I observed a group of six people facing a series of large video display screens. They barely noticed our entrance. Instead, the small gathering seemed lost in a concentrated collective effort, some jotting down notes while others typed instructions on computer keyboards, summoning various information displays to the waiting screens.

Rashid led me over to them. After introducing me as a researcher and journalist, he asked if someone would volunteer to update me on their efforts. A tall, thin, and intense-looking Black woman with elaborately braided hair quickly nodded agreement. She introduced herself as Miriam, a WSC Educational Consultant. Environmental sciences were her specialty, she said. Smiling briefly, she offered us the seats on either side of her so we'd have a good view of the forward monitors. "Would you like to see a visual representation of the state of the world's forests?" she asked me politely. I hesitated, knowing the news would not be good, but my curiosity got the better of me. "Sure," I said.

As the two of us sat down together, Miriam called up a multicolor display of the world's forests and their present conditions. "Dark green means healthy, dark brown indicates serious decline, and yellow-brown depicts complete loss."

Another touch on her keyboard activated an animated sequence, accompanied with dates in years, documenting the global forest's shrinkage over time. It was dramatic. I saw that one thousand years ago, forests covered thirty-two percent of the world's land area. There was plenty of green then. But now almost half the primal forests are gone, and in many countries, only about twenty percent or less of original forest cover remains. The great green forests had suddenly changed into a sickly yellow-brown, turning into deserts that continue to expand at a rapid rate. It looked like the world was fast becoming lifeless, without color.

"Shocking, isn't it?" she said, observing my quiet concern.

She then moved us from one continent to another through the deft manipulation of her computer mouse. Click. Click. Click. Everywhere it was the same—green gone to yellow-brown or desert-tan. "Scary," I said, depressed but not surprised at the sight.

"Our strategy is this," she explained. "First, we use the GlobeNet database to determine which forests are undergoing the most rapid decline. Then we try to assess the value of threatened ecological zones; this is the resource evaluation mode. Next comes the human evaluation. We identify the indigenous inhabitants of the area, and what patterns of land use and local ownership or tenure status might exist. We try to quantify how much wood is cut for local use and how much is destined for export."

"Legally recognized local ownership is probably minimal," I said.

"Yes. More like nonexistent. Then we examine the purchase agreements between national governments and logging companies."

"Not always aboveboard . . . no pun intended."

"Right again. Our undercover work shows that most governments sell their timber at a fraction of its market value—about fifteen percent—which means governments are massively subsidizing the timber companies. We found that questionable relationships abound between the industry and government representatives. Additionally, governments routinely disregard the intellectual property rights of the affected indigenous people—the original inhabitants of the land—by unilaterally selling plant, animal, and human genetic harvesting rights to international pharmaceutical companies."

"This is why our legal teams are so important," Rashid interrupted. "Our teams work with indigenous groups to help them gain some control over their forests. If sovereignty or ownership rights can legally be established for local communities, such entities as national governments and timber interests are then forced to negotiate with the residents who live there and are dependent upon the sustainable use of the resources. WSC advisory teams try to make sure that communities are adequately appraised of the value of their ecosystems. They help the community understand the importance of biodiversity and carbon credit values and the environmental, cultural, and eventually economic devastation that would occur with wholesale tree removal."

"I bet that's sometimes a dangerous business," I said.

"As a matter of fact," Miriam responded, "our representatives often encounter opposition from collusive national governments and logging interests. Jobs are at stake, they claim, as is desperately needed hard currency income to pay foreign debts. Sometimes this is at least partly true, but we know that much of the money is disappearing into bureaucrats' and bankers' pockets and is being used to purchase military equipment. The situation has appeared so grave that our original initiative was temporarily halted while the Global Policy Council met to debate the issue at length. Normally, the WSC holds a fairly neutral attitude, but a strong advocacy position seemed unavoidable in this situation. Too much was at stake."

"What happened?" I asked, really curious.

Miriam turned to me with a quizzical look on her face. "You haven't heard about our infamous Forest Media Action Project?"

"No, I've been out of the media loop for almost a year."

"We need to bring you up to date then. About nine months ago, the Global Policy Council decided to act aggressively, even if it meant challenging the sovereignty of certain nations, opposing powerful transnationals and— in the short run—possibly damaging local economies.

"The decision was not arrived at easily, though. When the first vote was taken, the council was split evenly on the action recommendation. Then the Wise Council of 13 responded by presenting a whole variety of people to speak for the forests. Their pleas for help were so poignant and persuasive that no one in the audience could remain unmoved. I remember a young Apache Indian man from the United States who tried to explain his tribe's personal kinship with trees. He said, 'They're people. They're our brothers. When they're gone . . .' He was all choked up. There was total silence in the room. He never finished his sentence. A Maya Indian added his perspective, 'Each tree that's cut is another child murdered. Each forest, a nation massacred. When the last tree is gone, so will be the last human. We've got to see it that way,' he said.

"All the speakers made their points with heart-rending clarity; they likened forest destruction on the present scale to the inevitable destruction of humanity. They warned that the loss of the Earth's forests would place all life on the planet in serious jeopardy. Fortunately, on the next vote the council issued a strong condemnation of what it termed 'forces of greed and instant profit that threatened to destroy the global life-support fabric.' Shortly afterward we were told to mobilize our top video producers, researchers, and writers and 'give it everything we've got.' Twenty million dollars were appropriated for a massive media campaign to take the issue worldwide to the public."

"As a result of all the public relations activities," Rashid continued, "a global movement was spawned to ban the conversion of rain forests to cattle ranches. Hamburger sales plummeted. The price of beef collapsed."

"Yeah," added Miriam, speaking proudly, "and people were horrified, outraged, and disheartened with what they

Saving the Tree of Life

saw. But they were also encouraged by the host of practical alternatives that we proposed. Our follow-up speakers urged an immediate boycott of all products delivered by outlaw logging companies and colluding national governments. We identified several large multinational corporations who were involved in the questionable logging practices, and an angry public reacted. Corporate sales crashed and exports from the guilty countries were halted. Consumers in industrial countries cut back purchases of cars, electronics, appliances, and furniture, reduced wood use, and canceled their subscriptions to magazines and newspapers that refused to use treeless paper. Recycling of paper jumped forty percent and purchases of alternative paper products exploded. Where timber harvesting was particularly abusive, local economies weakened and unemployment soared."

Rashid added, "But the WSC had wisely prepared itself for adverse consequences and offered to purchase some of the controversial timber concessions from logging companies or local governments at reduced rates. This accomplished, timber rights were then gifted back to the indigenous land owners, subsequent to establishment of legal tenure and the development and guarantee of sustainable use plans. Wood prices increased as markets shifted to reflect the higher value of timber products, which had to include new ecological standards. Consumers continued to reduce wood consumption, however, because they were better able to appreciate the overall value of timber."

Miriam screened a few short excerpts from their now-famous forest videos. I found it extremely painful to view the murky rivers, war-zonelike hillsides, and scalped mountains. "Threats to trees by logging are easily identified," she noted without taking her eyes off the video monitors, "but other destructive factors, perhaps even more catastrophic in potential, are not."

"What do you mean?" I asked.

"The forests are dying in the United States, Europe, and Asia, almost everywhere. We're witnessing a pandemic—a universal epidemic. Virulent forms of fungi are attacking white pines in New England; birch trees are dying at an accelerating rate in the Adirondacks; sabal palms are withering along the Gulf Coast; researchers have documented a ten-fold increase in the mortality of Sierra Nevada mixed conifer forests. And it goes on and on."

"Why?"

"A lot of reasons. Decades of clearcutting, excess ozone in the troposphere and insufficient amounts in the stratosphere, drying winds, a constant dousing of industrial chemicals, and climate change. A major culprit appears to be increased UV-B radiation. The link is pretty clear. When stratospheric ozone levels plummet over certain forest areas, tree needle and leaf damage increases. It's like the trees have AIDS. And not only are the trees adversely affected, but plant and animal life as well. We know, for example, that UV-B radiation scrambles the cells of frog eggs, preventing them from maturing properly. As a result, many amphibian populations are in decline or have disappeared entirely."

I could formulate no verbal response, but her alarming comments cut deep, very deep.

Miriam sighed and continued speaking. A tone of desperation was evident in her voice. "But this is only one aspect of the global crisis. There's also transportation, energy, food, women's rights, employment, population, and so on; and all are intimately interconnected and interwoven."

"I know. It's a bit overwhelming, isn't it?" I said.

"Absolutely."

"I haven't heard how the WSC is addressing the issues of food and population growth. In my mind, they're the really big ones. If we're unable to generate some creative thinking and bold actions regarding these issues pretty soon, we'll be looking at some serious global unrest occurring."

"I think you could say it's already begun," Miriam corrected me. "Many of the regional civil wars and refugee migrations we're seeing in Africa, Eastern Europe, and Central America are due, in fact, to the loss or degradation of cropland and the unmet food needs of rapidly growing populations. Food and population are, of course, intimately linked. But reducing population growth is an exceedingly difficult area to deal with because it's loaded with complex emotional, religious, political, and economic implications. But, we can't ignore it either. Our future is totally dependent on our ability to strike a balance between these two key components of life. Some of our programs might shock you. They're rather radical."

"I don't think anything less will make a difference," I replied boldly.

CHAPTER 24

A CRITICAL BALANCE

That afternoon, after a healthy lunch of vegetarian sandwiches served in the WSC cafeteria, Rashid, Miriam, and I returned to the conference room inside the communications center. As we sat around the large oval table, we laughed together and traded stories about how we found ourselves drawn into the work of attempting to educate others about the pressing problems of the world.

"It's always been in my genes," Rashid said. "I've felt born to use media to help make a better world. When I attended school in the United States, I heard the saying 'to whom much is given, much is expected,' and that really resonated with me. I come from a wealthy family so I take the call to service very seriously."

Miriam smiled tolerantly. "I wish I had the benefit of growing up in a wealthy family, but all my relatives are either dead or missing, victims of hunger and civil war in Central Africa. I was the lucky one, taken in by a generous British family and given a college education in England. I discovered I had a good mind for sciences, so this is my way of giving back. How about you, Tom?"

"Well, I sort of stumbled into all of this. My directives haven't been as clear-cut as yours. But yeah, I've felt a call too . . . to use my communications skills to benefit humanity. Sometimes it's been really faint, other times it's blaring in my head."

"How's the volume now?" Rashid asked directly.

"Very loud. So loud, in fact, I find it hard to focus on anything else."

"So, we'd better get back to business then."

"Okay," said Miriam, spinning around in her seat. "I'd like to look at food production and carrying capacity. These are areas in which I have considerable and painful personal experience. I'll define carrying capacity as the maximum number of a particular species that a given habitat can support indefinitely. Unfortunately, I think we're close to our limits already. And what's pushing the global habitat beyond its carrying capacity is us."

"Sometimes I see the situation like this," Rashid added. "If Spaceship Earth had a central control panel, lots of red warning lights would be flashing. Horns would be blaring incessantly. The captain would be assembling the crew members on deck and announcing that the very survival of each passenger was at risk."

"Do we need to consider abandoning ship?" I asked, hoping it was an extreme question.

"In some parts of the world people are already in the lifeboats, and have been for some time," answered Miriam succinctly. "Many fisheries, rangelands, forests, farmlands, and hydrological cycles have been pushed to their limits or are in decline. In places like Africa and Asia, food production has fallen way behind demand. People are moving into ecologically fragile areas and further degrading their environments and reducing biological diversity. When food support systems collapse and people are unable to feed themselves, the pressure builds, political instability increases, and violence results."

Miriam remained silent for a time, deep in thought. "Our data tells us that world grainland productivity is expanding at barely one percent per year, but world population continues to grow by 1.5 percent per year. And each year we add another ninety million more people who will need to be fed. Think about that for a minute!"

"Can't we expand the world's farmland?"

"Somewhat, yes—by better utilizing existing cropland, bringing idled land into production that's currently withheld for conservation purposes, and by moving onto more fragile areas. But we're also losing our arable land to industrialization: factories, highways, housing developments, shopping centers, golf courses, and so on. Industrialization is claiming some of the most productive farmland in the United States, Asia, and elsewhere because so much of it is located near expanding cities."

"And water is another critical factor," said Rashid.

"Yes," agreed Miriam, "productive farmland depends on water, and much of it comes from wells and irrigation. But water sources are drying up. In the United States twenty-one percent of the cropland is dependent on drawing down underground fossil aquifers, and water tables are falling rapidly."

"Clearly an unsustainable practice," I said. "So what's the bottom line?"

Miriam responded first. "The bottom line is—absent some dramatic technological breakthrough, like the sixties green revolution—the world's farmers won't be able to keep up with the projected increase in population. I don't see how the world can possibly feed an expected population of nine, ten, or eleven billion people—even if climate systems remain stable."

"It does seem doubtful," I said. "So if there's no new 'green revolution' in the making, and biological engineering can't do the trick, then environmental constraints like amount of arable land, soil fertility, crop yields, and water supply would determine what's truly sustainable. And there's the wild card of climate change. That could have an impact on world food production, and it's not likely to be all positive."

"Rising sea levels would take out one third of all the world's cropland and eliminate the homes of one billion people. We could have more droughts like the one back in 1995 that took a heavy toll on the U.S. grain harvest."

"Perhaps then, our energy decisions may be as important to our food security as our agricultural decisions. To me it seems a no-brainer that we need to do three things to redirect the planet toward a more sustainable path: protect our soil and biological diversity, make a shift to renewable energy, and stabilize or, better yet, reduce world population."

"Obvious to us, but not so easily accomplished," responded Miriam. "Population issues are dicey politically, even though it's been said 'there are no humane alternatives to solving the population crisis.'"

"And," I added, "I know the 1.4 billion people in industrial countries cause a much greater drain on world resources than those 4.6 billion people in the Southern Hemisphere. Practically speaking, the people of industrial nations are eating the developing world's lunch."

"Unfortunately true," Miriam agreed. "It's not an equitable situation. But to address this problem successfully, people need to understand how food and product consumption and population levels relate to local, regional, and global carrying capacity, and to their own quality of life. If we want to achieve population control, the education and economic security of women is critical."

Miriam and Rashid explained to me that in order to facilitate the transition to a stabilized population, the WSC produces a steady stream of educational tapes. Weekly teleconferences are held around the world, incorporating highly entertaining and imaginative presentations dealing with the principles and personal advantages of wise family planning. Millions of leaflets and books in different languages are distributed, but dramatic and explicit videotapes seem to get the message across best. Traveling theater groups and music video road shows have also proved especially popular.

"Look what we can do here—right from this room," said Rashid excitedly. He turned toward the keyboard on the table. A few mouse clicks on icons and a data screen appeared. "This is a log of health care requests and telemedicine interactions occurring in hundreds of communities. Those blinking lines indicate the ones doctors and health experts are working on—right now as we speak. This shows that the necessary help is being given to those in need."

"How do you suggest addressing the issue in industrial nations?" I asked. "They'll need a different approach, won't they?"

"Yes," Miriam responded. "As you've mentioned, here the problem is the global resource impact of each child. A typical middle-class U.S. child uses many times the natural resources of a child raised in Central America or Africa. The average U.S. energy use is equivalent to the energy consumption of 3 Japan-

A Critical Balance

ese, 6 Mexicans, 12 Chinese, 33 Indians, 147 Bangladeshis, or 281 Tanzanians. Our response has been to create the WiseChoice, EarthCare Program. Financial compensation is offered to anyone, male or female, who elects to remain childless. The fee is based on a percentage of the estimated dollar value of the lifetime natural resources needed by a child born and raised in a particular country. In countries such as the United States, the amount of resources used is considerable."

"I can imagine," I commented, "but tell me more about this program."

"To encourage the reduction of human population and related environmental impacts, the WiseChoice, EarthCare Program pays an abstaining individual a certain fee, prorated for the remaining length of his or her lifetime. Persons consenting early in life, at perhaps age fourteen or fifteen, receive more money than if they wait until age twenty or thirty, especially if they've already produced offspring. The later the decision, the lower the total amount of benefits received. Compliance is ensured through birth control implants or permanent sterilization. An individual can receive a maximum of two credits. Adoption is the recommended course for those who want children but who also desire to act responsibly toward all life on the planet."

"It really does come down to people and the choices they make, doesn't it?" I said to Rashid and Miriam as we paused for a break. "The salmon, the wolf, the mahogany . . . they took the long walk through evolution. They made the right decisions. They arrived here knowing how to live cooperatively with other species and within the carrying capacity of their own environments. Why are humans such a problem? Somehow we haven't learned how to do this yet. And sometimes, we don't make very good choices, do we?"

"Not all humans are so ignorant," Miriam corrected me. "Many indigenous cultures understood the need to preserve the critical balance between their population and available resource base. They maintained this balance for thousands, even tens of thousands of years. Sure, some of them overhunted, overcut forests, and exhausted local ecosystems, but look at the Australian Aborigines; they've been around for thirty-five thousand years without creating tons of toxic waste, miles of polluted streams, or vast radioactive wastelands. And the aboriginal homeland probably would be nearly perfectly intact today were it not for the intrusion of foreign colonization."

"This suggests," I said, "that humans did just fine before the advent of the Agricultural Revolution. Apparently we managed to survive for several million years without cars, television, computers, and indoor plumbing."

"It's true," Miriam said. "Tribal communities that remain relatively unimpacted by the outside world have been able to maintain reasonably healthy, balanced lifestyles for millennia. And their immediate environments are still pristine. You know, some anthropologists suggest that Native tribes generally had far more time for rest, arts, dance, and recreation than we do today. Look how much time and money we must devote to our machines—their purchase, care, and feeding. They require major portions of our lifetime effort for support. Sure, our machines do good things for us, but at what cost to us physically and psychologically?"

"Have we really progressed, then?" I asked her rhetorically. "We've taken the planet to the brink. In spite of all the wonderful things the WSC is doing—it's making an extraordinary effort for sure—but, well, is it enough? Or are the odds against humanity really rising to the challenge just too great? And to do it in ten years, which the experts tell us is about the maximum time left before major problems become irreversible? One would need to be a serious optimist to think so."

A hush fell over our group as we all reflected on the issues we had just discussed. I knew both Miriam and Rashid held strong personal feelings in this regard, but I was curious to hear how they might articulate them. I watched Rashid's formerly cheerful face change as if he'd been informed of a dear friend's death. His gaze became distant, his eyes moistened. I saw tears begin to form in his soft eyes. He inhaled deeply, and exhaled slowly.

"Of course it's late, very late," he said with calculated gravity. "But logic is inadequate. When I look at it rationally, I often begin to panic. A hopelessness grips me like some giant claw. It wants to squeeze the breath out of me. And I feel really angry, especially when I think about losing yet another species, and yet another stream, lake, or river slowly dying from the effects of toxic chemicals."

I paused for thought and began slowly, "I believe our intent and our actions can trigger powerful changes. I think we need to view ourselves as messengers. Unfortunately, much of the news can be rather discouraging and it can easily produce a kind of apathy or psychic numbing. Somehow we must find a context that motivates rather than merely depresses people."

"What do you suggest?" Rashid asked.

"I think by generating awareness—awareness of one's self and individual purpose in life. And how everything's interconnected. That whatever we do—both the good and the bad—affects everything else. Thus we have the power to make things much worse or infinitely better, depending upon the choices we make. I believe the power is really in our hands. It's not true that we're powerless as individuals.

"This kind of whole systems understanding is sometimes referred to as ecopsychology, deep ecology, or ecological literacy. Certain Native people I know would be quite amused by our obsession with fancy terms. They'd say it's just life. It's common sense, what they've always known by closely watching and observing nature. Also, I think people want to feel they have options and choices. We must create a vision of the future that's hopeful, but we also need to be realistic so people will feel motivated to take positive action. But major global action must come soon. If we wait ten or twenty years, it'll be too late. Still, I believe things might happen that we can't possibly predict at the moment."

"Are you expecting some kind of last minute rescue or reprieve?" asked Miriam.

"I think we have to do the rescuing, but there might be some unexpected circumstances, some extraordinary factors that will assist the effort. It's just a hunch I have."

"Maybe," Miriam added tentatively. "I know evolution

doesn't always work in linear, predictable ways. It has its cycles, its ups and downs. Plants, animals, trees, civilizations—they come and go. And sudden lunges, anomalies, and quantum leaps occur every once in awhile."

"So you think there's hope for breakthroughs, too?"

She paused, her attention turning inward. I could feel her mind working overtime. "Sort of. We need, I think, to create the circumstances for what some call 'evolutionary breakouts'—a generation of individuals who can cast off outdated ways of doing and being and recommit to life. We need a renovated version of Homo sapiens—an improved model—and a 'new story,' if you will."

"A new story? I like that. What kind of new story?"

"I'm not sure, but it must be a humane vision. One that's physical and spiritual. A bold new mindset. A radical new worldview. One that is able to imagine real solutions to our very real problems and to capture the imagination of people, lots of people, and fires them into action."

"Hmmm," I said, my mental computer calculating furiously. "I think you're onto something. Miriam. We need to bring together the physical and the spiritual, the political and the environmental. And somehow, we need to invite the whole world to envision and participate in this . . . *new story*."

CHAPTER 25

A NEW STORY

Six, seven, eight billion people colliding with the planet's environmental constraints. Carrying capacity. Sustainability. Evolutionary breakouts. A new story. Humans pushing the edge of all life on Earth. A whirl of provocative thoughts tumbled through my mind as I walked alone outside in the WSC gardens. I found the muted, afternoon sunlight intoxicating as it gently bathed the cornucopia of tropical plants that filled the grounds. As I walked, my thoughts circled back to the dedicated men and women I had met inside, struggling to help the planet grapple with its approaching apocalyptic destiny.

My cynical mind asserted itself. Do people really care about the fate of the Earth, of humanity? Do people care enough to want to make a difference? Or are they just too overwhelmed by it all?

Some people would say we're hopelessly materialistic. We want the cars, the dollars, the goodies of our high-tech world far too badly to seriously consider any alternatives. We'd rather die in front of our TVs and VCRs eating pizza and guzzling beer than exist in a world without such amenities; we've become terminally addicted to our technology and the high-stimulus, immediate satisfaction lifestyle it affords.

A mild depression began to take hold. I half-heartedly resisted it and shifted my attention to the sounds around me. The jungle is rarely silent. Always there is the insistent noise of parrots, monkeys, and an abundance of other creatures boisterously going about their business. Today was no exception. I marveled at the variety of secretive clicks, abrasive screeches, brash howls, and ear-splitting whistles that emanated from the forest. And I certainly couldn't ignore the sopping humidity that hung heavy beneath the high jungle canopy.

I felt a need to walk, but was drawn away from the open area where I stood. Instead, I was pulled toward the interior of the forest itself. At the edge of the clearing, a small path appeared, as if on cue. I followed it for perhaps a hundred yards. It wound serpentinelike through the dense undergrowth, rising and falling with the uneven terrain. To my surprise, it led me directly to a cluster of weathered and fragmented stone walls, barely discernible beneath the cover of thick vegetation. An old Maya ruin, no doubt. After all, I was in Maya country. A small temple, I concluded, upon inspecting the vague remnant shapes of masonry mounds and earthen depressions.

But one particular feature attracted my attention. Elements of an arched entranceway bid me advance more closely. A thousand years old and still standing! It demanded a closer look. I struggled through a tangle of twisted vines, carefully inspected the area for dangerous residents of the reptilian kind, and cautiously entered into the darkened space. Once inside, I sensed a refreshing coolness provided by the rock and earthen walls. Wiping the damp sweat from my forehead, I scanned the room's interior—about six-feet deep and ten-feet wide. Its ancient purpose remained inscrutable. For now though, it provided a welcome respite from the day's burden of mental activities. I leaned my back against the stone wall, the better to absorb its cooling grace. Slowly, I allowed myself to slump down into a comfortable sitting position.

I easily closed my eyes, leaned my head back against the wall, and allowed my mind to drift. Within seconds, I became conscious of an intelligence that beckoned me to listen, to open to its message. In my exhaustion, I could offer no resistance and readily succumbed. As I willingly relaxed into a semiconscious state, the intelligence that called to me began its extraordinary tale:

A New Story

Once upon a time the Earth and all its living things were in balance with each other, with all the forces that supported them. Healthy food and unpolluted water were plentiful. Virgin forests served as safe and secure habitats for myriad lifeforms. The forests also provided a rich and abundant source of fuel and essential life support materials for the evolution of the human species. For millions of years men and women existed in harmony with their environment.

And they learned many things during this time of seminal growth, chief of which was to appreciate the abundance and generosity of nature. These early humans learned to honor the spirit forces, which they believed served as their guardians. Men and women daily acknowledged these ephemeral patrons of life, sometime with grand ceremonies, but most often with simple prayers and offerings. These people are called the 'Honorers,' and their legacy of knowledge remains preserved in the rituals and cultural wisdom of the present-day nature- and earth-based people of the planet. They serve as good examples of what it means to be a true steward of the Earth.

But during the long journey—from amoebae to astronaut—certain members of the human family decided to experiment. They asked questions about their environment: How did it originate? What made it work? What comprised it and how could it be changed? And they asked about themselves: Who are we? How might we reorganize ourselves? What might it be like to gain and hold power over others and the forces of nature? These people are called the 'Experimenters.'

The Experimenters, because of their intense curiosity and cleverness, sense of organization, propensity to thought, and pronounced aggressiveness, have, over the course of seven thousand years, come to dominate the planet and all its members. But the Experimenters became distracted by their projects and thus have failed to properly maintain the four foundations upon which human life rests: food, forests, fuel, and population. These four basic compo-

nents must co-exist in proper proportion if life, as it is known, it is to continue.

The Honorers and the Explorers have now reached a critical crossroads. They must choose which direction they will turn. They might decide to continue traveling separately, as has so far been the case, or they could elect to venture forward as one unified group, sharing what they've learned and creating a "new story." If they decide to seek a shared destiny, a new balance for life might be reestablished, but this would require a major shift in attitude and considerable effort on the part of all participants. If they decide to go their separate ways, the Honorers remaining to themselves, and the Experimenters charging blindly ahead, the great human experiment will likely come to a painful and speedy end. The choice then becomes an Earth in ruin or an Earth in renaissance.

The voice ceased abruptly. I shivered despite the heat and quickly woke myself up. Was I dreaming? Did I really hear a voice? That story. Was it real? Of course it's real, I chided myself, or at least true. But wait a minute. How do I know it's true? Honorers and Experimenters? Yes, I could see it this way. I guess I'm a bit of both. I was born an Experimenter, but I'm learning the way of the Honorer, too.

The voice spoke of a shared destiny, the coming together of the Experimenter and the Honorer. If I can do it, so can others. And I think many are, in fact, doing so. I suspect they're acting quietly and working undercover. But perhaps now a more visible, more public profile is needed if we're to have an Earth in renaissance rather than an Earth in ruin.

How could I help this happen? Perhaps I might draft a map, a blueprint, a rough prescription for positive change, a call to action that might direct humanity in moving toward a positive future. Something that would alter the course of the PAPA's intent to resort to violence.

And so, newly inspired, thanks to the spirit of the ruins, I returned to my apartment. In the days that followed, I worked diligently to formulate my proposal. I'd address the

A New Story

four components of life mentioned by my mysterious mentor.

FOOD:
According to the information presented by Miriam, it seems seven, maybe eight billion people might possibly be sustained at a minimum level of sustenance if certain steps are taken. These steps would include:
- Instituting best soil conserving and farming practices along with aggressive erosion control and soil desalinization measures.
- Promoting maximum crop and biological diversity and use of open-pollinated seeds, and aggressive preservation of traditional seed stocks.
- Undertaking more aggressive agricultural research to help increase crop yields and develop more sustainable farming practices.
- Protecting and conserving water supplies and only withdrawing water on a basis that is sustainable.
- Preserving existing farmland and redistributing land to those groups and individuals best able to utilize it in a sustainable fashion.
- Equitable distribution and sharing of food among the entire world population.
- Affluent populations reducing their meat and dairy consumption by about fifty percent and adopting a simpler diet.

FORESTS:
"Without trees, there is no life," warn the indigenous people of the world. Though not scientists, they are nevertheless absolutely correct. And most scientists, I think, would agree. With only a quarter of the planet's land surface (excluding Antarctica and Greenland) remaining in tree cover, we must make every effort to conserve what is left. A global forest conservation plan would include:
- Preserving and conserving remaining virgin forests and intact forest systems.
- Replacing clear-cut logging with sustainable forestry

practices.
- Using environmentally benign substitutes for wood—for example, treeless paper—solar energy for heating and cooling whenever possible, and alternative building materials for construction purposes.
- Restoring secure land tenure to indigenous inhabitants of forest areas.
- Using wood products more efficiently and recycling lumber whenever possible.
- Insisting on full ecological and economic valuing of living forest systems.

FUEL and ENERGY:
Humans cannot survive long without energy and the many necessities and conveniences its provides. Yet relying on fossil fuels for eighty percent or more of our energy needs is affecting our health, depleting a valuable planetary legacy, and dangerously disrupting our global environmental support systems. We need to change the way we make and use energy. We can do this by:
- Switching from fossil fuels to a global solar hydrogen economy where energy generation and distribution are regionalized wherever practical.
- Establishing individual and community solar hydrogen farms on lands too degraded or not practical to use for crop production.
- Establishing manufacturing of renewable energy equipment in communities and regions throughout the world, thereby providing local employment and local energy generation. Ideally, these facilities will be worker owned and managed.
- Using sales of excess electrical power and hydrogen fuel as a means to provide revenues to communities where power generating facilities are located, and employing the excess heat from thermal power stations to warm greenhouses for supplemental food production.

A New Story

POPULATION and HUMAN SECURITY:

Clearly, population is the most intractable of our four critical foundation components. Whereas forest, fuel, and food can be successfully addressed given sufficient amounts of money and technology, population is about people, and any initiatives for change must take into consideration what individuals think, what they feel, and what they believe. And many differences of opinion abound regarding what comprises a right or wrong choice or course of action. A population stabilization and human security program will need to:

- Make health services, family planning information, and contraceptive services easily available to women throughout the world.
- Grant women the freedom to choose their mates, how many children to have, and the right to own land and property.
- Provide basic literacy education and economic development assistance to women, especially in developing countries.
- Provide gender awareness programs for men.
- Provide public education regarding the environmental importance and the quality of life benefits of small families.
- Provide social security programs for families in developing countries.
- Grant all men and women the right to full political, religious, and democratic expression.

Population means much more than mere numbers, I reminded myself. We need to make primary the notion of "human security." National security is something easily understood. That's why we're prepared to spend many trillions of dollars on weapons and armies. But human security entails such important aspects of life as peace, environmental protection, human rights, religious and racial tolerance, and social integration. Human security will need to be a cornerstone consideration in our plan for Earth in renaissance.

It's sketchy, incomplete, rough, but a good beginning, I thought to myself, as I edited the draft. What shall I call it? I needed a name that described the program's intent to shift political power and economic responsibility from a global to a regional focus, while encouraging a rapid move toward regional and global sustainability. After some rumination, a complicated but descriptive title emerged: Regional Environmental Self-sufficiency and Self-determination through Community Underwriting and Enterprise. It mercifully abbreviated to the nice, neat acronym of RESSCUE.

I now had a proposed plan of action. If adopted on a large enough scale, it might help turn the tide and indeed make a difference. The next step, then, was to present it to the WSC for discussion and refinement. But more critical was the necessity to convince the PAPA that RESSCUE could achieve their stated aims without requiring violent uprising and revolution. I would need to meet with President Singh. Surely with the weight of the WSC behind such a plan, she could prevail on the PAPA to reconsider.

I again looked over my notes. The recommendations did seem to address the physical needs for Earth in renaissance, but what about the nonmaterial aspects—the element of spirit? I had drawn up a decent program for the Experimenters, but what about the Honorers? Where do they fit in?

I wrestled with this question for hours, wishing Jenny and her people were here to help me. I knew they'd have lots to say. As exhaustion pressed down hard on me, I recalled the words I heard in the ruins. "They could travel as one unified group, sharing what they've learned." Unity seemed a key—and sharing and offering support for others. How, though, might the normally less visible Honorers be encouraged to join with the commonly dominant Experimenters to explore the concept of common purpose and "shared destiny" without sacrificing cultural diversity? After considerable thought, I realized all Experimenters possess Honorer origins. Perhaps if the Experimenters were helped to remember those distant origins . . . .

A New Story

Rising with the sun, I attempted to formulate a practical course toward a program of shared destiny that could be implemented between Honorers and Experimenters. I now had only twenty-four hours before the PAPA would issue its promised ultimatum. The WSC was alive with activity as buses, taxis, and shuttles unloaded men and women of all nationalities at the entrance foyer. A full assembly had been called to witness the pivotal event. Due to the heightened state of activity throughout the WSC, I had a difficult time making my way to President Singh's offices. Once I got there, her secretary ushered me into the office conference room. President Singh appeared minutes later, warmly receiving me, but her personal state of anxiety was palpable. "We don't have much time, Tom. I hope you've brought something I can use."

"It's not perfect by any means. I call it the RESSCUE Plan, but I think it might satisfy the PAPA's needs for a comprehensive approach to addressing the pressures and problems they face."

I spread my papers across the table in front of President Singh. She removed a pair of reading glasses from a nearby table and carefully scrutinized my documents. I stared absently out through the conference room windows from my seat next to hers, waiting tensely for her response. I feared she would be less than impressed. If that were the case, there would be no time to explore other options as too many wheels were now in motion.

I glanced back to President Singh's face. Her diplomatic demeanor gave no hint of her assessment. Upon finishing the final page, she, too, stared into the office patio gardens, lost in thought.

"It's very ambitious, some would say hopelessly ideal, but it does address the basic problems that concern the PAPA—and much more. Here at the WSC, we have most of the tools and mechanisms to promote and advance such a program."

"Yes, that's what made me think such a plan might be doable."

"But we lack one very important component."

"What's that?" I asked, worried.

"Public and governmental endorsement."

"I hoped the WSC could help with that."

President Singh lay back in her chair and frowned, either at my naiveté or the impossibility of the matter.

"That's not so easily accomplished. We've not been able to do that yet with the Share Tax. And I assume the Share Tax would serve as a source of funding for the RESSCUE Plan?"

"Yes, but I haven't calculated the costs yet."

"They would be quite considerable—more expensive than anything else the world community has undertaken."

"I'm not surprised."

President Singh rose slowly from her chair. A resolution and a resignation burned in her eyes. "I can try to discuss this with El Aguilar this afternoon. The WSC has a private, encrypted teleconference line. I can fax the written materials to him. I'll attempt to persuade him that with the full weight of the WSC issuing a call for global action on the RESSCUE Plan, the PAPA need not resort to violence. I'm afraid that the PAPA will see this as just one more paper proposal that lacks teeth to place sufficient pressure on global power brokers, while falling short of mobilizing public support for the PAPA cause. However, I'll give it my best. At this point we have only enough time for one last attempt."

I left President Singh's office, feeling less than hopeful. I wandered through the WSC lobby, dodging a high speed stream of incoming delegates in widely varying dress and chattering loudly in a dozen foreign languages. I thought I would try and locate Mr. G. Certainly he would be attending this major event. His office, though informed me that he remained on leave. I found this highly curious.

Throughout the day and evening, tension continued to mount in and around the WSC. The level of expectation escalated as the hours slipped away. I spent several hours before retiring, endeavoring to summon whatever spiritual forces I could imagine to inspire a peaceful resolution of the crisis. But I received no confirmation that my entreaties were

A New Story

received. I slept uneasily that night fearing that if the PAPA proceeded with their intentions, I would somehow be partly responsible for failing to stop the bloodshed that would inevitably ensue.

At 8:00 a.m., two room attendants opened wide the great carved doors of the All Peoples Council Chambers. A gridlocked crowd of perhaps four hundred people surged forward into the wide and empty aisles. I was involuntarily carried along with the torrent of colorful delegates, international visitors, and media representatives. Once inside the chambers, I rushed to find an empty seat. The hall was huge, having a capacity for two thousand people, but I could see it was filling rapidly. Indeed, in a matter of minutes almost every seat was taken. Room attendants struggled to prevent additional entries by slowly forcing closed the several sets of double entrance doors. Disappointed individuals were directed to upper balconies, which quickly filled as well.

I tried to remain calm, but the energy of the room, now bursting with so much human activity and flooded with brilliant sunlight from the sparkling overhead skylights, amplified the intensity of the experience.

An additional element of tension was created when it was announced over the public address system that a live video link would be established with Geneva, Switzerland. Apparently an emergency economic summit was underway in that city to discuss the recent deleterious effects on the global economy caused by climate change. A news release was circulated through the crowd that informed us that during the past three months large sections of Bangladesh and other low-lying coastal areas around the world had been permanently inundated. Thirty percent of the grain harvest in the United State and Canada had been destroyed by drought and pest infestations, and malaria and yellow fever had struck North American and European cities with major epidemics. Despite the tragedy of the events driving the meeting in Switzerland, I thought this coincidence timely; now the PAPA would be able to directly address those whom they believed to be their primary adversaries.

The murmur of crowd noise diminished markedly as the large curtains parted to reveal two huge video screens affixed to the wall in the front of the council chambers. To the left of the screens and below was located the president's box with its podium and microphones. Several tripod-mounted video cameras were partially hidden inside a covered room below the president's box. I surmised these cameras provided the live video feed from the WSC.

Then without warning, a hush fell over the crowd as one of the large screens flashed with static. Quickly a picture stabilized. It showed the exterior of a large, ornate building in Geneva where the emergency global economic summit was in session. A few seconds later, the image changed to a view of a dozen men dressed almost identically in dark suits and seated at a long, gracefully curved table. Behind them were mounted twelve flags from their respective countries. Commonly referred to as the G-12, these dozen men represented the most influential economic nations in the world.

On the second large screen, President Singh appeared, radiant and charismatic in a scarlet and gold trimmed dress. As she addressed the leadership of the G-12, her voice was powerful and confident, and offered no hint of the tension that gripped the WSC council room.

"Good morning from Belize. We welcome you to our important gathering. I and all my distinguished colleagues of the World Stewardship Council are pleased that you have agreed to join with us today to grant audience to the Pan American Peoples Alliance, as their concerns are shared by many millions of people throughout the world. We anticipate receiving the transmission momentarily. We ask you to please stand by."

Several seconds later, President Singh's image was supplanted by the now-familiar green quetzal bird overlaid across a Maya temple. The council chamber audience observed the screen with rapt attention. An image of nine ski-masked individuals appeared, with both men and women seated around a rectangular, rough-cut wooden table, on the surface of which lay a modern automatic rifle. The table rested upon a wide, polished stone platform, and the platform was positioned directly in front of a great stone pyramid. Jungle foliage bordered both sides of the pyramid. I squinted to try and recognize Eva Luisa and the other women I had met previously, but their ski masks effectively obscured their individual identities.

The camera held a wide shot of the scene. Then, slowly and deliberately, the man sitting in the center of the seated line of the PAPA representatives rose and walked around the table to the front, and faced the camera. The camera zoomed back to reveal the entire pyramid, which had the effect of adding an unmistakable element of mystical power. It was as if the PAPA had acquired the endorsement of the ancient gods and goddesses of the Maya.

The man introduced himself as El Aguilar, the designated spokesperson for the PAPA. El Aguilar stood quietly staring into the camera as it zoomed in to a close-up shot of his face. As if cued, he began to speak, "We are here today to seek a just and dignified peace. We speak for the hundreds of millions of poor people who suffer daily from the effects of the ecological destruction carried out on their lands by oil and gas exploration, mining, indiscriminate logging, and rampant industrial development. I speak for those who must contend with the aftermath of these activities, which includes agricultural plunder, hyperinflation, alcoholism, prostitution, political and economic isolation, rape, and poverty. From these lands, uncompensated tribute is exacted in the form of petroleum, minerals, coal, electricity, cattle, lumber, coffee, bananas, corn, sugar, cacao, soy, melons, sorghum, mango, tamarind, avocado, and many other valuable products and materials. These raw materials are the blood that is drained from the veins of rural communities. It is made to flow to many different parts of the world, yet the people whose lands provide these materials are left with illiteracy, hunger, and desperation."

As El Aguilar spoke, I could easily sense the growing unease that registered on the faces of the slick-suited men of the opposite screen. They shifted their bodies nervously, indicating to me an impatience and a probable anticipation of blame.

El Aguilar continued, "Now it is time to talk business, as you would say. First though, I would like to introduce you to some of our allies and supporters."

The screen displayed a prerecorded tape insert which depicted numerous armed groups of masked PAPA guerrillas positioned near power plants, hydroelectric dams, industrial centers, airports, plantations, and telecommunications centers. Long lines of marching units could be seen proceeding across fields and through jungles. It was an impressive demonstration of troop force.

"Our ranks of trained combatants now number at least three hundred thousand deployed throughout many countries. In addition, we have received commitments of support from five million indigenous people and two million men and women in other parts of the world. They have agreed to participate in nonviolent acts of civil disobedience to support our cause."

This statement definitely caught the attention of the G-12, as the representatives displayed a sudden animation. The camera then cut back to El Aguilar, zooming in tighter on his masked face.

"We are meeting together today to discuss the need for change in a highly inequitable global situation. We are also here because the PAPA has threatened violence if a change to a more compassionate human world order is not forthcoming. I will now speak to the matter of violence. The present economic system is violent. Laissez-faire economics, the global marketplace, NAFTA, GATT, Multilateral International Investment Agreements, and Free Trade policies are waging war against the Earth and all the people who care for it. We know the planet's natural resources are limited. Our stocks of forests, fish, and fertile soil are disappearing rapidly, sold to those who can pay the highest prices. Our natural resource legacy is being liquidated. Our national sovereignty is being auctioned off to distant investors. These are violent

A New Story

acts against people, against the Earth, against justice, against dignity, and against life. And it must stop! This capitalistically driven environmental and political violence can no longer be tolerated."

El Aguilar's words, though moving, caused me to become increasingly anxious. I sensed he was now mere seconds away from launching his guerrilla teams against the central infrastructure of selected countries. And I was confident that the military forces in the target countries had already positioned themselves to thwart any PAPA advance. Though the PAPA had apparently demonstrated surprising physical strength, at least in the videotape, I was convinced they could never prevail against the sophisticated technology and countermeasures of those countries supported and armed by the Industrial Nations.

But El Aguilar did not act as expected. The camera, still tight on his face, pulled back. El Aguilar changed the tone of his voice from one of anger to one of dignified assertion. And I realized the voice sounded strangely familiar, as well as the words.

"The violence must cease. Violence is the old way, not the new way. It serves only to cause greater pain and suffering. And to that we say ¡Ya basta! Enough! The PAPA will therefore take the first step and hereby renounces all violence!"

A collective exhale of relief filled the room. I sat straight up in my seat with astonishment. But there was more to come. El Aguilar pivoted toward the table behind him. The camera pulled back as he lifted the automatic rifle from the table, turned again and presented it to the viewing audience, the G-12, the WSC, and all the world to see. In a dramatic series of gestures he removed the ammunition clip, tossed it away, then rapidly disassembled the gun. He next unbelted his side arm and dropped it to the ground.

"We will no longer rely on our weapons of destruction as instruments of power. We discard them. We ask you to do the same with your predatory capitalistic practices. We ask you to step out from behind the veils of your exploitative trade, tariff, labor, and international financial agreements that do violence to the environment and its indigenous stewards. Here, too, we will take the first step by removing our masks. I ask that you, too, do the same for the sake of the Earth, for the sake of the people, and for the sake of the children and generations yet unborn!"

Even though El Aguilar already had all two thousand men and women at the WSC glued to the screen, this unexpected announcement heightened excitement even further. I doubt anyone even blinked in anticipation of the famous masked one exposing his carefully hidden identity. The camera tightened on El Aguilar's face. His hands moved slowly upward, grasping the corner of his ski mask. I held my breath. No words passed as the mask ascended, revealing . . . It was . . . No, it couldn't be! . . . It was Mr. G! . . . Suddenly all the pieces fell into place. His undefined background, his inside knowledge of the PAPA, his intimacy with Eva Luisa, his curious disappearance during the past week. The camera again pulled back as the other PAPA representatives now removed their own masks. I could just barely make out the face of Eva Luisa.

The room rang with the excited buzz of conversation, heads turning to each other, exchanging words of consternation. The G-12 members now appeared very alert, stunned by the PAPA's apparent major course change and El Aguilar's personal dramatics.

El Aguilar continued, "We know the Earth is suffering, losing species and valuable resources by the hour. People are giving up hope. Time is short. The PAPA is therefore committed to work with those who are willing to create a new vision, a new world, where all men, women, and children can live a life of full democratic rights and experience the freedom of political expression. We also demand that the sovereignty and independence of our villages be respected and legally upheld. Though we have cast aside our military weapons, we carry the potent arms of dignity, truth, and justice. With these powers, no one can defeat us."

I sensed a skepticism in the air following this remark. After all, history was littered with the corpses of noble men

A New Story

with lofty ideals. But El Aguilar had yet another bombshell to deliver.

"And to demonstrate the power of hope and collective possibility expressed in action, I hereby declare exactly one month from now a Global Day of Declaration and Reconsideration. It will be a day of walking and dreaming together, a day of peacefulness, of renewing our connection with nature and the Earth. It will be a day of remembering, of honoring our planetary life-support system, and considering our place in time."

El Aguilar paused, just long enough for his words to settle in. Then his voice shifted, expressing a deep seriousness. "And because our planet and so many of its people are now in great peril, it will also be a day of political statement. Four weeks from today the PAPA will call upon the people of the world to take a stand against injustice, poverty, hunger, disregard for basic human rights, and environmental destruction. Because the forces that oppress men, women, and children and destroy the environment are often the same ones that manipulate the world's governments, financial centers, and technology systems, we call for a day of economic noncompliance, a day of consumer disobedience.

El Aguilar now stared directly into the camera as it quickly zoomed tight on his face. "Avoid all uses of anything electronic or mechanical. Pull the plug. Turn off your electricity, if you have any. Watch no television. Make no phone calls. Drive no cars. Instead, go walking, visit with nature, or stay home. Sleep late, practice random acts of compassion and cultural nonconformity. Send a message to the transnational corporate pirates that they have failed to enslave your heart or your soul, that you remain a sovereign, free individual. Disconnect yourself from the global economy. Break the industrial society entrainment circuit. Go cold turkey with zero consumption, zero work. Buy nothing. Pay no bills. Dance, sing, play music, write poetry, and laugh. Make your day a celebration of life, of new possibility, of glorious change. Express your creativity."

Consternation began to register on the stern faces of the

G-12 as they pondered the implications of El Aguilar's radical, global economic paradigm-busting proposal. The WSC council room, however, erupted in a gloriously spontaneous display of deafening applause and uncharacteristic exclamation once the crowd had understood the stunning simplicity and power of El Aguilar's suggestion. Cries of endorsement in a hundred different languages charged the room. The applause continued unabated as delegates stood, hugged each other, laughed, and shook hands. Not a few delegates gazed skyward, their faces radiant with unchecked smiles, cheeks wet with tears of hope and joy.

Yes! The concept of a giant global gesture of individual public declaration was pure genius, I thought. It was something almost anyone could afford to do. People around the world could join with each other in solidarity, with dignity, in the hope for a better future for themselves and for their children. Billions of men and women could stand together and reject the scourge of planetary economic globalization and all its elitism, injustice, and environmental destruction. This could be the grand opportunity for Experimenters to recall their origins and for Honorers to step forward and share their wisdom. Perhaps this is just what El Aguilar had in mind. If true, the mysterious Mr. G was truly the shaman—the master magician and global shape shifter.

The video operators at the WSC video control next placed President Singh alongside El Aguilar in a split-screen format. President Singh raised her hands to return the room to order. As the crowd gradually quieted, she addressed the G-12 and the global audience.

"The WSC's mission has been to serve as guardian of the environment and to unequivocally support all those who consider themselves planetary stewards. Our delegates have long been aware of the inequitable distribution of wealth and the destructive plundering of nonrenewable natural resources of which the PAPA speaks. We agree with the PAPA that conflicts in today's world can no longer be solved at gunpoint. Instead, we believe that a creative global rechanneling of financial resources could help resolve the potential for violent conflict if invested wisely in health care, universal education, poverty eradication, renewable energy, self-sufficiency, environmental restoration, agricultural sustainability, population stability, and human security. Toward this end, we have developed a strategy we call our RESSCUE Plan, which attempts to do just this. The PAPA has endorsed this plan and will direct its members to serve as implementation leaders. Our prescription for the funding of RESSCUE is Resolution 636, the Share Tax, which as you know is awaiting endorsement by your countries."

The Geneva screen showed little movement, but clearly, the G-12 members paid close attention to President Singh's words. After all, the Share Tax would take money out of their constituents' pockets. As President Singh continued to speak, I sensed the presence of a new force that seemed to build around her, like she had suddenly contacted a potent source of spiritual power.

"The PAPA has no fear of bold action. Neither does the WSC. I therefore request that the G-12 and its affiliate financial associates—in particular the World Trade Association, the international banking community, and the transnational corporate community—respond in kind, with equally creative, positive action. I invite you and your representatives to participate with the WSC in a new partnership—a Confederation of Economic Justice and Earth Stewardship—which is vitally necessary if we are to address the towering challenges of today's world. But our noble ideas and deep personal commitments to systemic change will flounder if adequate financial resources are not forthcoming. The WSC and the PAPA therefore challenge you to assume responsibility for this very important component."

President Singh by now had everyone in the palm of her hand. The vast council room was totally silent except for the distant hum of air conditioning systems. I felt myself upon another expectant threshold. Another major announcement was imminent—of equal weight to El Aguilar's previously proposed Day the Earth Stood Still and People Took Stock. This seemed the moment the Earth stood still. President

Singh pressed on, carefully choosing her words, knowing that her next few statements were of profound importance. "I first request that all of you encourage your governments to ratify the Share Tax as soon as possible. And I challenge you to support the establishment of the Share Fund at the level of one trillion dollars annually."

A gasp rose from the room and I noted the sober faces of the G-12 members ripple with thinly disguised shock. But President Singh wasn't finished yet. "I realize one trillion dollars is a considerable sum of money, but our research demonstrates that this amount is necessary to successfully address the world's most pressing problems of human security and environmental sustainability. And the money is available. Each day almost 1.5 trillion dollars flows through the world's electronic markets, unregulated by governments. Each year, world governments spend eight hundred billion dollars on weapons and military activities. I therefore challenge you to divert fifty percent of military expenditures, four hundred billion dollars—to be placed into a Share Fund, which will be accessed by many organizations and countries to address their critical social and environmental problems. And I ask the World Bank to immediately forgive at least two hundred billion dollars worth of debt for developing nations. The balance of the one trillion dollars—or six hundred billion dollars—would be generated annually by the Share Tax. I propose that the G-12 banks serve as the trustees of this global reconstruction fund and work to ensure that the monies are properly collected, deposited into the Share Fund, and safeguarded. The WSC will administer a portion of the funds through its network of NGOs. The NGOs will then assume the responsibility to guarantee that revenues reach those individual projects, programs, organizations, and individuals most in need."

It was, indeed, a stunning proposal. I sat transfixed by President Singh's careful, methodical, and fearless presentation. She was, after all, asking the world's governments, bankers, and capitalists to surrender one trillion dollars of annual revenues. This was big bucks. A preeminently gutsy

A New Story

proposal! I sensed the G-12 felt the same, as I observed them squirming uncomfortably in their seats. Momentarily I was at a loss for words as I considered the vast scope and incredible potential of what was occurring here. Then suddenly, two words exploded inside my mind—*la serpiente*. Of course, here it was, right in front of my eyes, on the screen. President Singh had wielded the transformational energy of the serpent, and El Aguilar had exercised the overarching vision power of the eagle. Together they had become the twenty-first century embodiment of Quetzalcoatl, the Feathered Serpent. Together they had accomplished the sacred marriage of male and female energy in order to shift human consciousness toward a more balanced state. We had, in fact, all been offered a PsyEarth vision. Human soul and psyche could now be joined with nature to begin the necessary process of planetary healing. It was happening now, here, in this specific time and space while all the world looked on. Perhaps Quetzalcoatl had indeed returned to guide humanity into a new age.

President Singh continued to address the G-12 leaders. "We have established a framework of administration, decision making, and technology through the WSC that can successfully address the human and environmental needs of the people of the world. You, the governments, bankers, and capitalists of the world, are charged to provide the financial resources for the necessary economic, social, and environmental transformations of which we speak. The people of the world have now been granted the power to vote their approval or disapproval of the current world order through the upcoming Day of Declaration and Reconsideration proposed by the PAPA. The WSC media network will advise our audience, which can number about three billion people, to step forward on the appointed day and express their will. On that day, four weeks from now, the WSC will silence its network of computers, television, and radio stations, and we will suspend all our normal activities. We will join the rest of the world in disconnecting from the human-made grid of work and machines. Instead, we will sing, dance, make music, pray, laugh, be silent, honor life and nature, and evoke the power of change. We will envision our Earth in Renewal, bathed in the light of a new beginning."

President Singh paused to allow her words to be absorbed by the highly attentive audience. She looked down, then up, as if she had just received a message from some unknown source. "And we believe there is a place at the table for everyone. We invite you to join with the WSC, the PAPA, and all the people of the world to act decisively in the coming months and years to bring about the changes in our social, political, economic, and environmental quality of life that so many believe is so necessary at this time."

Loud, vigorous applause from the council chambers forced President Singh to pause for several seconds. As the room quieted, she continued speaking. "In the weeks, months, and years to come, we must stand united against all that would endanger this precious world in which we live. We dare not fail in our task, for upon our success depends the future of life on Earth. I therefore call upon all of you who would consider yourselves stewards of the Earth. I would ask you to come forth and demonstrate your willingness and worthiness to create a better world—a world where justice and dignity and hope for all is possible, and life is fully nurtured and universally honored."

President Singh bowed her head slightly, indicating she was finished. The image of President Singh and Mr. G remained on the screen as the council audience expressed its satisfaction with a ten-minute standing ovation. As I wiped away my own tears of emotion, I felt truly blessed that I had been able to witness this highly potent blending of male and female energies to make the case for a transformed world. Perhaps, I hoped with all my heart, a new story that would some day benefit all living beings had indeed begun to be written.

EPILOGUE

Several days of celebration and intense international discussion followed the tumultuous teleconference at the WSC. The PAPA and the G-12 sent high-level representatives to the WSC to negotiate terms for financing a human security and environmental restoration strategy. I was most pleased to hear the RESSCUE Plan had received a strong endorsement as a candidate blueprint for future action. And, of course, the ratification of the Share Tax was considered a priority item by both WSC and the PAPA. As the sometimes tense and angry negotiations moved forward, the hammer of enforcement—the Day of Declaration or what I like to call the Day the People of the World Stood Still and Said Enough!—proved essential to goad the governments and financial and corporate forces into a sufficient willingness to change.

It was truly an amazing day. The media reported that many businesses, public transportation systems, government operations, and even a few cities ground to a halt. Many roads were nearly empty and, for once, totally quiet. Hundreds of thousands of stores closed for lack of customers. In some communities, phone lines were silent for the first time since the telephone system was installed. Hundreds of millions of people stayed home from work. Parks and forests rang with the happy sounds of picnickers and campers. Countless men, women, and children could be seen sitting quietly, reading, examining flowers, playing games, and watching trees grow and waters flow. The Internet registered a significant decrease in activity. According to the pollsters, almost two billion people had participated in the event—four hundred fifty million from the Industrial Nations and nearly 1.3 billion from Third World countries. Overall, it was in fact a day of profound peacefulness and political statement, just as El Aguilar had envisioned. And governments, bankers, and the corporate community took careful notice.

Following the Day of Declaration I drove down to the PsyEarth Institute. I had traveled there to conclude my promised article for Jack and also to join with several other PsyEarth alumni who were returning for a fall equinox reunion. We had been asked by PsyEarth staff to participate in the training of the new recruits who would soon depart for their six-month wilderness sojourn in the mountains. It was thought our newly acquired wisdom might be useful to the neophytes as they prepared to embark on their own personal journeys into destiny.

But to be frank, I was looking forward to spending time with Jenny, who had agreed to serve another six months as a PsyEarth Institute wilderness field counselor. When we did meet, she welcomed me with a long, deep hug. Over the next few days, we walked together in the woods, both just being silent and excitedly sharing our experiences of the past few months.

She listened carefully and with intense interest to my tales of "unusual occurrences"—the visions I had received and the apparent appearance of certain spirit forces. Several days into our conversations, she invited me to participate with her on "night work" duties, her processing in other dimensional realms in support of the PsyEarth wilderness journeyers. At first, I was taken aback by the offer, not so sure I was up to such things. After all, what did I know about working in other dimensions? And I had agreed to partner with Mr. G to develop the RESSCUE Plan back at the WSC. When I expressed my confusion and doubt, she reminded me that I had already, on several previous occasions, entered into the "otherworld," and had demonstrated prior communication with other-than-human forces.

Of course, I quickly realized, I no longer needed to con-

Epilogue

sider myself of limited consciousness and abilities. So much had changed since I first approached the PsyEarth Institute nearly a year ago with considerable trepidation. I was a new man. I could work with Jenny as an equal. I'd come into my own. I knew now what I was about.

Suddenly, I felt Mr. G's presence surround me, but not as Mr. G. Rather he was El Aguilar, radiating the knowledge and power of Eagle. I felt embraced in an energy that was both full of potential and challenge and rich with support and compassion. I perceived I could, indeed, travel in the realm of spirit while remaining connected to the Earth. And immediately, I recalled the eagle feather Jenny had gifted me with, seemingly a lifetime ago. Yes, I would embrace the energy of Eagle. I knew immediately the power of Eagle was to be my destiny.

I turned toward Jenny. She patiently observed me in silence, awaiting my response. Yet I detected a slight smile attempting to animate her face. But something more was required of me, I sensed, as I stared deeply into her dark, wise eyes. Of course! Like President Singh, she is la serpiente! Eagle and Serpent must join together to create the fire and magic that will carry us both toward greater insight, ecstasy, and wisdom. And from this place of intimacy, beauty, and clear vision, we will learn how to help heal the world in potent new ways.

I stepped forward toward Jenny, opened my arms, and invited her into my vision, into my heart. Without words, she accepted.

To celebrate the ideals of the Day of Declaration and the new PsyEarth class, our group of forty people spent a day building a new fire ring inside a wide, circular grove of ancient, old-growth ponderosa trees about a quarter mile from the institute's headquarters. We dedicated the site to the emerging, compassionate human, and built a small altar of stone and wood on which offerings could be placed. That evening, we gathered around our new fire and renewed our intentions to heed our own inner voices and seek guidance to serve the Earth and all its species in the best way possible. Later, as the coals grew bright and luminous flames soared exuberantly toward a star-scattered sky, we danced together, honored the richness of our lives and relationships, and prayed. Prayed not just for ourselves, but for all people, all species—everywhere.

Strangely, though, I had the distinct impression that the dark forest interior surrounding us was filled with animal eyes, observing and perhaps remembering when humans danced in the sacred forest groves more often. I sensed those animal eyes were wide with anxious expectation, knowing full well their fate, too, now depended upon what specific actions we humans might take in the months, years, and decades ahead. I gazed skyward, admiring the delicate and gracious curve of a barely visible new moon. And silently I prayed that as long as we humans were entrusted as stewards of Mother Earth, we would remain true to our covenant to respect and protect all that is precious and in our care.

BIBLIOGRAPHY

Ausubel, Kenny. *Restoring the Earth: Visionary Solutions from the Bioneers* (Tiburon, CA: H.J. Kramer, 1997).

Bagdikian, Ben. *The Media Monopoly* (Boston: Beacon Press, 1997).

Benedek, Emily. *The Wind Won't Know Me* (New York: Knopf, 1992).

Bensinger, Charles. *Chaco Journey: Remembrance and Awakening* (Santa Fe: Timewindow Publications, 1988).

—. *Designing the New World: A Map for Change* (Santa Fe: Timewindow Publications, 1996).

—. *Solar Thermal Repowering: A Technical and Economic Pre feasibility Study* (Santa Fe: Advanced Energy Systems, 1993).

Boissière, Robert. *The Return of Pahana* (Santa Fe: Bear & Co. 1990).

Brecher, Jeremy, John Brown Childs, Jill Cutler, eds. *Global Visions: Beyond the New World Order* (Boston: South End Press, 1993).

Brown, Lester R., et al. *State of the World 1998* (New York: W.W. Norton, 1998).

Bynner, Witter, trans. *The Way of Life According to Lao Tzu* (New York: Capricorn Books, 1962).

Duvall, Bill. *Living Richly in an Age of Limits* (Salt Lake City: GibbsSmith, 1993).

Easwaran, Eknath. *The Compassionate Universe* (Petaluma, CA: Nilgiri Press, 1989).

Ehrlich, Paul. "Too Many Rich People: Weighing Relative Burdens on the Planet," (Cairo: International Conference on Population and Development, September 1994).

Eisler, Riane. *The Chalice and the Blade* (San Francisco: HarperSanFrancisco, 1987).

Glendinning, Chellis. *My Name Is Chellis & I'm in Recovery from Western Civilization* (Boston: Shambhala, 1994).

Gunaratana, Venerable Henepola. *Mindfulness in Plain English* (Boston: Wisdom Publications, 1993).

Hartmann, Thom. *The Last Hours of Ancient Sunlight* (Northfield, VT: Mythical Books, 1998).

Hawken, Paul. *The Ecology of Commerce* (New York: HarperCollins, 1993).

Heider, John. *The Tao of Leadership* (New York: Bantam, 1985).

Hillman, Ann. *Dancing Animal Woman* (Norfolk, CT: Bramble Co., 1994).

Johnson, Sandy and Dan Budni. *The Book of Elders* (New York: HarperCollins, 1994).

Little, Charles E. *The Dying of the Trees* (New York: Penguin Books, 1995).

Loftin, John D. *Religion and Hopi Life in the Twentieth Century* (Bloomington: Indiana University, 1994).

Mander, Jerry. *In the Absence of the Sacred* (San Francisco: Sierra Club, 1992).

Martin, Calvin Luther. *In the Spirit of the Earth: Rethinking History and Time* (Baltimore: Johns Hopkins University, 1992).

Mayes, Vernon O. and Barbara Bayless Lacy. *NANISÉ: A Navajo Herbal* (Tsaile, AZ: Navajo Community College, 1989).

Meadows, Donella H., Dennis L. Meadows and Jorgen Randers. *Beyond the Limits* (Post Mills, VT: Chelsea Green, 1992).

Morgan, Marlo. *Mutant Message Down Under* (San Francisco: HarperCollins, 1994).

Quinn, Daniel. *Ishmael* (New York: Bantam/Turner, 1992).

—. *The Story of B* (New York: Bantam, 1997).

Rael, Joseph with Mary Elizabeth Marlow. *Being and Vibration* (Tulsa: Council Oak Books, 1993).

Redfield, James. *Celestine Prophecy* (New York: Warner, 1994).

Roybal, Rose Lillian. *"Healing from Racism,"* (Boulder, CO: Winds of Change, Spring 1995).

Starhawk. *The Fifth Sacred Thing* (New York: Bantam, 1993).

—. *Truth or Dare* (San Francisco: Harper & Row, 1987).

Talbot, Michael. *The Holographic Universe* (New York: HarperCollins, 1992).

Todd, Nancy, Jack and John Todd. *From EcoCities to Living Machines: Principles of Ecological Design* (Berkeley: North Atlantic Books, 1994).

—. *Ocean Arks International* magazine, Falmouth, MA.

von Franz, MarieLouise. *Alchemy: An Introduction to the Symbolism and the Psychology* (Toronto: Inner City Books, 1980).

Weisman, Alan. Gaviotas: A Village to Reinvent the World (Post Hills, VT: Chelsea Green, 1998).

Audio and Video Tapes:

Caldicott, Helen. *Saving the Planet* (Boulder, CO: Sounds True Recordings, 1990).

Ereira, Alan. *From the Heart of the World: The Elder Brothers' Warning* (New York: Mystic Fire Video, 1992).

RESOURCES

As far as the author knows, none of the institutions cited in this text presently exist in mature form. However, it is the author's strong belief that if such institutions were developed and financially and organizationally empowered, humanity could move much more rapidly down the path toward sustainability. The author, therefore, encourages sympathetic individuals, groups, organizations, businesses, and governments to take whatever action possible to manifest or help to manifest institutions like those proposed in this book. The author also invites anyone having information regarding the initiation or development of such institutions to communicate with him so he can include contact and descriptive information on a future web site.

CONTACT: Charles Bensinger
P.O. Box 2685
Santa Fe, NM 87504
e-mail: psyearth@timewindow.com

A CALL FOR INDIVIDUAL ACTION

Individual initiative is the key to moving humanity toward a more compassionate, equitable, and sustainable world. Such initiative, though, is more likely to be successful if persons are well-informed and joined with others of like mind and heart. The following resources are offered to help readers become more personally active and make a difference.

GLOBAL NEWS AND INFORMATION

As global economies and social systems become increasingly interdependent, it becomes all the more critical for "planetary citizens" to become better informed about important issues and the changing state of the world. This is especially true for residents of the United States, as U.S. mass media is very selective in presenting international information. U.S. residents will need to dig deeper to find out what is really going on beyond their borders.

RESOURCES

EARTH COUNCIL
Apartado 2323-1002
San José, Costa Rica
Ph: +506-256-1611
web site: www.ecouncil.ac.cr/
Non-governmental organization created in 1992 to promote and advance the implementation of the Earth Summit agreements.

EARTH ISLAND JOURNAL
300 Broadway, No. 28
San Francisco, CA 94122
Ph: 415-788-3666
web site: www.earthisland.org/ei/
An excellent source of U.S. and international environmental news and information. Publishes a quarterly magazine.

EARTH TIMES
Box 3363, Grand Central Station
New York, NY 10163
Ph: 212-297-0488   Fax: 212-297-0566
web site: www.earthtimes.org
Global news and information. Publishes a bi-montly newspaper.

CORPORATE WATCH
web site: www.corpwatch.org/
Reports on activities of transnational corporations.

INSTITUTE FOR GLOBAL COMMUNICATIONS (IGC)
Produces EcoNet, PeaceNet, LaborNet, ConflictNet, WomansNet
Presidio Building
1012 Torney Ave, First Floor
P.O. Box 29904
San Francisco, CA 94129-0904
Ph: 415-561-6100
web site: www.igc.org/igc/
Electronic network of progressive activist organizations

INSTITUTE FOR GLOBAL FUTURES RESEARCH (IGFR)
P.O. Box 263
Earlville, Cairns, QLD 4870 Australia
Fax: 61-7-4033 6881
e-mail: igfr@peg.apc.org
Monthly electronic newsletter on global issues analysis.

POPULATION INSTITUTE
107 Second St. NE
Washington, DC 20002
Ph: 202-544-3300
web site: www.populationinstitute.org
Information on world population.

WORLD RESOURCES INSTITUTE
1709 New York Ave. NW
Washington, DC 20006
Ph: 202-638-6300
web site: www.wri.org./
Independent center for global policy research.

WORLDWATCH INSTITUTE
1776 Massachusetts Ave. NW
Washington, DC 20036
Ph: 202-452-1999
web site: www.worldwatch.org/
Global news and information. Publishes *State of the World* and *World Watch* magazine.

RENEWABLE ENERGY AND SOLAR HYDROGEN ECONOMY

Much is happening in renewable energy. Fuel cells are being moved rapidly toward commercialization and photovoltaic manufacturing output is doubling every few years. Wind power is really taking off. Hydrogen generation and storage technologies are receiving considerable research and development attention and plenty of investment dollars. The Third Energy Revolution (solar hydrogen) appears to be underway.

RESOURCES

AMERICAN HYDROGEN ASSOCIATION
1739 W. 7th Ave.
Mesa, AZ 85202-1906
Ph: 606-827-7915 Fax: 602-967-6601
web site: www.clean-air.org
Hydrogen workshops and newsletter.

AMERICAN SOLAR ENERGY SOCIETY (ASES)
2400 Central Ave. Suite G-1
Boulder, CO 80301
Ph: 303-443-3130
Web site: www.ases.org/solar
National organization of solar energy researchers and users.

BALLARD POWER SYSTEMS
web site: www.ballard.com
World leader in zero-emission fuel cell development for transportation and stationary power applications.

CENTER FOR RENEWABLE ENERGY AND SUSTAINABLE TECHNOLOGY (CREST)
web site: solstice.crest.org/index.shtml
Information on renewable energy and sustainable technologies.

DAIS CORPORATION
4326 Clairidge Way
Palm Harbor, FL 34684
Ph: 813-942-8353
web site: www.dais.net/
Manufacturers a new generation of small PEM fuel cells for recreational use, remote power, and small motor applications.

FLORIDA SOLAR ENERGY CENTER (FSEC)
University of Central Florida
1679 Clearlake Rd.
Cocoa, FL 32922-5703
Publishes "Photo Catalyst Report,"
Hydrogen, pollution detoxification, and alternative fuels newsletter.

H POWER CORP
60 Montgomery St.
Belleville, NJ 07109
Ph: 973-450-4400
Manufactures small PEM fuel cells for remote power use.

HYDROGEN & FUEL CELL LETTER
Grinnell Street
P.O. Box 14
Rhinecliff, NY 12574-0014
Ph: 914-876-5988
web site: www.mhv.net/~hfcletter/
Publishes monthly newsletter.

HYDROGEN WIND INC.
RR2, Box 262
Lineville, IA 50147
Ph: 515-876-5665
Manufactures low cost home and ranch electrolyzers.

PROTON ENERGY SYSTEMS
50 Inwood Rd.
Rocky Hill, CT 06067
Ph: 860-571-6533
web site: protonenergy.com/index.html
Manufacturer of PEM—proton exchange membrane-type water electrolyzer hydrogen generation equipment.

ROCKY MOUNTAIN INSTITUTE
1739 Snowmass Creek Rd.
Snowmass, CO 81654-9199
Ph: 970-927-3851
Research and educational foundation working to foster the efficient and sustainable use of resources as a path to global security. Specific focus areas are: energy, sustainable development, transportation, and rural communities. Publishes newsletter.

GENERAL ENVIRONMENTAL ISSUES

Everyone, from the youngest to the oldest, needs to become environmentally literate—as the health of our economy, our society, and ourselves, depends critically on the health of our environment. Get involved ASAP in some area that interests you. Plenty of help is needed.

COLLECTIVE HERITAGE INSTITUTE
826 Camino del Monte Rey, #A6
Santa Fe, NM 87505
Ph: 505-986-0366
Mission is to conduct public and media education to promote a solution-oriented culture of environmental restoration. Produces annual "Bioneers Conference."

GREEN DISK ELECTRONIC JOURNAL
P.O. Box 32224
Washington, DC 20007
Ph: 888-GRN-DISK
web site: www.igc.apc.org/greendisk/
A bimonthly electronic environmental journal. A compendium of resources on environmental issues.

NATIONAL AUDUBON SOCIETY
3109 28th St.
Boulder, CO 80301
Ph: 303-442-2600
web site: www.earthnet.net
Mission is to conserve and restore natural ecosystems.

NATIONAL WILDLIFE FEDERATION
1400 16th St. NW
Washington, DC 20036-2266
Ph: 202-939-3011
web site: www.igc.org/nwf/international
Mission is to conserve wildlife and other natural resources.

OCEAN ARKS INTERNATIONAL
Center for Ecological Design
233 Hatchville Rd.

East Falmouth, MA 02536
Ph: 508-563-2792
web site:www.vsp.cape.com/~bjosephs
Ecological Design and "Living Machines." Publishes newsletter.

SIERRA CLUB
85 Second St.
San Francisco, CA 94105-3441
Ph: 415-977-5500
web site: www.sierraclub.org/index/
Mission is protecting wild places of the earth and responsible uses of the earth's ecosystems. Publishes books and magazines.

UNION OF CONCERNED SCIENTISTS
Two Brattle Square
Cambridge, MA 02238
Ph: 617-547-5552
web site: www.ucsusa.org
Advances responsible public policy in science and technology.

ZERO POPULATION GROWTH
1400 16th St. NW, Suite 320
Washington, DC 20036
Ph: 202-332-2200
web site: www.spg.org
Organization dedicated to slowing population growth.

BIOREGIONALISM

Bioregionalism encourages people to learn about the ecological interrelationships present in the particular geographical area in which they live. Bioregionalism encourages people to fall in love with nature. It is also about bringing people together to build community, to organize politically, to network, and to celebrate the joy of life.

BIOREGIONAL ASSOCIATION OF THE NORTHERN AMERICAS
P.O. Box 31251
San Francisco, CA 94131
Ph: 415-285-6556

email: bana@igc.org
Grassroots organization working to create a bioregional network/organization that includes Alaska, Canada, U.S., Mexico, and Central America.

INDIGENOUS ISSUES

Because Native People have neither had a voice in the media or held sufficient political and economic power, they often find themselves and their resource base seriously exploited. Yet Native People provide the world with much valuable cultural and biological diversity and often serve as critical guardians of our planet's physical support system. If they are to continue to perform this important service, they will need the political, financial, and physical support of the non-Indian community.

DIRECTORY OF NATIVE AMERICAN WEB SITES
http://info.pitt.edu/~lmitten/indians.html
Listing of Native American resources.

INDEX OF NATIVE AMERICAN RESOURCES ON THE INTERNET
http://hanksville.phast.umass.edu/misc/NAresources.html
Listing of Native American resources.

ZAPATISTAS SOLIDARITY SITE
www.ezln.org/links.html
Excellent listing of web sites and resources re: Mexican indigenous issues—in English and Spanish.

POSITIVE FUTURES GROUPS

Many groups and individuals are working to build a better future for themselves, their communities, and their planet. The power in this movement is in its networking and selfless sharing.

GLOBAL ECOVILLAGE NETWORK
web site: www.gaia.org/
Directory of international communities and ecovillages.

NEW CIVILIZATION
P.O. Box 260433

Encino, CA 91316
Ph: 818-725-3775
web site: www.newciv.org/ncencino/INDEX.HTM
Grassroots organization working to create "improved civilization." Offers Time/Money/Credits for volunteer work. Focus areas: organic food, sustainable community, eco-house design, and renewable energy.

NEW CIVILIZATION NETWORK
Flemming Funch
7448 Oak Park Ave.
Van Nuys, CA 91406
web site: www.newciv.org
Network of international grassroots groups and individuals for positive change.

SOULFUL LEADERSHIP

We need much more of this. Everywhere. At all times—at home, in schools, in government, in the business world. Soulful leadership is about right work and right action—living wisely and with integrity—serving yourself and others, creatively, impeccably, and mindfully.

MAKING A DIFFERENCE COLLEGE GUIDE
Outstanding colleges to help you make a better world
Author: Miriam Weinstein
SageWorks Press
P.O. Box 150488
San Rafael, CA 94915-0488
Ph: 800-218-4242
Directory of environmental and service learning based college programs in the United States.

SHAVANO INSTITUTE
P.O. Box 17904
Boulder, CO 80308
Ph: 303-440-4153
web site: www.shavano.org
Offers programs to advance new initiatives in ecological leadership and sustainable community. Focuses attention on "outer environment" of ecological systems and "inner environment" of soul and spirit.

ABOUT THE AUTHOR

Charles Bensinger is a technical consultant specializing in renewable energy, electronic media, ecovillage design, environmental education, and intercultural collaboration. He is president of NewWorld Energy Systems, a company that advises clients on renewable energy project development and energy-related public policy. His clients have included community colleges, private companies, federal agencies, and southwestern Indian tribes. He is presently working on solar hydrogen applications for public education and practical demonstration. His previous books include *Chaco Journey* and *Mayan Vision Quest*. Charles lives in Santa Fe, New Mexico.

BOOKS OF RELATED INTEREST BY BEAR & COMPANY

BREAKING OUT OF ENVIRONMENTAL ILLNESS
Essential Reading for People with Chronic Fatigue Syndrome, Allergies, & Chemical Sensitivities
Robert Sampson, M.D. and Patricia Hughes, B.S.N.

MAYA COSMOGENESIS 2012
The True Meaning of the Maya Calendar End-Date
John Major Jenkins

MEDITATIONS WITH THE HOPI
Robert Boissiere

MEDITATIONS WITH THE NAVAJO
Gerald Hausman

PROFILES IN WISDOM
Native Elders Speak about the Earth
Steven McFadden

SACRED PLACES
How the Living Earth Seeks Our Friendship
James Swan